# Blue Hill

# Blood

# ELIZABETH GRAY

*Blue Hill Blood*
Copyright © 2015 Elizabeth Gray

Cover Design: All By Design
Photo: Dollar Photo Club
Editor: Premier Romance Editing
Formatting: Champagne Formats

ISBN-13: 978-1516936199
ISBN-10: 1516936191

# DEDICATION

To my bloody soulmate and husband.
There's nothing I wouldn't do for you.
Nothing.

"If I got rid of my demons,
I'd lose my angels."

~ Tennessee Williams,
*Conversations with Tennessee Williams*

# PROLOGUE

## The Past

*G*rayish green.
*Decaying.*

Once, last year in the seventh grade, I was sent to detention for disrespecting my teacher. But, quite honestly, she was the one whom had disrespected me. During the middle of a test, I had to pee. She told me I was under no circumstances to leave. And I didn't have any desire to pull my wiener out and pee in the trashcan in front of my class, which would have been much worse I might add. Instead, I simply stood up and walked out of the room.

When I returned, I had earned myself a ticket straight to detention.

The walls in the detention classroom were grayish green. Sickening. Even though I was supposed to be studying quietly, I found myself staring at the putrid walls. Wondering about them. Wondering who painted them. Wondering if they could see me as I watched them. All four of them with invisible eyes.

Four walls that were pulsating and throbbing with ragged, dying breaths it would seem, threatening to suffocate me with their oppressiveness as I sat directly in the middle of their impenetrable cage. Of course nobody else could see, but I was sure the walls were talking to me.

*Hissing.*

*Threatening.*

*Foreshadowing what's to come.*

They wanted me to see their suffering—to understand that they were alive, for now, but their existence would soon be snuffed out.

By the time the last bell rang, I dragged my weakened form from the despotic room. For an entire year the thoughts of those walls haunted me. And I certainly never disrespected Mrs. Lozier again.

Now, I'm brought to the present. I'm a fourteen-year-old man-boy staring at his sixteen-year-old sister's decaying flesh.

*Grayish green.*

*Hissing.*

*Threatening.*

*Foreshadowing what's to come.*

Just like those walls so long ago.

But she's not dead, yet.

"You act like I'm going to disappear right before your very eyes," she teases, her breath ragged and labored.

I drag my eyes away from her vibrant blue ones, blue eyes that don't match the hideous, failing body she was cursed with.

"What color?" I evade, my fingers effortlessly moving and twisting my Rubik's cube. I've mastered the complicated cube and like pleasing her with the color of her choice.

"Green."

Always green. At least this green doesn't match her skin. Just once I want her to choose blue, the same blue of her wiser-than-sixteen-year-old eyes.

"How about yellow?" I grumble and set to twisting the cube over and over again.

A ragged sigh rushes from her lips and I flick my gaze over to her as I absently work the puzzle.

She's dying.

They call it Leukemia. Cancer.

Mom and Dad have taken her to endless doctors, dumping every last dime they had to their name into finding a cure for my sister.

But, there is no cure.

Only death.

Her once mahogany, lengthy locks have long since fallen out and batches of muted brown cover her pale scalp. Many nights I hold Dad's razor in the shower and wish I could shave it all away—to erase the evidence of her impending death.

"Boom," I tell her as I hand her the cube.

A smile, so beautiful it crushes a piece of my heart, graces her chapped lips as she takes it from me. "Green." A happy sigh.

Pride blossoms in my chest. She may not have long in this world, so when I can provide her one sliver of happiness, it overwhelms me.

We didn't always have this relationship—she and I stretched out on the bed together talking of futures that will only ever happen for one of us. In the past, we fought like any other normal brother and sister that are two years apart would. I antagonized. She whined. Typical.

But now?

Nothing is typical.

Everything is on the brink of nothing.

A slam of a door somewhere within the house makes us both jump and my sister reaches a bony hand for mine. Her protectiveness over me causes my vision to blur for a moment with tears as I realize it won't be long and we'll no longer have these moments.

She squeezes it. "They won't fight as much once I'm gone."

Our parents. Two people that loved every part of the other until the illness. Then, the stress consumed them. I'm pretty sure they would be divorced already if it weren't for my sister, Helen. It's like they're holding on to their marriage for her.

"Henry, I promise."

Her words are meant to comfort me but I don't care if our parents fight or not. If they fought every second of every day, I'd take it if that meant keeping my sister—if that meant going back to days where I would pull her ponytail or push her into the pool fully clothed.

"Don't make promises you can't keep," I say softly as I take the cube back from her.

She breathes heavily again and my heart clenches into a

painful fist in my chest.

"What color?" I ask gruffly.

"Red," she says, surprising me.

With newfound determination, I set to twisting the puzzle to a color she's never before requested. The shouts beyond the walls, although growing in intensity, are normal. Comforting even, because we've come to expect them each night.

"I love you, Henry." Her words take me by surprise and I pause to look at her.

Blue eyes that match mine shimmer with unshed tears. It's a sucker punch to the gut and I swallow thickly. "I love you too, Helen."

Normal fourteen and sixteen-year-old siblings don't talk the way we do. But normal kids our age aren't losing their only sibling either. Screw those idiots.

A shrill, terrified scream pierces the air and I sit up quickly. Helen's eyes have widened but my weak sister remains lying down.

Seconds later, Mom bursts through the door and slams it shut behind her, pushing the tiny lock on the knob. Her brunette head is a wild mess and her face is a tearstained crimson. She's in an absolute hysterical state.

Almost an instant after, the door rattles from its frame as something heavy crashes against it. *Dad.*

"Henry, call 911," Mom instructs, her hands violently shaking as she points to the telephone on the end table.

I'm confused but when another pound on the door makes her shriek, I roll off the bed and snatch the banana yellow phone receiver from its cradle. While I dial the police on the old rotary phone, Mom crawls onto the bed beside my sister.

She tugs her into her arms and whispers soft assurances that make Helen cry.

I'm furious.

Furious at my father for scaring my sister.

"911, what's your emergency?" the operator asks in a bland tone. It makes me want to crawl through the phone and choke some life out of her.

"I—it's my dad. He's upset and angry. We're locked in my sister's bedroom," I say as I shoot my mom a questioning glance.

But she's too wrapped up in Helen.

I don't know what the heck to say to this operator.

"Young man, if this is a prank—" she starts but is cut off when a foot smashes through the door, causing both my mom and sister to cry out in fear.

"This is not a prank! Send someone now," I yell.

My dad reaches a hand in and unlocks the door. When he steps inside, I don't recognize him. Sure, Dad gets different when he drinks, which is a recent occurrence for him— something he never did before Helen's illness. But tonight?

Tonight, my dad is a monster.

"He's got a gun," I choke out.

The operator rambles on but I'm too frozen in terror to understand a word coming out of her mouth. Everything happens in such slow motion.

"David, stop this," Mom pleads as she holds Helen up against her breast, reminding me of how she would hold me as a small child after a nightmare.

This nightmare is real.

"Goddammit, Janet," he growls and stumbles a bit. "I told you. No mother should watch her child die a sick, unfair death. She's being punished for fucking nothing."

"Please," she begs through hysterical tears.

I stand there staring at the monster with the yellow phone glued to my clutches, not knowing what to do to calm him.

"Daddy, this isn't right," Helen tries but Dad silences her when he raises the gun.

His sudden movement startles me into action. "Dad, no!"

"I love all of you. Please forgive me."

Those are the last words.

Last freaking words.

His gun is pointed at my mother and his hand sways but he steadies it to fire the weapon.

I scream or is it Helen?

The moment Mom's blood splatters all over my sister's pastel purple headboard, I cease to function as a normal human being.

I'm a tree.

Rooted into the brown, aging carpet.

Immobile and useless.

Dad doesn't hesitate before moving to aim the gun at her. The angel. *My sister.*

*No!*

The words aren't real.

Trees can't speak.

The moment the shot pierces the air, my heart implodes.

It is nothing.

I'm still staring at the horrific scene before me, with the frantically babbling operator on the other line of the yellow banana phone I'm clutching, when he raises the gun at me. Holding out a shaking hand, I silently beg my father to stop.

But he doesn't stop.

He fires again, this time at me.

I feel the heat of it as it clips my shoulder.

So this is what a gunshot wound feels like?

Burning.

Stinging.

But not the worst pain I've ever felt. No, the worst pain was seconds before when I watched my sister's blood mix with my mother's.

It seems like it should hurt worse—somehow match the pain in my heart. Stumbling forward, I fall onto the bed, face first over my sister and mother's unmoving legs. My fingers delicately reach out to touch their soft flesh—first my mom and then my sister.

An anguished sob rips from Dad's throat.

So sad. And filled with remorse. But I don't miss the relieved gasp after.

He really thinks this is the only way.

"I'm sorry, son," he garbles out as he rolls me onto my back.

Shoving the hot barrel of the gun into my gaping mouth, burning my tongue and the back of my throat in the process, he forces me to stare up at him. His dark blue eyes rage wildly with a demon behind them.

This man is not my father.

Not the man that taught me to ride my bike.

He is not the same guy that once explained to me why morning wood occurs despite our mutual overwhelming embarrassment.

This guy is a monster.

Another shot fires and this one explodes in my head.

Teeth shatter in my mouth.

My brain seeps onto my sister's legs.

I'm dying.

But at least I'll be with her. Helen.

The last thing I see is Dad shoving the gun into his own mouth.

The blast should be deafening but I can't hear it—I can't hear anything anymore. His brain paints the ceiling a vibrant shade of red and I stare up at it.

*Red.*

*The same color as the Rubik's cube.*

It's like she knew all along.

# CHAPTER 1

## The Present

*H*is fingers slip around her throat and the blood pulses through the vein just under his thumb. This is the moment—the moment where their life flashes before their eyes. All the horrors they created. The sadness they endured. Moments of joy. Each and every one of those memories scroll up and away from them like credits after a long movie.

Sometimes, he steals it away from them though.

He robs them of this moment.

But tonight?

Tonight he's feeling generous.

His eyes devour her face as he gently squeezes her throat. Her eyes flutter momentarily closed but then reopen, continuing to dart back and forth, gobbling up every morsel that was her life before it's snuffed out for good.

"There, there. Take your time," he urges and runs his nose along hers, inhaling her scent. The salt from her tears mixed with her panicked sweat and a faint lingering of her floral perfume has him wanting to lick her flesh clean. To taste the very essence of who she is.

Another tear rolls out in defeat. She's no longer fighting against him but instead closes her eyes, needing that last bit of human connection before she's gone. Once again, he's a giving man and grants her what she needs.

"You're so beautiful," he murmurs, "Watching your life silently drain is exquisite and I want to prolong it. But you've given up, haven't you? I'm not that greedy that I'll keep a death that you know you desperately crave, just out of your fingertips."

Her now red eyes blink open and the breaths that were earlier rushing past her purple lips are now few and far between. He wants to steal them and drink them.

"Almost there," he tells her in a singsong voice as he tightens his grip around her neck. With her hands bound ruthlessly by the unyielding duct tape behind her, she's worthless to squirm away. He literally holds her life in his hands.

When her eyes roll backwards, his dick grows hard. Every fucking time whether it be a man or a woman, the brief moment before they die, it turns him on. He knows that as soon as he leaves, he'll be eager to stroke out his release.

She's gone now, well, at least in consciousness, but he knows her heart still beats—even if only barely and sporadically.

*His grip never loosens and when she lets out a final gasp, he wants it. Pressing his lips to hers, he inhales the lingering taste of toothpaste mixed with impending death. It's absolutely delicious and intoxicates his soul.*

*He feeds off the taste of her departure from this world.*

*If he were in to necrophilia, he'd fuck her lifeless body. Sometimes he considers what it would feel like. Perhaps one day he will.*

*Not today, though.*

*Today he wants to watch her expire and then go home. He is greedy and doesn't want to share his high with anyone, not even her corpse.*

*"You had a nice life," he whispers, kissing her once more. "Thank you for your gift."*

*When he releases her throat, she doesn't move or respond. She doesn't smile like she did earlier when she answered the front door to him. Not one single part of her responds to him.*

*Just as it should be.*

"Hank."

I blink away my daze and lazily drag my head to the sound of the voice. Her voice. The voice I love more than any other. "Hmm?"

"You've been staring at your computer for a solid hour. Have you managed to get any words down today?" my wife, Leesa, questions with her hip cocked to the side.

My eyes skim over her body that's clad in fitted yoga pants and a tank top. Her long, messy auburn hair is piled up on top of her head and out of the way while she cleans. She looks good, even after seventeen years of marriage and having birthed our two children. I'm lucky to have this woman.

She's spent the day scrubbing our house from top to bottom in an effort to stay out of my hair while I work. Since the kids are in school, I should use this time to write without distraction.

Only today, I'm doing more staring and less writing.

"Five hundred and forty-nine words," I grunt in defeat. During these moments, when the words come out as molasses, slowly trickling from the jar of my mind, I become frustrated.

"When's your deadline?" she questions, tossing the dirty rag she was dusting with onto the table and walks around behind me.

I groan as she begins kneading away the tense knots in my shoulders. Leesa presses her thumbs into the trigger points on my back that flare up from time to time having spent so much of my life in front of the computer.

She doesn't push me to answer but instead massages me into a relaxed state. I would be lost without her.

Finally, she slides her arms around my neck and kisses my ear. It's her thing, kissing my ear. That's how I knew she would be mine forever.

"Six weeks," I tell her after some time.

Her fingers tug at the hearing aid in my ear and she gently removes it, silencing half of my world in the process. When her lips find the shell of my mangled ear that three surgeries still couldn't get right, I close my eyes. Hot breath tickles the inside as she whispers things only she can hear. I don't have to hear the words to know they are meant to soothe and encourage me. This is her way and I love that about her.

She tucks my overgrown hair behind my ear in order to gain better access. My hair stays in a constant state of shag because no matter how many times someone stares at my grotesque ear or asks me a question about it, I never can seem to shake the horrors of how it came to be that way. If the ear isn't visible, neither is my deeply suffering soul. I can hide my ear, along with the pain of my past, under my unruly almost black locks.

Leesa claims she loves my hair long like this because it gives her something to hold on to when she kisses me. I know better though. She doesn't like their questions either. My wife hates the shitty-ass mood it puts me in afterwards.

Once she's finished whispering the unknown to me, she situates the hearing aid back in its place, and with it, I can once again hear the fan of my laptop running in front of me. A dog barking in someone's backyard nearby.

"A lot can happen in six weeks, Hank. You work better under pressure," she tells me in a reassuring tone.

I groan and stand from my desk chair, stretching my arms above my head in an attempt to loosen some of the stiffness in my frame.

"Five hundred words a day isn't going to finish this novel, babe. Every single word, I overthink and obsess over. It isn't normal slow writing—it's more like writer's block with a crack in the wall. Instead of no words passing through, they trickle out," I say in response.

She steps into my space and I envelop her in my arms. A faint scent of furniture cleaner mixed with her body wash permeates my senses. Tugging on the entanglement that is her hair, I tilt her head back. Her full lips part open and I want to taste them.

"You know we can't," she whines, bringing voice to my impending thoughts. Thoughts that involve her naked, riding my cock.

"Just this once," I beg with a crooked grin that I know makes her weak for me.

She rolls her eyes. "You're a *New York Times* and *USA Today* bestselling author. You didn't get there by me giving in to your every whim," she chides. "You got there, Hank, because I know how your brain works. If we make love, the festering passion to release those words will die the moment you climax. And then where will you be?"

With a grumble, I steal her lips and kiss her hard enough for her knees to buckle. She's right though. The moment I pump my seed into her, I'll feel sated and lazy. My overactive brain will cease to function and I'll be happy spending my day in bed with my wife.

I need to hold on to the fire of those words.

Fuel them and let them rage on.

My agent, Linda, already emailed me earlier today asking where we stood on this novel. I couldn't tell her that I'm only a third of the way in and hate half of those words. Instead, I fired off a curt reply that she'd be the first to know once I had something worth reading.

"You're right. You're always right," I tease as we release each other.

She walks back over to her discarded rag and I plop back down in my desk chair. Running my fingers through my thickening facial hair, I stare back at my screen.

The words wiggle and dance before me, almost as if to

mock me.

Rereading the last five hundred words I wrote, I sigh in frustration. This book is about a killer on the loose in a small unnamed, at the moment, coastal town. I'm having trouble identifying with the characters, or the victims rather, and have been scratching my head all day in an attempt to figure out how to understand them better.

Leesa loses herself to cleaning while I stew over which direction to go next. The main character in my Kill Town series, Eli, is one that I have fleshed out over the years. This is his sixth book and it is highly anticipated by the public. He's morphed into his own persona and basically writes himself.

It's all of the other characters that are being fucking wish-washy as hell.

I click open my web browser and search for images of the beautiful east coast in an attempt to draw inspiration. It does nothing but distract me—festers a craving to vacation there instead.

Finding a picture of a fisherman standing on a dock, decked out in rubber coveralls, I ignore the scenic background and focus on him. White squirrely hair and wily matching eyebrows. His weathered lips are pressed into a firm unsmiling line. He appears to be unimpressed by his bounty of fish that he drags all trussed up behind him.

Garrett. He looks like a Garrett. My mind begins to un-click puzzling pieces and I sear the image into my brain before toggling back over to my document. I become a man possessed as my fingers take over and record what's now playing in my head.

*"Store's closed," the old man grunts out as he slams the lid*

to the bin where he keeps the live bait.

Eli approaches him and attempts to disarm the grumpy man with a charming smile that's typical of him. He wears it easily and without any effort.

"That it is," Eli tells the old man, "But, sir, are you looking for help still? I saw the sign in the window."

His agitated eyes briefly skim over Eli's appearance. Eli is out of place in his tucked in teal Polo shirt and pressed khakis. With each step toward the man behind the counter, his loafers squeak on the damp, tiled floor.

"Boy," he snaps, irritation written all over his face, "You don't know real work. Go find a job selling insurance or some shit. Now get out of my hair before I drag you out by your pretty little collar and dump you in the goddamned bay."

Rage blooms in Eli's chest at having been treated like an annoying child by the man. He's had enough of his own father treating him that way, without any means to defend himself. This man has no right.

"Have you no couth? It surprises me you maintain a business because your customer service skills are utterly lacking," Eli bites back, his shoulders squaring.

Blood rushes through his veins as he sizes up the old man. He didn't intend on killing him but now he knows it is necessary. In an attempt to evade the snooping police back in Springfield, Massachusetts, he fled to the eastern coast to start anew. Finding work that would keep him under the radar for a while meant applying at seedy establishments such as this one.

The old man is nothing but a white trash piece of shit compared to Eli. Eli knows of his value in this world, both as the son of financial mogul, Lawrence Firth, and as the stalking lion he has become.

Because of his place in the socioeconomic world, Eli is used to a certain level of respect, despite the fact that it comes because of his asshole father. He's entitled to people treating him as if he holds a key to their future.

And he does, in more ways than one.

He approaches—

"Dad! Whitney called me a whore on the bus," a shrill voice cuts right inside of my skull and inserts itself, squashing Eli and Garrett's world in the process.

I blink out of the daze from being finally consumed by my words and turn to see my thirteen-year-old daughter Callie, with one sassy hand on her hip looking pissed as hell.

"Why would your sister call you a whore?" I question in disbelief and rub my fingers through the scruff on my cheek, scratching the never-ending itch of the cheek that is made almost a hundred percent of skin grafts from my ass.

My semi-beard is another way to hide parts of me. And while the hair doesn't grow as thick as the other side, it still hides the pink, gritty flesh that was meant for my ass and not my face.

Callie bursts into tears and rushes for me, dropping her backpack along the way. Climbing into my lap like she's always done since she was a baby, she curls into my chest to seek comfort. I glide a hand over her shaking back and pat her.

"Whitney didn't mean it. Do you even know what a whore is?" I question, humor lacing my voice.

She shakes her head no and I'm thankful for her innocence.

"What happened?" Leesa demands with a concerned glint in her eye as she rounds the corner. Upon seeing Callie in my lap, a smile tugs at her lips. We all know Callie is a Daddy's girl.

"Whitney called her a whore."

When she stares at me incredulously, I simply shrug my shoulders as if to tell her, *You deal with it.* The front door slams, rattling all of the windows around it, and I ignore the shiver that runs down my spine.

Slamming doors are always a trigger to the past that haunts me. My family doesn't know of half of my triggers and I would prefer to keep that away from them. I can control how I react to those memories. But I don't want them trying to manipulate their lives—who they are—to accommodate me.

"I called her a bore, Dad," Whitney snaps in exasperation upon entering my office.

Leesa regards her with one of those warning looks she's so good at, being Mom and all. I remember my own mother mastering that look.

"Calling her a bore, still isn't nice," I say in a stern tone.

Whitney glares at me and I wonder if Helen ever used to stare at Dad that way. The thought of his coffee colored hair and maddened blue eyes causes my stomach to sour. If Callie weren't in my lap, I'd be hunting down some antacids.

"Dad, she needs to woman up and stop being such a baby."

Leesa frowns at me and I mirror her expression.

"Go do your homework, Whitney," Leesa finally sighs in

frustration. "You can apologize once you've cooled off."

Whitney makes a kitten-like growl that only fifteen-year-old girls seem to know how to do and storms away. Now that she's gone, Callie turns her head up and grins at me through her tears.

"Can we play a game, Dad?" she asks, tugging at my heartstrings.

My brain begs for me to get back to my novel but Callie is pretty damn good at mastering my heart.

"Cal, honey, Dad has a deadline. Why don't you help me in the kitchen so he can work? You two can play a game after dinner. He'll need the break by then anyway," Leesa says in a firm tone, immune to Callie's charms.

She grumbles but obliges. Before climbing off my lap, she presses a kiss to my scruffy cheek. God, I love that kid.

"Thanks, babe," I sigh in relief as I accept another kiss, this time from my wife. "Always looking out for me."

And it's true. Leesa and I met in college where we both studied Secondary Education. We'd both had to take one of the same classes and instantly connected. It was that year that I fell in love with her and shared with her the ugly parts of my past. She showed compassion, not pity, and loved every part of me, even the mangled ones both inside and out. It was also her that discovered my talent for writing and pushed me in the direction to publish.

Writing has been therapeutic and I'll forever be grateful for her encouragement.

"I love you, Henry McElroy," she says with a smile, "but stop looking at me with bedroom eyes and get back to work. I'll make you a cup of coffee."

Her playful tone soothes the parts of my suffering soul that ache daily. But as I watch her ass jiggle on the way out of my office, I groan knowing that she won't be soothing *that* ache until I finish this damn book.

# CHAPTER 2

"Go fish, got my wish," Callie giggles as she tosses her pair of cards down and effectively wins the game in the process.

"You cheated," I tease.

She pouts her lips out in a cute manner and frowns at me. "Dad, I don't cheat. Whitney cheats."

Whitney hisses out a "whatever" from the couch. Her fingers tap furiously on her iPhone, no doubt telling the whole world of Facebook what an awful family she has. I make a note to log in and check on her account later.

"Girls," Leesa says upon entering the den, two wine-glasses in hand, "Time for bed. It's getting late."

Both girls groan but eventually leave us to complete their bedtime routine.

"You look tired, Hank."

She motions with her head for me to come sit with her on the couch. I slide off of the barstool and saunter after her. Even though she's wearing a simple pink pair of pajama bottoms and matching top, I find myself wanting to tug them off of her—to find release inside of her.

"I'm exhausted," I reply honestly and plop down beside her. I pull her close to me and we both sip our wine, enjoying the silence without our bickering children.

"Are the words flowing again? Callie was full of energy earlier and talked my ear off while we cooked. I hope you managed to tune us out."

I chug my wine and revel in the way it burns the flesh inside of my throat. Ever since the attempted murder-suicide gone wrong, where I was the only one left breathing in the bloodbath that was my family, I've had to adjust to certain things in life. Like wine. It is just about the only alcoholic beverage that I can consume without pain. The tingle of the plum colored liquid as it swishes past the inside of my reconstructed cheek, and part of my throat, is just enough to remind me of how I incurred the injuries in the first place. Soon, though, it softens the blunt edge of the sword that is my past with its inhibition squashing abilities.

"I reworked what I'd already written. It didn't sound right," I complain, a small lie.

She sips her wine and pats my thigh through my jeans. "I'm sure it was perfect. You know you need to work on getting the story down first and then fixing it later."

I don't want to tell her it's because the characters, even ever reliable Eli, have gone silent. That means failure on my part and I hate failing her. In an effort to feel productive, I fucked around on Facebook and reread my words from today about a hundred times.

"If the pressure is getting to you," she says, her words one ginger step after the other, "I could always go back to work. The school will find a place for me."

Anger explodes inside of me. Over my dead body. "Absolutely not," I snap.

She tenses at my reaction and I pull her possessively against me.

Four years ago, when I made it big and signed a major book deal, she quit her job. Not because we had a sudden surge of money padding our accounts, but because of *him*. The principal at the girls' school was a prick. A prick that thought he could steal my wife right out from under my nose.

Sure, I was engrossed in making a name for myself. And she was sorely neglected. However, it didn't give him the right to think he could put his hands on her. When she came home in tears one afternoon, explaining that he touched her ass in a suggestive way, I was overcome with rage. I wanted to kill the motherfucker on the spot.

Instead, she wanted it to simply blow over.

And in an effort to protect her and keep her close, I made her quit. Teaching was her passion but she makes an amazing housewife and our marriage has never been better.

"The pressure isn't too much. You know how I get. Sometimes my mind slams all of the doors shut and I'm stuck trying to figure out which one to reopen. It'll happen."

I hope she doesn't sense the stress in my voice. When I get like this, only one thing truly helps and that only draws us apart.

"I browsed online earlier," she says, "and came across this cute inn in Blue Hill."

Chugging the rest of my wine, I ignore the burn and set the glass down on the table. "I don't need to leave, baby."

Her hazel-colored eyes peer into mine, searching for truth. "They say it's perfect for writers and artists, off the beaten path but still houses a colorful and vibrant mix of interesting people. It might help with your character development."

My wife. She knows me all too well. Last year, I ended up traveling to a small town outside of Portland, Oregon in an effort to finish another troubling book. The words poured from me—beautiful and pure—the moment I turned on my computer at the bed and breakfast. It was that book, the one that I somehow managed to reach deep inside for and retrieve the most passionate of my thoughts and ideas, that hit number one on all lists for six straight weeks and still remains in the top twenty. *Adair Village Blood* will now be made into a movie.

"Hmmm," I evade as I nuzzle my nose against the soft flesh of her neck. Pressing a soft kiss there, I smirk when she gasps.

"As much as I want to let you haul me to the bedroom, Hank, I won't allow you. In fact," she chides with a tsk, "you should be getting back to work now that the girls have gone to bed. I'll come for you in a couple of hours."

I groan playfully at her and reluctantly stand, knowing she's right. There's too much to write and not enough time.

"Two hours, baby. Then come get me."

*Smiles. All goddamn day long. Eli wants her smiles gone. She brightens up this darkened world and he wants to punish her for that. It isn't her place to bring joy to a place that reeks of hate and ruin. His fingers twitch at his sides to hurt her—to erase that fucking smile forever.*

*Pushing through the door to the coffee shop, he flashes her his signature grin. Her green eyes meet his and her smile grows increasingly bigger at seeing the handsome man. If this shit-shop weren't full of goddamned people he'd choke that smile off her face right this instant.*

But, I need more time.

*He'd already be in some prison yard getting fucked in the ass by some big-ass redneck if he went around killing anytime he pleased. Instead, he bides his time and later indulges in the perfect murder. A murder that'll have his dick hard for days and his own damn smile lighting up every room he enters.*

*"Grande drip," he tells the woman, a hint of playfulness in his voice. His intentions are to flirt with the woman. To disarm her with his charms.*

*"Uh, sure, room for cream?" Her voice is breathy and he finds himself watching the vein in her neck pulsate rapidly. She's nervous at having to talk with the brutally handsome man.*

*Eli has always been able to land any woman he wants. His chiseled jaw with a dark shadow of hair ever-present is seem-ingly a magnet for women. As he watches their pulse, their eyes skitter over his rugged, handsome face. It's when he quirks up one corner of his mouth and gives them a knowing smirk, they tend to fall completely over him.*

*"The cream is my favorite part." His words are suggestive and the woman's cheeks blaze crimson as she diverts her gaze back to the register.*

*"Four eighty-seven," she responds, eyes still drawn down.*

*He pulls out a twenty and hands it to her. "Keep the change, beautiful."*

*Green eyes find his again and he watches as confidence slowly seeps into her features. The woman is no doubt beautiful. Dark hair pulled back into a ponytail, small, perky tits hiding behind her apron, and a virtually make-up free face have her appearing to be much younger than her age, perhaps only that of sixteen. But her Delta Zeta T-shirt underneath her apron gives her true age away.*

*"Thank you, mister," she responds politely and then smiles.*

*He bristles at the smile but doesn't let his annoyance show. "Please, call me Patrick," Eli lies.*

*"I'll call you when it's ready, Patrick."*

*"How about I call you after your shift and take you to dinner?" Eli flirts back.*

*Her cheeks are flushed and she briefly skitters her gaze behind him. Those assholes can wait. He's on a mission.*

*"Maybe," she responds meekly and tosses another nervous glance at the idiot in line behind Eli who is impatiently grunting.*

*He nods curtly at her and strides away. Sliding into a table meant for two, he drags his gaze back over to her. The blush is gone and she seems frustrated dealing with the impatient fucker that stood behind Eli in line. He has the urge to valiantly slit the man's throat for the woman but then he remembers he's no hero. Eli is the monster in his story.*

*"Patrick," a bored worker calls out as he places the coffee on the ledge.*

*Eli pops up from the table and walks over to the window. When he glances back over at the woman, her cheeks once again blaze but she bravely forces a smile. He likes her strained smiles much better. They get his dick hard.*

*Grabbing his hot cup, triumph surges through him to see that "Candace" has written her name and number on his cup inside of a heart.*

*Stupid girl.*

*Eli looks back at her and shoots her a look that promises so much; sex, love, adoration. And stupid "Candace" fucking falls for it. Her panties are probably wet from his attention. He can't wait to steal away her smiles forever.*

*With a wink her way, Eli saunters out of the coffee shop to plan for his date.*

---

"You're staring again."

I drag my eyes away from my screen and take in my wife's sleepy appearance. Her hair is disheveled and I realize it's after three in the morning. I've been in the zone for several hours but much to my dismay, my word count is small.

Seven hundred and three words.

Fucking hell.

"This book is going to kill me," I complain with a dry voice and stretch my arms above me attempting to ease the kink in my neck.

She frowns and crosses her arms over her chest. The maneuver makes her tits lift and if I weren't so tired, I'd take her to bed now and make love to her. Book mojo be damned.

"Hank," she sighs, "You need to get away. We both know it's necessary. The kids and I will be fine."

I groan in protest but know she's right. Ever since she mentioned Blue Hill, I can't get it out of my head. Before I started writing this evening, I browsed the internet for information about the small coastal Maine town that's only a four hour drive from where we live in Manchester, New Hampshire.

"I have a title," I admit and turn my laptop to her.

She approaches me and wraps an arm over my shoulder as she reads the top of my Word document.

"*Blue Hill Blood.*" Her words are resigned and I hate that. I don't want to admit it either but we both know this is what will seal *Blue Hill Blood*'s success. It worked for *Adair Village Blood.*

"What do you think? You were right about the scenery, town, everything. It's a perfect writer's retreat and a hub of inspiring characters."

Her sigh is a ragged one but my wife is ever supportive. "I think it's perfect. And, it's just close enough that the girls and I can come for a visit when we get to missing you."

I tug her into my lap and playfully bite her tit through her tank. "You ladies will hardly notice I'll be gone. I'm sure it will be constant dance parties with Bieber on repeat."

She laughs and hugs me to her. "Dear God, I hope not."

We fall silent and my mind begins to open several doors at once. My former loose plot begins to fade as a new one materializes, fit with new characters and scenery.

"Thank you, Leesa. I can never thank you enough for all that you are to me," I murmur as I squeeze her to me.

"I love you more than anything. You know that. I'll do whatever I can to make you happy. Always, honey." Her words saturate my soul and I soak up every last drop. Besides my grandmother, whom I ended up living with after the *accident*, Leesa and the kids are the only true, loving family I have. It's times like these that I ache for my parents and sister. Had the illness not started a ripple of events that eventually took Helen, I know without a doubt she'd have been good friends with Leesa and an amazing aunt to my daughters.

"Go on to bed," I finally say when I hear soft breathing coming from my wife. "I'm going to check my Facebook page and Twitter before bed."

She yawns but climbs out of my lap, leaving me to finish up for the night.

Opening up Facebook, I see that I've missed a few messages from eager readers. One catches my eye and I decide I should respond to it.

*Dear Mr. McElroy,*

*Why are you keeping the release date of the next book a secret? And furthermore, the title? Your avid readers are impatiently awaiting the next release. Will Eli get caught in this book? Are there more books planned for the future?*

*Yours,*

*Your biggest fan, C.*

Before responding, I take the time to add my book to Goodreads since I now have a title. I've yet to come up with a synopsis so I simply state:

**Eli Firth avoids the police and finds solace in the mysterious town of Blue Hill, located in coastal Maine. Has Eli changed his evil ways since the police are on to him, or does his new location give him a fresh breeding ground to wreak havoc on the innocent lives in the charming town? Blue Hill is about to rain red with blood. Catch the sixth installment of The Kill Town series, *Blue Hill Blood*, on November 12th. Official synopsis to come.**

Responding back to the reader, I am sure to include the link to the book on Goodreads. I decide that I'll also tease my following of over five hundred fifty thousand fans with a snippet from the book.

*Two hours.*

*Eli watches the clock as each second ticks by, the next one slower than the last. His body thrums with excitement and he can barely contain his need to show up early for his date. Of course, that won't do. He needs to prepare.*

*His eyes skim over the filthy living room and he grimaces. It wasn't his choice to stay at the old man's—whom after looking at his license, he discovered to be Garrett Thornby—shitty house. The fisherman's home had the potential to be something beautiful and the location had a great view of Peters Cove. But the lazy fucker couldn't pick up a damn thing to save his life. Every surface was inch-thick with a layer of grime and dust that most likely dated back to the late eighties.*

*He desires to allocate some of his limited amount of cash toward a maid service because he isn't accustomed to being around such filth. The dirt and trash that litters this house makes his skin crawl. However, he can't draw any attention* to the fact that he dispatched the old man. And, Thornby's basement is a perfect place to hide the bodies until he's ready to dispose of them properly. Being that the man was a career fisherman, his basement houses many chest deep freezers. It is almost too perfect really.

Now, Eli will simply have to deal with the grime. Perhaps he can roll up his sleeves one day and take on cleaning the mess himself.

A dark chuckle erupts from his chest and he shakes his head.

Yeah fucking right.

With an entitled sniff of his nose in the air, he stalks over to the phone book and begins thumbing through the pages in search of cleaning services. He'll find someone—perhaps some Spanish speaking immigrant—to do the work under the table.

Eli Lawrence Firth doesn't clean.

He kills.

# CHAPTER 3

"Hank," Leesa says with a gentle voice, "I think you should wake up. Your phone has been ringing off the hook. Linda's been calling and insists it's urgent."

I rub a fist into my eye to attempt to force the sleep away. "What time is it?" I ask gruffly.

"Just after eight. I'm sorry, honey. I wouldn't have woken you but she won't let up."

Grumbling about my literary agent that has no respect for those of us that sleep until noon each day, I take the phone from Leesa and fumble until I find Linda's number.

"Jesus, Henry! You can't just go off the grid like that," she rattles into my ear upon answering, effectively grating on my nerves in the process.

"I wasn't off the grid," I grunt, the agitation in my voice loud and clear, "I was sleeping."

She sighs heavily into the phone and I'm thankful to see Leesa mouth that she'll make me some coffee. I nod at my wife and focus on my babbling agent.

"—Fourteen thousand, eight hundred and thirteen shares on Facebook." That part sticks out in my head and I perk up to listen more intently. "Hashtag Blue Hill Blood is trending on Twitter. It's a mad house. Why didn't you tell me you'd come up with a title? And the excerpt. Brilliant, Henry, absolutely brilliant."

With a heavy sigh, I listen to her ramble on while I tug on my jeans from yesterday. Forgoing a shirt, I pad barefoot into the bathroom and take a piss while she fills me in.

"The publisher is thrilled with the hype surrounding this new book. They've asked that you provide small snippets every few days to keep it going," she says with a little too much excitement for eight in the damn morning.

My stomach sours knowing the snippet took hours to get out of my head and onto my Word document. The idea of having to produce them regularly has unease flooding my system.

"I don't know—" I start but Linda cuts me off.

"Henry, I get it. You're old school. But, this is how the self-published authors are making and keeping their presence on social media. We can take a lesson from them. Your excerpts don't have to be long—just enough to tease the reader," she explains. "But while it may seem as if I'm suggesting it, I'm not. Consider this a have-to. Your publisher is specifically requesting for you to do this."

I'm just staggering out of the bathroom when Leesa meets me with a steaming mug of coffee. I mouth "thank you, beautiful" to her and accept a kiss and the coffee before she scurries off to get the kids ready for school.

"Fine. I'll do it," I agree with reluctance. "Oh, and I'm driving out to Blue Hill this afternoon."

Linda squeals into the phone and I have the urge to hang up on her. When I hired her many years ago, I was sold on her ability to come up with fresh ideas and the fact that she was an absolute go-getter, unlike myself. Her skills complemented my lack thereof. But sometimes she's a little too fucking peppy for my liking.

"Last time you went to the scene of a novel, we signed a movie deal. This book is going to kill *Adair Village Blood*. See what I did there?" she laughs. "Kill. Get it?"

"Linda," I warn. "Are we done? Some of us need to shower."

I hear the pout in her voice at not having been baited by her joke. I'll laugh after my third cup of coffee but not a moment before.

"Yes, grumpy, we're done. I'll forward you their email and send a short note to the mayor of Blue Hill. We want them to welcome you and give you the access you need in order to write the best story possible. Is Leesa booking your stay or is your assistant doing that?"

I sip my coffee before answering her. "I fired Chris last week. Idiot wasn't doing a goddamned thing but I was paying him handsomely to do jack shit. Leesa will book it. Take care, Linda."

She starts chattering some more but I hang up. I'm pretty sure she can email the rest. I take another sip of my coffee before crawling back into bed. This crap will be here for me to deal with when I wake up.

---

*Eli stares into the mirror and admires his reflection. Dark, brooding eyes that pass for smoldering glare back. There's a fine line between sexy-as-sin and psychotic. He knows that the handsome stature that hides his edginess is what disarms the women and has them crawling into his arms.*

*He chuckles just remembering the shock of some of the women in the past. How he would start kissing them with his hands all over them in an eager manner. And how sometimes he'd slide his hands down under their panties. Eli wanted to know if they were wet for him. They always were.*

*Stupid bitches.*

*He would dip his finger into their hot, dripping cunts and see how aroused he made them. Then, he'd slip his hand back out and choke them to death with the same damn hand, their essence lingering when their life no longer did.*

*Groaning, Eli realizes he needs to get rid of his hard-on before he picks up Candace. She'll be so eager to fuck him but the poor girl will never get the chance. If only these women knew what hid behind his beautiful face—the fact that he was an evil man hell-bent on destroying them.*

*He checks the clock on the dash of his car. Fifteen more minutes and Candace will be within his grasp.*

*The woman is no different than the other women he prefers to kill. His type, if you will, are all the same.*

*Dripping with fucking innocence.*

*Eager to please.*

*Naïve to a fault.*

*It always pleased him to rob them of a good life. For, at one time, he was robbed of a good life by a woman much like Candace. The thought of Marla sends a quiver of hate rippling through him. He shouldn't think about her when so close to picking Candace up. Marla makes Eli see red.*

*Bloody fucking red.*

*Eli realizes his grip on the steering wheel is making his knuckles turn white and that he's been holding his breath. With a rush of air, he exhales and curses.*

*"Stupid bitch."*

*But now, he can't stop thinking of Marla. Waist-length, chocolate locks that she'd keep hidden away in a neat bun, elongating her neck in the process. A neck that he used to whack off thinking about biting and marking.*

*When Eli was sixteen, he'd pleasure himself over and over simply by conjuring up an image of her in his head. He became obsessed with Marla and found ways to talk or flirt with her. And much to Eli's delight, Marla would flirt back. She'd flash him innocent smiles that would light up his father's dark home.*

*Speaking of his father, he was the one who decided one day that Eli was to never date the help. That night, Eli punched a hole in the wall of his bedroom closet over his father's orders. Marla was so perfect for him, even if she was a few years older than him. He knew that despite his father's wishes, he would have her one day. Without his father's approval, he would marry the girl and have a bunch of fucking babies with her because she was just that perfect.*

*But it didn't happen that way for Eli.*

*In fact, quite the opposite actually.*

One day, after all of the other staff had gone home except for Marla, he asked her for help. Being the naïve bitch that she was, she willingly went into his room. Yet once there, he remembers the way she nervously scanned his bedroom and eyed his bed with suspicion as if he was some creep.

But she still fucking smiled at him.

Even though she seemed nervous to him, some sense of eagerness danced behind her eyes. Eli was a virgin and wanted to make love to the woman that was going to be his wife. It would seem that perhaps she felt the same way about him too.

A knock on the window of his car startles Eli from his memory of Marla. Candace peers down at him and grins. The past still hangs thick in the air and for a moment she is Marla. Everything inside of him explodes with the desire to punish the bitch for trying to ruin his life.

"Get in," Eli demands through the glass of the window in a gruff tone.

Her eyes widen at his tone but, much to his surprise, she rounds the car on wobbly legs and climbs in on the passenger side.

So she's one of those women—the kind that likes to be told what to do. Good, because he's about to get really fucking demanding.

Stupid bitch.

---

"All packed."

I blink away the haze of Eli and Candace to regard my wife. While the story still hangs thick in the air, I'm thankful for the break.

"What time is it?" I question as I rub the weariness from my eyes, not bothering to look at my computer.

"Half past noon. I made you a sandwich before you go and a Thermos of coffee. You'll need to leave soon so you aren't driving at night. You know how I worry," Leesa says from my office doorway.

I drop my hands and drag my gaze over to her. Today, she's dressed in my favorite pair of jeans and an off-the-shoulder cream-colored sweater. It kills me knowing I can't drag her upstairs and make love to her before I go.

"Such a tease," I chide as I stand and stretch.

The vixen flashes me a satisfied grin, knowing that her outfit pleases me. Stalking over toward her, no longer tired, I slip an arm around her waist and haul her to the nearest wall. My lips find hers and we kiss with greed. She moans when my cock flares to life and presses painfully against her. But, before things escalate further, I tear my mouth from hers and admire the lusty gaze in her eyes.

"I love you but you drive me crazy sometimes." I laugh and shake my head as if it bothers me. It never bothers me. In fact, I think this is why our marriage has lasted seventeen years. We've never lost the physical spark between the two of us. I will always want her and, it would seem, she will always want me. I'm surprised we only have two children versus a whole litter of them.

"Just wanted to give you something to think about on your drive," she tells me innocently, batting those long dark lashes at me.

A growl of need rumbles in my chest but I back away from her and storm into the kitchen. I sit down and devour the chicken salad sandwich, just now realizing how starved I was after having missed breakfast. She follows me into the kitchen and dumps some chips on my plate.

"Want me to make you another one?" she questions.

With full cheeks, I nod and watch her ass as she sashays back over to the fridge. An ass like that belongs to a twenty-one-year-old, not a thirty-nine-year-old. But, hell, you don't see me fucking complaining.

I munch on the chips and sip on my Coke while she sets to making me another one. When she hands it to me, I ravenously eat that one as well.

"One more?" Her laugh is cute.

"Nah, I'm watching my figure," I joke, standing to deposit the plate into the sink.

She takes it from me and kisses my scarred cheek. "You look great. Now go change and get on the road, mister."

"If I didn't know any better, I'd say you're trying to get rid of me," I tease and furrow my brows together as if I'm angry. "Who is he?"

Leesa rolls her eyes and sets the plate into the sink. "It will always be you. Always has, always will, Henry."

I tug her to me and hug her tight. Everything in me screams to stay here with my family but my deadline looms and I'm beginning to find my groove with the story. Leaving to write in retreat is the only way I'll make it. The story has everything in it to be as successful as *Adair Village Blood* and I'm looking forward to watching it evolve.

"Leesa, if this story goes big, I'll take a break. I know I've been absent, mentally, and I'm sorry." I sigh into her hair, but then inhale her unique scent.

Her fingers trail along my back as she lifts her head to look at me. The tiny crow's feet at the corner of her hazel-colored eyes only serve to make her more beautiful. Matching near-invisible wrinkles around her lips indicate she's spent a lifetime, mostly with me, filled with laughter and smiles. This woman owns my damn heart, every twisted piece.

"Writing is your therapy, baby," she says in a firm tone that she uses on the kids. "I would never take that away from you. We love you just the way you are. After you send your draft off, we'll spend some quality time together, all four of us. Then, when the itch consumes you again, we'll let you do your thing. Nobody here is complaining. The girls and I support you a hundred percent."

I press a kiss on her pert nose, which thankfully both girls got, and flash her a crooked grin. "I don't understand how I got so lucky. At one time, life was pretty damn bleak. Then, along came an angel. Thanks for being my angel, Lee-sa."

She stands on her toes and finds my lips with hers. I grab on to her curvy ass and hold her to me while we kiss unrushed. After a few moments, she breaks away and regards me with a serious look.

"Your life was a mess, Hank. You were dealt a bad hand. When we met, I saw that I could help you. Behind the pain and hurt, you were someone that needed to be loved. I wanted to be the one to love you. It was worth sifting through the horror to find you, deep inside. You're perfect to me," she offers, dragging her fingers over my scarred cheek and gently touching my mangled ear. "Every single part of you is perfect. And completely deserving of love—of having a family that was selfishly stolen from you. The girls and I will always be here for you no matter what."

Emotion from her words hangs thick in my throat and I have to force my gaze away from hers in order to blink away threatening tears. Twenty-five years later and the mere mention of how my father brutally murdered my entire family in front of me, and it still guts me. Every damn time. As I mentally force those lingering memories back into the haunted door I never open in my mind, I think of *them* instead. Leesa, Whitney, and Callie. My girls. All perfect in their imperfect ways. All mine and nobody is ever taking them away from me.

"You sure you don't want to fuck?" I grumble in a teasing voice, an attempt to erase the emotion from it, and look back down at her with a smug grin.

She laughs and swats me on the back. "My God, Hank! You're impossible. Now go change."

I reluctantly tear myself from her warm grasp and saunter away from her. The sounds of her cleaning up can be heard as I make my way into our bedroom. Tearing off my shirt, I walk into the bathroom and find myself staring in the mirror.

The smile she put on my face only moments ago falls as I inspect my reflection. A pink, still-angry scar on my shoulder reminds me vividly of my father's first attempt to kill his only son. It was on my left side, just inches from critically injuring me. Oftentimes, after the accident, I used to scream to God, in my head because my voice didn't work for a long fucking time. *Why me*? I wanted to know why he left me alive to watch them die in such a heinous way. How was it fair to leave a fourteen-year-old boy without a family? Sure, I had my loving grandma. But I lived my teen years without a father guiding the way. Without a sister to confide in. Without a mother to nurse the heartache of breaking up with a girlfriend, not that I ever really had any.

Running a palm through the dark hair on top of my head, I lift it up and peek at my ear. The hearing aid, one that was specially designed to fit my ruined ear, hangs on for dear life, offering me sounds that can't be heard without it. I pluck it out and set it on the countertop. A ringing takes the place of Leesa clattering dishes around in the other room. The ringing is familiar—the sound I first heard when Dad pulled the trigger with a gun shoved in my mouth. It haunts me and I find that I like sleeping with it on, even when the hearing aid digs into my scarred flesh.

I swallow down the stress of the memories still lingering and open my mouth. The damage inside my mouth was the worst. Dad's hand must have slipped when he shot off the firearm, because instead of reaching its intended location, the bullet obliterated my teeth on one side in the back where it blew through my cheek, destroyed the back of my throat, and traveled out the side of my head, nicking parts of my ear in the process. Destroying it further. My brain, the original target, was completely unscathed. Yet, had I not already placed the call to 911, they'd have never gotten to me in time, for I'd have drowned in my own blood.

But they did get to me in time.

They managed to, even in the late eighties, find a way to reconstruct my body. It took hours and hours' worth of life-saving surgery, but it worked. I came out living and breathing, even if I did need the assistance of tubes and ventilators in the beginning.

I was a Frankenstein of parts—parts of my own flesh rearranged and moved to cover the uncovered portions. Cadaver bones were eventually added to places in my jaw that no longer existed and were used to drill screws in for dental implants. And finally an artificial hearing device was added to aid me in hearing fully.

My appearance changed, but I was still alive.

One slip and the original intent of the bullet missed my brain and took out half my face instead.

Problem is, though, my brain *was* affected.

The blood.

The brain spatter on the walls and headboard.

Their slack faces, devoid of life.

That shit fucked my brain up more than any bullet ever could. Instead of blasting my head into matching chunks on my sister's legs like that of the rest of my family, the bullet instead, infected my mind.

I was infected with anger and confusion and devastating loss.

And because of the bullet's destination, it took months and months of surgeries and physical therapy before I was finally able to talk about the mental anguish I'd endured. However, by then, I was no longer interested in talking.

The terrible door inside my head was instead getting slammed shut and I took great pride in nailing plank after plank over it to keep from ever opening it again. I had managed to control keeping my pain at bay by pushing away all memories of that fateful night. Why talk about it when it would just reopen the wound?

The accident made me different.

And every now and again, I allow myself to peek inside. Seeing Helen's smiling grayish-green face soothes an ache in my suffering soul. One smile is all I'll allow before I slam the door back shut.

"Everything okay, Hank?" Leesa questions in what seems like a whisper through the ringing from the doorway, concern etched on her face, causing the wrinkles to become more prominent. And here I thought she got them from smiling. Now I wonder if I gave them to her over the years.

Plastering on a false grin, I drop my pants and boxers to the floor. I walk over to the shower and turn it on.

My voice has a slurry drawl to it from only being able to hear from the one ear. "Babe, everything's perfect."

# CHAPTER 4

## The Past

Beep.
*Blast.*
Beep.
*Blast.*
Beep.

My eyes are thick and heavy but I force them open. Confusion seeps into my head and pulls on the wiring of my brain. I have no idea where I am or how I got here. The room seems white but is still so blurry. The beeping is all I hear now but it seems muffled, as if someone stuffed cotton in one of my ears. When I go to lift my hands, panic seizes me when I realize one is bound across my chest and the other is restrained.

*Beep. Beep. Beep!*

The beeping noise matches that of my overactive heart.

Where's Mom? She always comforts me when I'm scared, even at fourteen years old. It doesn't happen that often, but when it does, she's always there for me. Stroking the overgrown hair out of my eyes. Promising that everything will be okay.

Is this a dream?

I certainly can't feel much. My ear is numb. My face is numb. Hell, the only thing that isn't numb are my toes. I wiggle them in a fierce way to try to wake up the rest of my body.

And my eyes, they're still playing tricks on me. White and blurry.

But wait, I see some movement just ahead. It is then I realize those are my toes under a nondescript snowy-colored blanket with boring blue stripes. As I continue my staring of my toes, things begin to clear, if only slightly so.

I think I'm in a hospital bed.

When I go to swallow, I feel inhibited and I wonder if I'm having a memory of when I was a small boy and had my tonsils removed. But my legs are longer and thicker under the plain blanket. Surely this is a dream.

My attempts to relax are futile because my heart won't cease the marathon it's running in my chest.

The muted beeping matches that of my heart which is really starting to unnerve me.

*Help.*

The word I attempt to say only comes out in my head.

Nothing can be heard over the soft beeping.

I snap my eyes shut and attempt to force myself into another dream, one that isn't so horrifying. However, when I reopen my eyes, I now find a nurse peering down at me. A small, sad frown draws her lips down. She can't be any older than Mom and for a moment, I take comfort in her presence.

*I want my mom.*

She must see the panic in my eyes because she approaches hesitantly. Her small hand slides over that of my right, restrained one and she squeezes it. I like the caring way with which she does it but I prefer Mom's touch.

*I want my mom.*

When I try to tell her this, I'm once again unable to get the words out.

"Shhh, don't try to speak." Her words are so soft I nearly miss them.

Don't try to speak.

Don't try to speak.

My eyes dart back and forth in a wild manner which I hope conveys that I need answers. Once again, her eyes are sad and full of pity. It hollows out my gut and I become nauseous. Slamming my eyes shut, I force down the feeling of wanting to puke. Moments later, I feel a cold compress on my brow. It helps rid me of the sickness and I'm thankful for the reprieve.

"I'm going to give you something to relax," her almost singsong voice states.

I want to relax—to wake up in my reality, not this nightmare.

*I want my mom.*

Something cold rushes through a vein in my arm. With it, a tingly sensation begins dancing its way through my body. I like the way it feels. It is as if it runs the worry out of my heart and replaces it with contentment. Everything becomes warm aside from the chill on my forehead and I feel my body drifting somewhere I want to be.

She strokes my hand again and I try in a futile attempt to smile. I'm pretending it's Mom, not the nurse. Mom comforts me with imperceptible soft words but I simply know what she's saying. I'm completely fading into nothingness.

*Helen.*

*Mom.*

*Dad.*

Before I can grasp onto them, I'm stolen into a perfect, black oblivion.

"Henry?"

A whisper.

"Henry?"

The faint calling of my name is unsuccessfully attempting to draw me out of a blissful place I was hiding in. I recognize the older feminine voice but I don't want to deal with it now. Last time I opened my eyes, I was in a hospital room. If I wake to that again, I'll have to face memories that are secretly tucked away in a corner of my mind, hopefully never to be accessed again. Right now, I'm safe in the black void of my brain.

"Henry." This time louder and firm.

The fog is quickly fading and I almost sob from the loss

of it. When I force my eyes open, I'm met with the same white room, this time less blurry than before. In protest, I slam my eyes back shut. I cannot face this.

"Henry," she says again. "It's me, Grandma."

Her voice, so similar to that of my mom's, is the only reason I'm reopening my eyes. This time, she's crouched over the bed, concerned eyes skimming over my appearance.

"Listen, Little Guy." As my vision clears, tears spill out over her cheeks and she runs a thumb across my forehead. "You were hurt."

The way she calls me by my nickname has my heart aching from the nostalgic feeling. For, the last time she called me Little Guy, was right before puberty when I was, in fact, still a *little guy*. But, at fourteen, I tower over my grandma who now refers to me as "Hank" or "Henry."

But not today.

Today, she calls me Little Guy.

"I'm so sorry," she sobs and presses a kiss to my forehead before sitting back down in the chair that's been pulled up to my bed. Her wrinkly hand wraps around mine and she squeezes it. I feel my own tears rolling down my cheeks.

"Don't try to speak. Just squeeze my hand once for yes," she chokes out. "Do you remember what happened?"

I stare back down at my toes and refuse to answer. A door inside of my head rattles at her words and I desperately hold it shut.

"Okay then, maybe now isn't the time to tell you. Perhaps you'd like to rest some more?"

Squeezing her hand slightly, I give her the yes she wanted from before.

"I'm so sorry, Hank. Everything is going to be okay. We'll work through this together. I'm still here and I'm not going anywhere."

Tears flood my eyes but go unshed. *I'm still here.* Because they're not. A bitterness creeps its way through my veins on a direct route to my heart. With every breath through what I'm understanding is a tube down my throat, realization rushes through me. Even though I am purposefully blocking out the memory of the event, it doesn't change the fact that they're gone and I'm not.

*I'm still here.*

The thought causes my stomach to churn but just the thought of vomiting with a tube down my throat is enough to send me into a panic attack. Beeping, matching that of my yet again racing heart sends a nurse rushing into the room. There's a flurry of muffled voices and then, once again, the chill enters the vein in my arm.

I'm growing to love the sensation. The quickly numbing feeling that blankets my mind with obscurity. With each passing second, the present and past fade away into nothingness. I float in an easy realm of nonbeing.

It warms and soothes me.

It's much safer here.

Nonexistence and emptiness.

*I'm still here.*

* * *

Nine weeks.

Nine *long* weeks.

Numerous surgeries behind me have left a faint light

at the end of my proverbial tunnel. The doctor says I'll go home soon. Wherever that is. Home certainly isn't with Helen and Mom and Dad. It would seem that the state of New Hampshire claims my new home is with Lynette Farris. Mom's mother—my grandma.

I remember every Sunday going to Grandma's, well, until Helen got sick, and we'd stuff our faces with her home cooking. Grandma was a whiz in the kitchen, her specialty being chicken and dumplings. The simple thought of her cooking causes my tummy to grumble. The gastrostomy and tracheotomy tubes still remain until my three month appointment. Because there was no significant nerve damage, Doctor Willis promises I should be able to eat after my appointment. But even then, my eating will need to be soft and mostly liquid-based considering half of my teeth are still gone. It doesn't matter though, I'm eager to taste something warm in my mouth. To drink a glass of water. Anything.

My shoulder is healing up nicely and physical therapy has helped with the mobility. The bullet went clean through the part of my chest between my collarbone and shoulder. But that's the least of my problems at the moment.

"How did it make you feel to see your father do those heinous things to your family?" my psychiatrist, Dr. Matthews, questions toward my good ear. They want to wait until my ear has healed further, after my second surgery, before fitting me for a hearing aid.

Even though I am supposed to be able to speak some through the tracheotomy tube, I won't. Instead, in a perturbed fashion, I wave toward my notebook on the table. Grandma brought it to me after our first encounter. She wanted to be able to communicate with me.

I can tell Dr. Matthews is irritated but she steps away from me and retrieves the notebook and pen. After situating it on my lap and handing me the pen, she waits expectantly.

With a messy flourish, I write: *What do you think?*

This time, her sigh is loud enough for my good ear to pick it up. A smile tugs at my lips. Annoying her thrills me.

"Perhaps I should come back later," she huffs. "You know, Henry, an awful thing has happened to you. And being sarcastic is a defense mechanism. However, for you to heal, you're going to need to be honest and come forth with how you're feeling."

I shrug my shoulders in response and try not to wince from the lingering pain because of the wound there.

"I'll be back this afternoon. Think about what I said and be prepared to talk about this," she tells me sternly.

*Thanks for the warning*, I scribble.

She doesn't reward me with a response and stalks out of the room. When she's gone, I turn a page in my book and write how I truly feel:

**You took them and left me all alone. I hate you for that, Dad. You were supposed to protect me but you ruined me. My mind. My heart. My body. My soul. How could you do that to me? MOTHERFUCKER.**

I trace the lines over and over the last part until the pen tears through the paper onto the next sheet. I hate what he did—how he took away my life in an instant. Now, he's probably in hell separated from Mom and Helen, burning for his sins. And me, I'm stuck in purgatory—somewhere between life and death.

"Little Guy," Grandma calls from the doorway, warming my frozen, blackened heart. Thank God for her because if I were all alone, I'd beg them to kill me.

My eyes light up upon seeing her and she rewards me with a comforting smile.

"I brought you some books," she says and my heart responds. The reading is an escape since they don't give me the good drugs anymore.

*Which ones?* I quickly write on my pad.

She laughs at my eagerness and I want to laugh too. If only laughing were that easy. I do enjoy the tightness in my chest, a signal of true happiness in such a bleak time.

"Well, I picked this one up at the library. It's never in stock but it is one of my favorites. Let's see," she mumbles as she digs through her bag, "John Irving's *The World According to Garp*."

I haven't heard of it and eagerly take it from her to read the back. It promises a tale of wild characters and weird events. Seems like my kind of book.

"Oh, and this one is a classic. It's called *Alas, Babylon* by Pat Frank. It's an apocalyptic story," she tells me. "It was required reading back when I went to school. But even though it was required, the class enjoyed it immensely."

Taking the book from her, I turn it over and immediately become interested in the book. I'll be reading this one first.

*Thank you, Grandma*, I scrawl out.

She smiles and kisses the top of my head. "Of course, honey. When you finish those, I'll bring you some more."

She sets her bag down on the table and fishes out her

knitting supplies. This is my favorite part of the day. Grandma never pressures me to talk about the things that hurt. Instead, she knits while I read. Every once in a while she'll tell me something funny about her neighbor or something Felix, her cat, did.

It's serene and calm. My grandma's presence is soothing and I almost feel normal. Almost.

"Beatrice made cookies for you," she grunts loud enough for me to hear with my good ear. "I told that old bat to use her brain. The old biddy's been told a hundred times you aren't ready to eat, yet she keeps baking stuff. I'm tired of being nice to her. So, today, I told her to shove those cookies where the sun don't shine."

My eyes widen and I gape at her.

"Oh dear heavens, I didn't say that but I was sure thinking it!"

The muscles in my stomach clench as I withhold a belly laugh. It hurts my throat to laugh but one sneaks out in a sniffling hissing manner through my tubes.

*STOP*, I write through my amused tears.

She flashes me a wicked grin and nods. "Fine. But as soon as those tubes are gone, I've got stories out the wazoo to make you laugh until you cry."

*I love you, Grandma.* My written words are small but she sees them.

"Oh, Little Guy, I love you more than anything in this entire world." I believe her and not because I'm the only thing left in her world to love. But for the fact that I can feel the love the moment she enters the room. Her presence is a salve to my battered and bleeding soul.

She settles into her chair and begins furiously knitting what looks like a masculine scarf. I can only assume it is for me and I can't wait for the day I can wear it, hiding the scar of the tracheotomy.

Lifting *Alas Babylon*, I flip through the pages and begin reading, quickly getting swept up in the story.

And for the next two hours, until visiting time is over, all is right in the world.

# CHAPTER 5

## Present

"That'll be four twenty-seven. Cash only."

I've been in a daydream for the past couple of hours on the drive reliving parts of my past that I'd rather not. Needing a change of scenery, I pulled over at a decrepit service station to stretch my legs and grab a drink.

The cashier is young, possibly eighteen or so. Searching for characteristics that could be useful in my story, I stare at him as I pass him a ten. His acne is horrible. It makes me realize the scarring on my cheek hiding behind my patchy dark hair is beautiful in comparison. He pops his gum in an annoying way as he hands me my change. Boring as hell. I hope the people in Blue Hill are more interesting.

Mumbling out my thanks, I snatch my tea and Twinkies before heading back out to the car. Once settled back in my seat, I rip open the snack and devour it. Lingering thoughts of Grandma hang in the air and I close my eyes to bring forth an image of her. She was the light of my life, even after I married Leesa, until twelve years ago when her life ended. Grandma died a natural death and for that I was grateful. Had cancer, the evil bitch that was destined to steal my sister, taken Grandma also, I'd have lost my mind.

But cancer didn't end Grandma.

At the age of eighty-one, she passed peacefully in our home. After she had grown too old to take care of herself, Leesa and I moved her into our house. It was difficult caring for small children and an elderly woman but we were all closer because of it. I cherish that I was able to spend those last moments with my grandmother.

I polish off the rest of my snack and wash it down with my tea before putting the car back into drive. Thus far, the drive has been scenic. With the change of seasons, leaves are beginning to turn slightly brown, mixed in with the perpetually green trees, still bushy from an unusually rainy summer.

Fiddling with my iPhone, I put on some classic Aerosmith that Helen and I used to listen to together. It's easy to get lost in the nostalgia of it. We argued over music pretty much every day but always agreed on Aerosmith. It was another one of our "things" that I try to hold on to. Leesa knows every single detail of my past including this about me which is why she always surprises me with concert tickets, signed albums, and once, she even got all four of us tickets to

American Idol where Stephen Tyler was judging.

Leesa is good to me. Better than good. She's my angel.

Speaking of my Leesa, my phone chirps mid-song and I'm more than eager to drop the raspy, screaming voice of ol' Stephen for that of the sultry one of my wife.

"Miss me already?" I tease as a greeting.

Her chuckle floods my system and I drink from it.

"Always, baby. But that's not why I called."

The staid nature of her voice sends a ripple of panic pulsating through me but I quickly squash it away and get to the heart of the matter.

"What's wrong?"

She sighs in resignation. "Nothing's wrong. In fact, everything's perfect. I did a little more research on Blue Hill after you left."

A thick bubble of emotion forms in my throat. My Leesa—always doing whatever it takes to nourish the starving artist that I am.

"And?"

"The sheriff, Holly Norton, she's only been doing it a couple of years. She'd taken over when the old sheriff died from a sudden heart attack," she says, the smile in her voice evident. "So, she's a bit of a novice."

The flicker of excitement takes root and begins to thread itself through me.

"Hmm," I say, unable to keep the eagerness out of my voice. "Sounds like the makings for a perfect story."

She laughs but it seems hollow to me. "I also pulled up some of the businesses around town. The most popular bar in town, The Pelican, is owned by a guy named Billy that's been to jail fourteen times for domestic violence on his wife of twenty years. Guess who his sister is?"

The creative wheels in my head begin spinning. "Holly Norton."

"Jesus, Hank. It's almost as if you made these people up," she says in a breathy tone filled with pride. "One of the bar regulars, Joey Matlock, is the deputy—always drunk according to buzz on the Blue Hill Police Facebook page and happens to be best friends with Billy."

"God," I praise, "I'm glad you research for me, babe. You're really good at that shit."

"Oh, and the mayor is something else. Ian Walsh is his name, he's not much older than you. He can't keep his pecker in his pants. Apparently, he's had multiple complaints of sexual harassment that haunt him but somehow he remains in office. Rumor has it that he knocked up a teenager but miraculously she's no longer pregnant. I bet he paid for an abortion," she speculates.

These real life characters are saturating my brain and new leads with my story begin to form. I'm so engrossed in taking mental notes that I nearly slam into a car that fishtails about a hundred feet directly in front of me.

"Shit!"

I yank my wheel hard to the left and narrowly miss the car that I see is still spinning when I finally manage to find it in my rearview mirror.

"What is it?" Leesa screeches.

"I'm not sure. A car lost control. Look, I'll call you when I check in at the hotel—text me the details. Love you," I blurt out and hang up.

I pull my car off on the shoulder and begin backing up until I'm near the now stopped car. As soon as I push open the car door, the smell of burnt rubber assaults me and I can only assume the driver had a tire blowout.

With a slam of the door behind me, I trot over toward the car. As I approach, two wide eyes stare back at me through the windshield.

"Are you okay?" I question.

Once I round the car to the driver's side, the sight of the girl peering back at me causes my stomach to drop.

Blue eyes.

Blazing blue eyes stare back at me.

I know these eyes.

"H-H-Helen?" I stammer, my lips failing me and I barely get the name out.

The girl shakes her head at me and lightning fast, she slams her hand down on the door lock. I can barely stomach the look on her face. The same fucking look my sister had on her face when my dad aimed that gun at it.

*This isn't real.*

*Helen is dead.*

"Go away, freak!" she hisses and fumbles for her keys that are in the ignition.

*Freak.*

The insult stings, even more so coming from her. *My Helen.*

She waves a canister of Mace at me through the glass.

Running a shaking hand through my hair, I tug at my unruly dark locks before pinning her with a knowing stare. "You're not Helen," I tell her in a firm, gruff tone.

When she flips me off and begins dialing on her cell phone, I become angry. Who is this Helen-lookalike-brat to treat me like shit for wanting to help her?

"Fine," I snap and storm back toward my car. "But you're going to want to get your goddamn car out of the road before you cause an accident."

I stride far away from the girl, that's no more than sixteen or seventeen and looks so much like my sister that it flays my heart, without casting a backwards glance. But, as I reach for the handle of my car, she shouts after me.

"Wait!" she groans. "I'm sorry. It's just…"

I turn to see her half hanging out of her car. Flicking my gaze down the road, I make sure no cars are heading our way. "What?"

She sighs. "Alexandra, well, if you're my mom. Alex to everyone else."

*Not Helen.*

I fold my arms over my chest and toss her an expectant look, careful not to focus on her eyes that remind me so much of my dead sister.

"Do you want a ride to a service station to wait for a tow truck? I just passed one not too far back."

Her eyes widen and she chews on her bottom lip, clearly trying to decide what to do. "Um, I don't know. What if you stuff me in your trunk and kill me?"

I gape at her incredulously. "Suit yourself. I was only trying to help, not kill you," I grunt. "Unbelievable."

She lets out an exasperated sigh and twists a lock of her hair around her finger in a nervous manner before her shoulders sag in resignation. "Sorry, sir, it's just…I don't know what to do," she whines. "My mom. When something happens, I call her and she helps me. She's a cop and has drilled into me to never take a ride from a stranger—which you are. Apparently she's too busy to talk to her daughter though."

"I think your mom would worry more if I left you out here to get smashed by a semi-truck that will undoubtedly round that bend at any time." I drag my gaze away from her to peer in that direction.

Fear flashes over her features but then she sets her jaw and lifts her chin in a brave manner. "Okay, fine. Please help me. But I swear to God, if you try and do anything, I'll Mace the shit out of you."

The last part she says in a playful tone that has my anger simmering down from the boiling rage I was consumed with only moments before. I let out a chuckle and approach her, arm extended. "I promise I won't do anything Mace-worthy. I'm Henry. And I have a daughter close to your age," I say in an effort to make her feel more comfortable.

She eyes my hand warily but approaches the rest of the way. "Nice to meet you, Henry."

When her hand closes around mine, the softness in her touch jackknifes its way through my heart. *So Helen-like.*

"No longer strangers," I smile tightly. "Now, let's get your car over to the shoulder before someone gets hurt."

When I finally force myself to let go of her hand, I glance over her attire. Short, frayed jean shorts are molded to her and a tight red T-shirt stretches over her breasts—an outfit Helen would turn her nose up at. Helen always preferred long skirts or corduroy pants, nothing revealing.

Dragging my gaze away from her to back down the road, I mutter, "You steer while I push."

Her apprehension of me quickly fades away and by the time we've pushed her car over to the side of the road, she no longer seems afraid of me.

"Do you know how to change a tire?" she questions, hope filling her voice, as she once again tries dialing her mother. "I wouldn't have to call a tow truck then."

I'm not eager to get dirty and sweat my ass off but I want to spend a little more time with her. It's not that I'm some fucking pervert but a part of me believes she's Helen and isn't ready to let her go yet.

"Yeah," I grunt. "But you're helping."

When she laughs, my knees buckle and I nonchalantly grab onto the side of the car to keep from falling. The laugh is so familiar—*so Helen*. It trickles its way in through my ears, both the good one and the mangled one, wreaking havoc on my soul along the way. Memories that have been kept behind the solid door in my head blast out as it swings wide open.

*I remember showing her how I moonwalked better than Michael Jackson.*

*I remember her answering all of the Jeopardy questions before the contestants ever had a chance.*

*I remember us arguing over which was better, Coke or Pepsi.*

There were many giggles on Helen's part—always amused by that of her younger brother.

"Sir, er, Henry?" fake Helen questions, interrupting memories of the real Helen.

Bringing my eyes to her own shining blue ones, I try not to devour her features like some pervert, because I'm not. I'm far from it. But, seeing her, this girl that resembles my sister that died so tragically, I can't help but stare. Chocolate colored hair hangs in loose waves down her shoulders in a style Helen used to wear before the chemotherapy stole it all away. Even her pink lips are exactly as my sister's were. They draw up in a half smile that causes me to me flash her a grin of my own.

"Don't call me sir. I'm not even forty yet."

She rolls her eyes in a way that reminds me more of my daughter Whitney than that of my sister Helen.

"You sound like my mom but she's forty-one. Still old."

"Watch it, Alex." I grin at her but force myself to look away so that I don't make her uncomfortable. "Pop the trunk and watch this old man change a tire in fifteen minutes."

"Oh, this I have to see," she giggles and bounces back over to the front seat where she left the keys in the ignition. From behind, her ass hangs out of her shorts and I smirk knowing that Helen would have never in a million years touched that outfit with a ten-foot pole.

Shaking my head, I stride over to the trunk that bounces open. When I peer inside though, all playfulness falls flat. "No tire. Shit."

Since her car is a compact, newer model, there's no spare tire—only a small box filled with fix-a-flat crap that is utterly useless considering her tire is in shreds.

I take a deep, cleansing breath and turn my head to look at her. She's come to stand beside me and a bead of sweat rolls down her temple. My finger twitches to swipe it away, but I don't. Instead, I drop my gaze to her pink bottom lip that's pulled between her teeth—*so Helen*—and I also see that her dark eyebrows are pinched together in frustration.

Studying her features, I realize that despite her resemblance to Helen, she bears some differences. Instead of Helen's smooth, pale complexion, Alex has a smattering of freckles that a frequent beachgoer would have across her nose and cheeks. She also wears a lot of makeup for someone her age, even though I really have no idea how old she is, unlike my sister who wasn't allowed to wear much.

"You're going to have to call a tow truck after all. Not much I can do," I admit with a huff.

Her sapphire eyes fly to mine and she widens them. "Will I have to ride with some creepy tow truck guy since I can't get a hold of my mom? Can't you just take me to her work? It's not far from here. You're not a stranger anymore," she reminds me with a smile.

Her plea is one that reminds me so much of my daughter that I cave. Not to mention, even though Alex is different than Helen, I still want to spend more time with her.

*I'm not some perverted freak.*

"Where are you headed?" I probe before agreeing, not wanting to seem eager.

She smiles and flashes me her white teeth that had to have cost a fortune to make so perfect. I'll need to remember to ask Leesa when Callie will get braces because I want her crooked teeth to be as nice as Hel—*er*—Alex's. Whitney still has a metal mouth but I have no doubt she'll look great after they come off.

"Blue Hill, another twenty minutes up the road."

It's in this moment that I know I was destined to come to Blue Hill. Running into Alex wasn't an accident. Fate has worked her magic and aligned the planets in such a way to give me a tiny morsel of something I loved so dearly.

*My sister.*

"I was just headed that way." I motion toward my car and wag my eyebrows at her. "You sure you don't want to ride in the trunk?"

A laugh bursts from her and she flips me off. "Asshole."

I slam the trunk down and throw her a mischievous grin as we head away from her car. "I hope you like Aerosmith."

<hr/>

Turns out, she hates Aerosmith—go figure. Another reminder that the girl that's now popping her gum beside me in the car is not, in fact, Helen. I'm thankful I have on sunglasses and that she's distracted with texting so that I can steal glances at her. My eyes trail along her toned, bare legs and I search for the small birthmark Helen had on her upper thigh. When we were small kids, she hated to wear swimsuits because the mark embarrassed her. But, once she grew boobs, the boys weren't interested in her legs. And Helen's ability to make friends with anyone insured the girls wouldn't care either.

*No birthmark.*

*Not Helen.*

My heart aches with realization and anxiety mushrooms inside me.

What am I doing?

I'm sitting here wishing for this young girl to be my

dead sister. It's sick. And even though I know it isn't her, I'm still drawn to her. I want her in my bed, talking of music and futures, just like old times.

The emotion bubbles in my throat and I cough. "How old are you, Alex?"

Her gum popping stops and she props a now bare foot up on my dash. "Just turned eighteen this past spring. The semester at my college has barely begun and I'm already headed back home. It's sacrilege to miss the annual Labor Day Blue Hill Fair, you know," she laughs and shoves her hand in my face so I can see her red, white, and blue painted fingernails. "Plus, my friend Poe needs me to help him run his pie throwing booth."

*Woman, not girl.*

She's been rambling and I've hardly paid attention to a word she's said. I'm too busy sneaking peeks at her plump lips and upturned nose and those goddamned blue eyes that she's hidden under oversized sunglasses.

"Mmm." It's all I can manage.

I drag my gaze away from her so that I may catalogue the details of downtown Blue Hill. Rows of multicolored shops line the streets, all adorned with charming window displays and bustling people. Bookshops, restaurants, and stores—they all thrive with visitors eager to spend their money—and the artistic, people-watching obsessed man that I am craves to sit and watch them all for hours. To take notes of their expressions and listen to their conversations. I'm inspired to write about each and every one of them while sipping on warm tea and overlooking the sparkling water on the bay. Leesa nailed it with finding this town, like always,

God love her.

"Turn there," she points and starts yelling, "Well damn! She *is* at the station—that Tahoe is hers. I can't believe she ignored my calls and SOS texts!"

Her shrieks pierce my heart as they remind me of the first time Helen started losing her hair. She wasn't upset, she was pissed. I remember slinking back into the corner of her room and watching in horror as she slung everything off of her dresser into the floor with our mother sobbing out pleas for her to stop. It wasn't until Helen chucked her hairbrush out her bedroom window that I was able to do what Mom couldn't. I physically tore her away from the window and dragged her over to the bed. That day, her anger melted into sorrow and I was the one to hold her through it.

I inhale a ragged breath before letting it out in a rush and force thoughts of my sister out with it. Meeting Alex has fucked with my head.

"End of the line," I grunt in annoyance as I park into a spot near the front of the Ellsworth Police Department. "It was nice meeting you and—"

She stops me when she places an innocent hand on my jean clad thigh. I'm not turned on by the simple gesture, but something happens, *and I like it*. An electric current buzzes through me at her touch. Her pink lips curl into an evil smile that never once crossed Helen's sweet features.

"Not so fast, old man. I'm taking you to meet Mom. I bet she won't ignore my calls again knowing I hitchhiked with some random dude," she smirks.

Her hand is gone and my body recoils at the loss. She moves to climb out of the car before she can notice the shudder that passes through me and the erratic rhythm speeding up my breaths. It only takes a second before I'm slinging open my door and following after her.

*I have to go with her.*

*How could I not?*

# CHAPTER

## The Past

I'm a monster.

A hideous fucking monster.

*He* did this to me.

Rage sears through me as I fist both of my hands at my sides. The action causes my still aching shoulder to smart in pain and I wonder how bad it would hurt to punch the glass between me and the person I've become. My reflection in the bathroom mirror is murderous, the black pools of my eyes overflowing with hatred for my father.

Instead of looking away—running from the truth of who I am now, I face myself head on. The truth is, I'm a freak—a Frankenstein of parts all over my face and body. I'll never have a girlfriend or lose my virginity. I'm destined to suffer in this new body because of *him*.

The thought of never having the future of a wife and kids like Helen loved to go on and on about infuriates me. She wanted me to live for the both of us—to have all the dreams of family and children like she did. With a roar against the twistedness of destiny, I slam my fist into the glass and it splinters at the impact, sending a few shards into the sink below. A hundred eyes and mangled ears taunt me as if I'm peering at a painting in a horror museum.

Blood trickles from my knuckles but I ignore it as I lose myself to my newest task. With a newfound frenzy, I pick at the mirror. The glass cuts and slices my fingertips as I pluck piece by piece off. Grandma is going to be pissed, but at the moment, I don't care. After what could be minutes or hours, my skin becomes so torn and bloody that it's hindering my task and I finally hunt down my pocket knife to continue the removal of the mirror. It isn't until I've ripped off every damn piece of that glass that I'm satisfied.

Now, my reflection is nothing.

*I am nothing.*

No longer a monster.

The yellow glue that still remains on the hideous orange and red floral wallpaper is now what I'll see when I come in here each time to pee or shower. A satisfied smile tugs at my lips but then my cheek aches so I purse my lips back together in a way that hurts much less.

"Little Guy?" Grandma's voice penetrates the cloud of my fury and my shoulders lose some of their tension.

Turning toward her, I frown. Her normally chipper and

72

somewhat feisty demeanor has morphed into one I don't recognize. As her eyes fall to my gory hands and then the bathroom demo behind me, her skin pales. If I didn't know any better, I'd think my grandma was afraid of me.

*Of the monster...*

"Oh, Hank," she whispers, her voice taut for a moment.

I wait for it—wait for her to be upset with me. To want to wash her hands of me like my father tried to do. Have I disappointed her to the point of wanting to rid herself of me for good? I feel it's only a matter of time—just like Dad was so easily able to do.

A long pause hangs thick in the air before she finally plasters a fake smile on her wrinkly lips. "How did you know I wanted to remodel this bathroom? We'll go tomorrow down to the hardware store and pick out a paint color more suitable for a young man. This tacky wallpaper will be gone before you know it," she says in a honeyed voice.

I stare at her but don't respond. This isn't unusual for us. Grandma never pushes me to speak but does shove that notebook in my hands each time my mood darkens. It's therapeutic and I think she realizes how it calms me after. Even though it's only been a few months since I woke up in that hospital and even less time since I've come to live with her, I've been through eight notebooks.

Eight notebooks filled with everything from mindless doodles to hate-filled rants against my father. Eight notebooks with poems about brunette angels and short stories where I've rewritten the story of my life to end happily. Eight notebooks that have been my voice when I've been too scared to use my own.

"Now, the shag carpet is still in good shape and it's hard to find shag anymore. I'm not changing it," she chides, "so, stop bleeding all over it. Let's get you cleaned up and perhaps you can draw me a design of what you'd like your bathroom to look like."

I nod and follow my grandma, careful to cradle my hands against me as not to drip on the carpet. Once we make it into her bathroom, she has managed to find her strength in dealing with me.

"Gladys, up at the church, said she needed someone to tinker with a few of her things to see if they can get them working again." She rummages through a cabinet until she produces a medical kit. "And she mentioned an old typewriter, a lawnmower, and a radio. I told her you'd probably enjoy making a little spending money and could use the distraction when you're not working on your studies."

I roll the idea around in my head. Before Helen got cancer, Dad and I worked on the refrigerator any time it would go out. He even let me help him rebuild the transmission in his old pickup. But I was never really mechanical. Yet the idea of doing something to keep my mind busy is tempting.

Grandma sets to cleaning my cuts and bandaging them as she continues, "Is that something you'd like to do, Hank?"

Without hesitation, I nod which earns me a sweet smile from her. "Good, I'll give her a ring shortly. Why don't you go work in your notebook while I get supper started?"

Another nod and I'm starting back toward my room.

"Hank?" Her soft voice causes me to pause. "I love you."

Her words—full of unconditional love—warm me to my very being. She loves the monster both inside and out. I can

74

count on my grandma no matter how jumbled my head gets.

Turning back to her, I try out my voice. "I love you too, Grandma." It's gravelly and nothing more than a whisper, not really sounding like my own.

A sob explodes from her as she hurries to me and pulls me into a tight embrace. Her words are a choked chant, over and over again.

*Good boy. Such a good, good boy.*

If I'm so good, then why do I feel like every day is a struggle to stay sane? Every second of every day, my thoughts lead back to that night. To the blood. To the terrified expressions on my sister and mother's faces. *To the beast that killed them.*

I inhale the scent of my grandma, a floral perfume that seems unique to her, and I smile. She thinks I'm her good boy and I *will* be good for her. Every single day I'll chase off those demons that flash dark thoughts in my head and hold onto the light that is Grandma.

The newest hearing aid works miracles. I've been through so many lately that I didn't have high hopes for this one. But, when the doctor showed me how to use it and found a way for it to fit comfortably in my mangled ear, I was shocked when I heard noise. Not just voices, but noise. I'd relied on my uninjured ear to hear the important, louder stuff, but having the newest hearing aid, I'm able to hear whispers and birds chirping outside.

So today, as my grandma and my latest therapist, Dr. Andrews, "talk" in the other room, I can hear them.

"Now that he has a working hearing aid and the bulk of

his surgeries are behind him, I believe it will be beneficial for him to go back to school," Dr. Andrews, a man with a nasally yet high-pitched tone, suggests. He reminds me of a boring, squeaky rat. "Homeschooling is great for someone like Henry who's been through such trauma, but at some point, you're going to have to reintroduce him to the public."

I grimace at the idea of anyone aside from the doctors and Grandma's church friends seeing me. While they all look at me with pity, the kids at school, I'm afraid, will stare at me as if I'm a diseased dog.

"But what if they tease him, Ronald?" Grandma questions, mirroring my thoughts, her own voice raising in pitch from anxiety. "He's so fragile and we've come so far with him. I don't want him to regress."

Dr. Andrews clears his throat and speaks low enough that I find myself scrambling off my bed and over to the open door to have a better listen.

"He'll have to learn to cope. Kids are mean—there's no doubt about that. My own children have been teased and bullied. But that's life, Lynette. Henry will need to talk to you when that happens. We'll coach him on how to handle the reactions of others upon seeing his appearance. I promise, he's going to turn out okay."

Dread has already consumed me at the prospect of attending school again. I won't do it. I *can't* do it. How am I supposed to attend a high school where my older sister isn't warning my teachers about her wily younger brother? How am I supposed to walk the halls after school knowing she won't be waiting outside for me to walk home? How in the hell am I supposed to focus on my schoolwork when the kids will be staring at me as if I'm a science project and the teachers will be trying not to make eye contact knowing all I've lost?

I can't do it. I'll tell Grandma that I'd rather die than go back into that school. I'm so lost in my head worrying over what they want me to do that I don't notice when Dr. Andrews leaves. It isn't until Grandma wanders into my doorway that I snap out of my haze.

"Little Guy?" My resolve falters the second the pet name falls from her lips and I'm already beginning to cave, especially the moment I see her hopeful expression. "You know I always want the best for you. But, sheltering you isn't the best for you. One day you're going to go on to have a family of your own and do great things. Unfortunately, that's not going to happen with me keeping you under my wing. Time to spread those wings on your own, Hank. You're strong. The strongest person I know. It's time for you to go back to school and face reality. I'll be here every step of the way, but it's time."

She tilts her head and pins me with a firm stare. There's no negotiating on this one I'm afraid because that would mean going against her wishes. And I love her so damn much that I won't disappoint her—this much I know.

"But I'm a monster," I rasp, still not used to speaking much.

Tears well in my eyes and anger flashes over my grandma's features—an expression I'm not used to ever seeing on her.

"Nonsense. You're my good boy, Hank. Those punks have another thing coming if they think they can mess with you. Hear me?" she demands. "You are handsome. You are smart. And, Little Guy, you're meant to be in this world. There's a place for you that was a part of God's plan. I'm not going anywhere."

I swallow down the emotions threatening to spew from me and nod. Grandma is all I have left and has promised to be there for me. I'm her good boy and won't let her down.

# CHAPTER 7

## The Present

"Where's Mom?" Alex demands with a shout as we enter the station together.

A plump receptionist with greying hair peers over her bifocals to greet the Helen lookalike but doesn't seem pleased with her arrival. "Well, Miss Alex, lovely seeing you. Your momma is with someone at the moment." Her tone is bored and I already dislike the woman.

Alex curls her red, white, and blue fingernails around each of her hips and cocks one to the side. The woman is pure fucking sass—not like my sister at all.

"Dottie, tell her I hitchhiked since she wouldn't answer her damn phone."

I snort at Alex but quickly swallow it down when the receptionist turns her attention on me and scowls. She scrunches her nose and her face contorts into a soured expression. "With him?"

Alex flicks a glance my way and winks at me as if we're partners in crime. "Yep, I hitchhiked with Scarface."

The nickname should bother me but a laugh bellows through me and echoes throughout the somewhat quiet lobby area. Poor Dottie's eyes have widened and she seems positively horrified.

Playing along with Alex, I shrug my shoulders. "I offered to stuff her in the trunk but she politely declined."

Alex cackles and I join in because this—*her laugh*—reminds me so much of Helen and I want to hear more of it.

"I, uh…" Dottie stammers, her face burning bright crimson, "I'll be right back."

I watch the woman stand on clumsy feet and then waddle down the hallway in a rushed manner, away from me and my lunatic sister—*er*, friend.

"Dottie is such a bitch," Alex huffs and flashes me a sweet smile. "You know I was kidding right?"

Her blue eyes have narrowed and I can feel her gaze sliding over each uneven and pink inch of the scarred flesh on my cheek, which I poorly attempt to hide under my facial hair. I want to turn away and not have her see what my father has done to me, but I can't. I'm frozen in place and my skin heats knowing I am a fucking sight.

She purses her lips together and approaches me. The sugary scent of her bubblegum invades my nostrils and my mouth waters. When she raises a tentative hand toward me,

I flinch.

"I'm not going to hurt you," she murmurs so low I almost don't hear. But I feel it. Her words soak through to my brittle heart.

I can't move my eyes from her compassionate face. Blue eyes peer into me, rather than at me. Her small nose flares slightly with each breath she takes. Parted lips barely contain the millions of questions brewing in her head. All bitchiness toward Dottie and sassy-ass attitudes are gone. She's curious about me—clearly seeing that there's a story behind the scars—and she wants to know that story.

When her fingers connect delicately with my cheek and then graze toward my ear, a shudder ripples through me. Her touch is nice. *Familiar.* Aside from Leesa, the kids, and Grandma, nobody has ever made their concern for me so flagrant. But with Alex, she fits right in with all those that care.

"Your ear," she gasps and runs one fingertip along the edge up under my unruly hair.

My chest is about to explode, barely able to contain my labored breaths. "It happened a long time ago," I tell her, my voice husky.

Her eyes find mine again and this time they're shimmering with unshed tears. "I'm so sorry, Henry."

*I'm so sorry, Henry.*

Slamming my eyes shut, I allow visions of Helen to dance behind my eyes. God, after all this time, I still fucking miss her so bad it hurts. Sure, I miss Mom too, but Helen was my best friend.

"Alexandra!" an older woman's voice gasps.

Alex's hand jerks away from me and I pop my eyes open. "What?" she snaps back, attitude back in full force.

Alex has folded her arms across her chest and glares past me. I swivel around to see whom she's talking to and I nearly topple over.

*Helen.*

*All fucking grown up.*

"H-H-Hel—" I start but the woman stops me with a dismissive wave of her hand.

"*Sheriff* Holly Norton," her tone is authoritative and she makes no means to shake my hand.

I'm still shell-shocked. If Helen had the chance to grow up, this could be her. A beautiful woman looking stunning and fierce in a navy, tailored police uniform with her dark locks pulled into a neat bun protecting her equally beautiful college-aged daughter. The fact that both cancer and my father stole this away from Helen nearly cripples me.

"Mom," Alex grumbles. "This is Henry. He rescued me when I had a tire blowout."

Holly's face burns a violent shade of purple before she explodes. "You took a ride from a stranger? My God, Alexandra, you've been in college, what, three weeks and are already doing wild shit? Why didn't you just call a tow truck instead of taking a ride from some—"

"Some what, Mother?" Alex seethes. "Some nice man that helped me get my goddamned car out of the middle of the road before I got smashed to pieces by a semi? I didn't know what to do and I was scared. When you didn't answer the phone and he showed up, I took the help. I was prepared to Mace him though."

I break out of my trance and a shake my head in exasperation. "I'll get going. It wasn't my intent to upset you, Sheriff. I have a teenage daughter of my own and would have wanted someone to help her in the same situation. I'll be going now."

I start to leave when Alex huffs. "Mother, tone down the bitch-o-meter. Henry's a good guy. In fact," she flashes me a grin, "I'm taking him over to Luna's for some pie after this. You know, to thank him for being such a good citizen. Being a cop and all, maybe you should thank him too."

Holly doesn't seem convinced but forces out an apology. "I'm sorry. I was just startled with the two of you standing so close. She's my baby and I worry," she states, tone still guarded. "But you're way too old to date my daughter, so don't be getting any funny ideas."

I laugh, "You'll never have to worry about that. Besides, I'm married. Seventeen years."

Alex's cheeks blaze and I swear she seems hurt by my comment.

Who would want to date someone that looks like their sister, anyway? I surely don't.

Holly's stiff posture relaxes and for the first time, she smiles at me. "Well then. Are you passing through or are you staying here in Blue Hill?"

I open my mouth to explain why I'm here when a tall, fit man in a sleek business suit emerges from the hallway where Holly came from. His dark hair is styled in a messy way on top of his head and his lips are curled into a smug grin.

"Holly, always a pleasure," he growls out as he passes the sheriff. But when he notices Alex, his smile becomes wolfish.

"And if it isn't little Alex. Really good seeing you, darlin.'"

My body coils and I feel as though I am a rubber band being stretched to its limit. Only a matter of time before I snap.

"Ian." Alex's gaze falls to her feet.

The name is a familiar one. My conversation with Leesa earlier revealed that a man named Ian was the mayor of this town. Perhaps this is the same Ian.

"Don't leave town," Holly barks at him as she strides over to flank Alex. Something about Holly's protective demeanor has me itching to punch the living shit out of Ian.

"New boyfriend?" Ian questions Alex as he approaches her. I don't like the way he berates her with the question and steps into her personal space. He's begging for an ass whipping at this point.

Wanting to drag his attention away from her, I blurt out, "No, I'm here on business. Henry McElroy. You can call me Hank."

Ian snaps his head over toward me and beams. "*New York Times* and *USA Today* bestselling author Henry McElroy? *Adair Village Blood* Henry McElroy?"

I nod and get a shocked reaction from both the Helen wannabes. "One in the same. I was just headed to the…" I tug out my phone and read the last text Leesa sent. "Sunny Inn."

Ian, no longer interested in the women, strides over to me and presents a Cheshire grin along with his outstretched hand. I don't trust the idiot as far as I'd like to throw him. "Mayor Walsh. We've been expecting you. Your agent Linda called my office with the good news."

My thoughts are confirmed about his identity. Flickering my gaze over to Alex and Holly, I see they're both watching our exchange with interest. Reluctantly, I shake his hand.

"Linda's always on top of things." I haven't much else to say to the man.

He narrows his gaze at me. "The town is thrilled to have you here. If you need anything at all…" He tugs a card from his breast pocket and hands it to me. "Call me. We'd love to have you join us at the fair this coming weekend. I'll be making a speech and you'd be a fantastic special speaker."

The thought of getting up in front of hundreds of strangers to display my scars for all to see nauseates me.

"I'm on a tight deadline that doesn't leave much time for playing," I reply, praying he'll drop the fucking subject. If Linda were here though, she'd have already signed me up for this shit because she'd say it was good publicity.

"Nonsense. It's not playing—consider it networking. Surely you can sacrifice an hour of your time."

I groan inwardly and steal a glance at Alex. Her anxiety levels must be through the fucking roof and I don't miss the fact that she wears the same panicked expression Helen wore when Dad entered her bedroom with a gun in his hands. If I agree to this dickhead's demands, maybe he'll leave and Alex can go back to being herself.

"Fine, yes. Email me the details," I tell him with a dismissive wave.

Ian holds my stare for a moment before nodding. "Good. Call if you need anything."

He starts toward the door but chooses to walk unnecessarily close to Alex and it rubs me the wrong way. My fists clench beside me as I contemplate how much shit I would get into if I leveled his ass in the police station lobby.

"See you at the fair, doll," he mutters as he passes Alex.

Once he's gone, Holly starts to slide an arm around Alex to hug her but she shrugs away from her mom, plastering on a fake-as-hell smile.

"I promised the great writer pie and pie we shall have. Come on, Scarface."

Holly frowns but nods, no longer agitated by my presence. Apparently Ian, the damn mayor, is the enemy in these parts. "Fine, be safe and come by for dinner later. I get off at seven. Bring Poe if you want," she hollers after us.

It isn't until we're outside and back in my car that Alex speaks up. "So, are you going to tell me how you got those scars?"

Her dark brow is arched in question and I fight the smile that's tugging at the corners of my lips. Helen used to give me the same look. *So, are you going to tell me who left an empty box of Wheaties in the cabinet? So, are you going to tell me who stole Dad's Playboy magazines from his closet? So, are you going to tell me what's going on with you and Jeanie from next door?*

"Are you going to tell me why you hate the mayor?" I challenge back.

She pouts and shakes her head, indicating that she doesn't want to talk about it. Fair enough. I'm not exactly eager to spill out the fact that she looks exactly as my dead sister did and that I'm becoming obsessed with her.

"Just go, old man. Poe's shift doesn't end for another half hour so if we book it over to Luna's, he'll give us a free slice of pie."

This time, I pat *her* thigh and it doesn't seem wrong to me. I crave to touch her. Goosebumps rise under my palm on her bare leg and she gasps.

"For the record, Alex," I declare. "That Ian is an asshole."

Her hand covers mine and she squeezes it.

No words are needed.

---

"The people here are even better than those I encountered at Adair Village," I say to Leesa on the phone as I watch Alex through the glass of the diner from the parking lot.

The diner is a small brick building with green awnings over each of the windows and flower boxes just below them. It's quaint and cute. And while it's a tiny restaurant, it's a town favorite as cars litter the lot, each one eager to partake on the famous pie. This is a place I know my girls would enjoy—with Callie asking a million questions about the juke box inside and the animated pictures of food painted on the windows. Even Whitney would be intrigued with the views overlooking the picturesque, choppy blue waters of the Mt Desert Narrows and the lighthouse on Sand Island that's visible from the booth Alex is sitting in.

My eyes are drawn to her again.

Leesa rambles on but I fixate on her—*Alex*.

Her sweet smile with a dimple that sometimes shows up on one cheek when she's really tickled about something. Blue eyes that shine with so many outward emotions that she fully displays for all to see. Her hands flailing wildly as she tells a story to her friend Poe.

I'm not impressed with the lanky fellow but he cares about her, that much I can see. He's head over fucking heels in love with her and she's so damn oblivious. When we first went into the diner, I thought he was going to kick the shit out of me, judging from the murderous look on his face. But once he discovered I wasn't some old-ass boyfriend of hers, he simmered down. He still doesn't trust me. That's okay, though, I still don't trust him.

"Hank?" Leesa questions, concern lacing her voice.

I drag my gaze away from Alex and focus on my wife. "Sorry, people watching. My point is, ideas are bouncing around in my head like mad. Once I check into the inn, I'm going to sit down and write for the rest of the night."

We chat for a few minutes and I even say hello to the girls who are now home from school before we hang up. I start walking back inside when something off to the side of the brick building catches my eye. A man, pointing a camera at me.

This won't do.

"Can I help you?" I bellow.

He lowers the camera and has the sense to appear terrified as I trot toward him. "No, sir, uh, oh my God. It's really you." His terror melts and he beams at me.

"Pardon me?"

"You. Henry McElroy. I'm a huge fan of your work," he chatters. "I saw on Facebook that you were headed to Blue Hill. I live in West Virginia but my aunt lives near here. You're my fucking idol, man."

My posture relaxes and I smile back. "Glad to hear you like my work. Why in the hell are you over here taking sneaky pictures of me? If you're a fan, as you claim, you'd know I'm not at all into having my photograph taken."

His face falls at having been called out. "I, uh, you're right. Shit! I'm so nervous and didn't think I'd actually get to talk to you…" he trails off.

I frown but shake it off. "No big deal, as long as you don't post them anywhere."

He nods profusely. "Of course. You have my word. My mind is just reeling," he laughs, "This is unfuckingreal. So, in *Adair Village Blood*, did Marcy's character really take after the town's homecoming queen? It's so cool that these characters are loosely based on real life people. That's why I hauled ass up here the moment I saw on Facebook where you were headed. I wanted to be a part of it. See these people first-hand. Really get the full Henry McElroy experience."

I look away from the enthusiastic man and back toward the window where Alex watches our exchange with a curious smirk. Holding up a finger, indicating I'll only be a minute, I wait for her nod before turning back to this man.

"What's your name?"

"Me? Holy shit! Will I be a character? Crap, I should have thought up a cool fake name. Nobody wants to read about a Clive Winston Ryker the third. I'm the one that messaged your Facebook page about this book. I'm a super fan of all of your work, you know."

*Actually, that's exactly the type people love to read.*

As Clive continues to ramble on about my books, I study him. He's about my size but not as fit. Where I have some muscle tone, he is a bit flabbier and has a belly that pokes out. His dark, greasy brown hair is a wavy mess on his head and he could use a haircut—as if I have any room to talk. The man can't be any more than twenty-five if I had to guess. When my eyes land on his hand, which he flails in the air in an exaggerated fashion, I cringe at the sight of long, dirty fingernails.

"Right?" he questions, snapping me from my visual inspection of the character before me.

"Hmm?"

This is the problem with people. They go on and on as if I hear most of what they are saying. What they don't get is that as a writer, I'm always plucking things from real life to add to my stories, and I'm too distracted by my visual cataloguing to ever comprehend a word they say. And old Clive here is making my author brain scream to write him all down.

"Listen, Clive, I have a shit ton of work to do. Not to mention, my friend is waiting on me. Maybe we can have coffee one day this week and talk more," I suggest mildly. "I'm staying at the Sunny Inn."

He follows my gaze to where Alex is no longer visible in the window. Where the fuck did she go? Unease ripples through me. I don't like her out of my sight.

"Oh, her. She's beautiful. Does your wife know you're on a date with a hottie?"

His question angers me, causing me to whip back around to look at him. I prowl toward him until we're nearly chest to chest. The lingering summer heat has sweat rolling down his brows and his eyes widen at my aggressive move.

"The young lady is a friend and I'm not on a date. Delete my damn pictures and forget about coffee," I snarl. "Mention my wife again and you're a dead fuck. Got it?"

Clive blinks in rapid succession and has the sense to look terrified. "I'm s-s-sorry. I didn't mean any d-d-disrespect. To each his own. None of my business. P-p-please, Mr. McElroy, I apologize for speaking out of line. Reconsider coffee with me." His words are a stuttered mess.

The idiot truly seems remorseful so I huff and step away from him. "We'll see."

I leave him gaping after me as I stalk back to find Alex in all of her Helen perfect glory. Ian, Holly, Clive, Poe, and, hell, even Dottie.

This is exactly what I needed.

This town is perfect.

# CHAPTER 8

*E*li's mood improved once Candace started chatting about her childhood. *The woman, who he discovered is almost twenty-two, is as innocent as they come. She grew up with two loving parents, excelled in school, and never steered away from her straight and narrow path.*

*Too bad he was going to drag her off the path altogether...*

"What are you hungry for, beautiful?" *The compliment rolls off his tongue like melted butter.*

*He glances over and waits for her reaction. And, as he knew she would, she blushes at his words.*

"Um, whatever you want."

*Fucking agreeable. Mindless. Innocent. Stupid fuck.*

"What I want is you," *he tells her, his voice dropping to a deep, suggestive tone.* "But something tells me you aren't ready to be dessert just yet."

He suppresses a laugh when her chest begins to heave and she tugs at the hem of her skirt, attempting to pull it closer to her knees. Too bad, angel, I've already seen those milky thighs.

"Oh, maybe um later?" she suggests, peeking at him from under her long lashes. Her attempt to flirt would be cute to most men. Eli isn't most men.

"I'll hold you to that. How about that crab restaurant down by Pier 57?" he quips.

She nods like a fucking bobble head and his hand itches to clasp around her throat. To choke the shit out of her so she doesn't move that goddamned head in such an agreeable fashion ever again.

Dinner is nice and conversation flows surprisingly well considering Candace is going to die tonight. On many occasions, Eli would forget that he was going to end her life in a matter of hours. She willingly agreed, no fucking surprise there, to come watch a movie at his place after dinner.

"Wow, nice place," she lies as she enters his space.

He rolls his eyes and drops his keys on the freshly dusted—thanks to Louisa—entryway table. "It'd be nicer if you were naked."

She pops her mouth open and he winks at her. "Sorry, Candace, I'm a little too bold for most women's taste. Am I too bold for yours?"

Panic flashes across her features. Not fear from Eli but fear of letting go of her guarded innocence. He wants to own it.

"No," she whispers, "I like it. I like you."

She thinks she's brave.

Eli knows otherwise.

*Her body quivers ever so slightly, revealing her inner fear. Candace is afraid of Eli and that gives him an erection.*

*Maybe he'll fuck her.*

*"Come with me," he growls. "I need to taste you."*

*Her squeak only fuels him. He wants to come all over her face as he chokes the life out of her. Tonight, he's going to allow himself the ultimate pleasure. Candace is different and he likes that about her.*

*They clasp hands and he guides her up the rickety stairs into the old man's bedroom. Once inside, he kicks the door closed and regards the pretty woman that resembles that bitch Marla.*

*God, he wants to hurt Candace like he did that night with Marla.*

*"Strip for me, angel," Eli orders with a sexy rumble.*

*Candace sucks her breath in but obeys like the good little brat she is.*

*"Mmm, suck my cock baby," he growls.*

*Her eyes widen but she quickly schools it away and replaces it with a look she must deem sexy. Stupid woman. She looks like a fucking whore.*

*Eli unzips his pants and lets them fall to the floor. Once he's pushed his boxers down and freed his average-sized dick, he raises a brow at her. "I don't have all night, gorgeous. Can't you see how much I want you?"*

*She visibly pushes her nervousness away and prowls toward him. It's all fucking forced but he doesn't give a shit. Eli hasn't come in so long and Candace is pretty enough.*

*He strokes his cock and waits for her to put it in her stupid little mouth. Eli nearly comes when she falls to her knees and drags an unsure tongue along his cock.*

*"Yes," he hisses as he tangles both hands in her dark hair. This feels so fucking good to him—he hasn't been laid in a long goddamned time.*

*The stupid bitch is an amazing cocksucker. Perhaps the innocence was an act to get men. Either way, the dimwit would pay.*

*And soon…*

*"I want to hurt you," he blurts out, against his wishes when she deep throats him. He's not one to tell anyone his feelings. But with Candace, Eli feels free.*

*"Do it," she murmurs. "Hurt me."*

*Her permission thrills him and he wants to do it now while he's hard as fuck. In a flash, his hand is around her throat and he's dragging her away from his cock and onto her back on the bed.*

*"You like it rough, baby?" he croons.*

*She whimpers and the dumb whore nods. Stupid fucking bitch! Eli craves to hurt her.*

*His grip tightens and he watches with delight as her eyes roll back, a satisfied smile tugging at her lips.*

*Stupid!*

*Stupid!*

*Stupid!*

*Slipping his hand up under her thigh, he pushes it up against her chest and enters her forcefully. She cries out but soon begins squirming like the needy bitch she is.*

*God, she feels so fucking good.*

*But Eli always needs more.*

*His fingers dig into the flesh of her neck and her face grows more and more purple by the second. He wants her to struggle and fight but she doesn't. Instead, a tiny smile remains on her now engorged lips.*

*She likes this.*

*His dick begins to soften because she should be clawing at him or trying to escape his grip. A small breath hisses from her parted lips when he squeezes harder. Her eyes roll back in her head—quite possibly from pleasure versus lack of oxygen.*

*He sees it written all over her face. She trusts him to take her to new sexual heights. What the fuck is wrong with her? He's not Christian Grey.*

*When she begins to shudder beneath him, he realizes with horror that she came. The bitch came and he can't even stay hard. She's stolen the entire experience away from him.*

*"Just fucking die already," he spits out.*

*Her eyes pop open and her defensive mechanisms finally snap into place. She scratches his arm deep enough to draw blood and he bellows from the pain of it.*

*But this is what turns Eli on and his dick thickens accordingly.*

*Watching Candace die with his cock deep inside of her is thrilling. Typically, the thrill comes from the kill alone. But tonight, he's about to have the biggest orgasm of his life. With a long, drawn out moan, he comes fast and furious inside of her tight heat.*

*He doesn't worry about an unplanned pregnancy from no condom because she'll be dead anyway.*

*He doesn't worry about STDs because this girl is practically a virgin.*

*He doesn't worry about anything because he is in his el-*

ement.

"Mmm, good girl," he groans as he thrusts the rest of his seed into her. Her eyes fall closed and her body becomes limp beneath him. For a moment, Eli is confused because it typically takes them longer to succumb to death.

He falters and relaxes his grip, hoping to prolong her life until he tells her she can die, not when she decides. Candace takes a shallow gasp and her eyes crack open, confusion written all over her face. She must have passed out.

When he grips her neck again, her eyes widen and the clawing begins once more. His dick still twitches from his epic orgasm and yet, he thinks he could come again.

How long can he draw out her death?

He's lost in his thoughts and doesn't notice when her hand stops clawing and slides between their thighs. In an instant, all pleasure flies out the window as blinding pain sears through him.

Candace has his balls in her hand and is squeezing them as if she is trying to rip them off. His grip on her neck is gone as he howls out obscenities. As he attempts to pry her fingers off his precious jewels, she surprises him when she clocks him in the nose with her other fist.

"Argh!" he chokes out.

It isn't until she releases him and rolls out from beneath him that he finds a reprieve from the pain.

He cradles his nads and is helpless to move until the pain dissipates. But Candace doesn't hesitate, much to his dismay, and bolts off the bed.

"You're a psychopath!" she rasps out before running out of the bedroom.

*Eli winces as he attempts to sit up and removes his hands to inspect his balls before going after her. Stupid bitch drew blood and he grows dizzy from the sight of it. He's snapped out of his daze when he hears the front door slam shut.*

*Shit!*

*He scrambles off the bed and locates his pants from the floor. Eli pulls them up over his messy genitals and tears after her despite not taking the time to find his shirt or shoes. The stairs are taken two at a time as he bounds after her. When he blasts through the front door, he pauses for a hair to listen.*

*"Help!"*

*Her scream is not far off and he sprints off in the direction of her voice. Eli isn't getting caught because some stupid bitch doesn't fight fair. It's against all the laws of life for a woman to purposefully injure a man's balls. When he gets his hands on her, he'll enjoy torturing the shit out of her before killing her. She'll deserve it, of course.*

*"Help!" he hears it again and as he runs through the wooded area around the house, he spies a porch light in the distance of a nearby home.*

*He picks up his pace when he hears pounding on the door ahead. Another fifty feet and he'll have her in his grasp. As he grows closer, he sees her naked ass jiggling as she beats on the door and screams.*

*Eli slows only for a moment when the door flies open and a fat old lady opens the door in her housecoat. She seems shocked to have the naked woman shoving past her into her house.*

*"Bad move, bitch," Eli growls under his breath as he flies through her yard and up the steps.*

*Now both women have to die.*

*He'll start with the old bitch.*

The old woman doesn't have a chance to defend herself before Eli tackles her to the ground.

*One.*

*Two.*

Three slams of her head against the porch floor is all it takes to dispatch her.

*On to his next victim he goes.*

A yappy dog goes crazy from behind a door upstairs but Eli isn't deterred. His focus is on Candace as she makes a frantic effort to dial on the lady's rotary phone for help. She's barely gotten to the second number before he rips the entire damn thing from the wall.

"Help!" she shrieks, her voice no longer weakened from being choked.

Eli takes great satisfaction in backhanding her hard enough to send her careening into the center island in the kitchen. A pained moan escapes her as she attempts to regain her bearings.

But Eli doesn't allow her any more time.

*She's already wasted so much of his.*

"Game over," he tells her as he tangles his fingers in her hair. With one quick movement, he bashes her head onto the tiled countertop. Three bashes, as he well knows, will kill her, but one is only enough to daze her. It's the second crack of her head on the hard surface that knocks her out and makes his job of carrying her back to his house to finish the job much, much easier.

I'm dragged from my intense writing by the chime of a text coming through on my phone. Stretching out my stiff muscles for having been sitting at the chair in my room of the overly quaint and ridiculously decorated bed and breakfast for far too long, I reach over to see who's messaging me at nearly midnight.

*Leesa.*

The smile on my lips is immediate and just thinking about her makes me homesick.

**Leesa: I love you and hope you're finding the inspiration you need to write. Goodnight.**

She didn't want to bother me by calling, knowing I could be writing, and the thought warms my heart. As soon as this book is done, I'm going to buy her something special or take her on a long vacation—something to show my appreciation.

Earlier, at the diner, I was on the verge of telling her about Alex. Leesa has always been supportive when it comes to my past and therapy. But for some reason, I worry that she'll disapprove of my wanting to spend time with the young woman. It's not that I think she will be jealous or anything—more like she'll make me face the reality that Alex isn't Helen.

And I know this.

But having Leesa tell me this will end my brief moment of pretend.

I want to fantasize for a bit longer. In fact, I already promised Alex I'd have breakfast with her.

My thoughts drift back to Alex and this afternoon. She was curious as to whom I was talking to and said it was "weird" that I had fans. I laughed it off but it is really fucking weird to know someone watches your every single move. Helen would have thought it was weird too…

A growl rumbles from my stomach and I take notice that I'm starving. The restaurant in the inn closed at nine but I was too much into the throes of writing to stop for dinner. Now, I realize I've made a mistake and will have to get out to pick something up from a twenty-four hour fast-food joint. A bean burrito sounds good right about now.

Before I go though, I type out another teaser post on Facebook, per Linda's recent demands:

*Now both women have to die.*

*He'll start with the old bitch.*

*The old woman doesn't have a chance to defend herself before Eli tackles her to the ground.*

*One.*

*Two.*

*Three slams of her head against the porch floor is all it takes to dispatch her.*

*On to his next victim he goes.*

I smile at how easily that section flowed while writing it. In my mind, the old woman was that receptionist from the police station, Dottie. She'd really gotten under my skin with how she treated me, as if I were a monster.

So, when the story needed a victim to answer the door in Eli's story, Dottie's judgmental face popped in my head and I gladly wrote her demise, careful not to go into too much detail of the way her blue eyes remained dulled and open after.

I chuckle as I hit the post button, making sure to hashtag Blue Hill Blood and share the post to Twitter.

The teaser is small but if I know my readers, they'll eat that shit up which will only make the anticipation for its release that much more great. Before I head out to grab a bite to eat, I text Leesa back.

**Me: Things are great, baby. I miss you so much it hurts. I'm going to eat something and then crash. I'll call you tomorrow.**

She responds with hearts and mine thuds in my chest. The love this woman showers me with is undeserved but I greedily accept it anyhow.

Standing, I swivel my hips back and forth a few times to stretch and then scoop up my keys from the dresser on my way out to go feed my craving.

# CHAPTER

## The Past

Ogre. Pig face. Vagina face. Scarface. Frankenstein. Pizza face. Phantom of the Opera. Ugly. Freak face. Retard. Scary. Dead boy. Loser. Fuck face. Nasty. Sick. Ass face. Disgusting. *Monster.*

"How was your day?" Grandma asks as I walk through the front door.

My fists are balled and I want to bust every mirror in this damn house. "Fucking terrible."

She frowns and her wrinkly lips purse together, clearly unhappy about both my bad language and my day. "I'm so sorry. Is that one boy still picking on you?"

Adam's shiny blond hair materializes in my head and

the desire to rip it all out strand by strand is overwhelming. I hate Adam and his goons. I've only been back to school for three weeks and they are relentless with their teasing.

A nod is all I can muster as I stalk past her and dive into the chocolate pudding she's left out for me at the bar. The good thing about Grandma is she waits by the front door each day when I get home with snacks and hugs. If I didn't have her pulling me off the proverbial edge of my mind, I'd have leapt off weeks ago.

"Want me to speak with the principal?" she questions as she follows me over to the bar where I've plopped down at.

"Nope. It'll just make it worse."

I don't tell her I have dreams of making him shut up. Dreams where I am my father and Adam is me. Dreams where I cut his tongue out, dicing it to bits with my pocket knife, and then feeding back to him bit by bit.

"Little Guy? Tell me what you're thinking." She braces her hands on the countertops and faces me head on, lighting the darkness that pulsates through me.

*If only she knew…*

"You don't want to know."

Her face contorts into a frown. She reminds me so much of Mom when I was in trouble that I'm gutted. I drop my eyes down to my bowl to escape the pain.

"Henry, listen to me. I want to know everything about you. It's the only way I can help you."

Dragging my gaze to meet her concerned one, I blurt out what I was thinking. "Sometimes I wish I could shut him up, Grandma. I think of hurting him."

Her eyes widen marginally but she seems prepared for

my answer. When she suddenly hustles out of the kitchen, leaving me alone with my dark pudding and darker thoughts, I fear she's abandoned me too.

Just like everyone else.

Today's probably the day—the day I've finally pushed her over the edge.

She'll send me away to some nut house.

Then who will love me?

I'm staring at my pudding for what could be seconds or years. Time is an irrelevant yet punishing force. This purgatory I've been sentenced to is unrelenting and I pray that it will end soon.

Grandma reenters the room carrying a typewriter. When she sets it on the countertop, she smiles at me. I don't smile back.

"Why do you have Gladys's typewriter? I fixed that weeks ago and it worked perfectly," I say with caution.

She pins me with a stern look. "I bought it from her. She wasn't using it and it could be put to better use here," her voice softens. "And I thought since you'd taken to writing in the notebooks, perhaps you might like to try your hand on the typewriter."

"The notebooks work just fine," I grunt, still in a sour mood from my school day.

A sigh rushes from her but she doesn't surrender. Helen got that quality from our dear grandma. The thought makes me nauseous as I try to block out all thoughts of my slaughtered family as often as I can.

"I want you to kill Adam."

I nearly choke on my pudding and gape at Grandma

who regards me with a serious look.

"What?" I sputter out. I mean, as much as I have visualized killing Adam, it isn't something I could go through with.

*Could I?*

His idiotic grin completely wiped from his stupid face as I—

"Not literally, Hank. On here," she taps the machine, interrupting my thoughts of killing him. "You're an avid reader, have always had a vivid imagination, and the notebooks have been therapeutic. I think if you could get your anger out in the form of a story, it could help you."

I can't believe she's seriously proposing this but my mind already reels at all of the ways I could kill Adam in my story. The possibilities are endless. Chopping him up into tiny little pieces and feeding him to the big fish in the pond at Gladys's house is one way. Beating the living crap out of him with my fists is another. Pushing him in front of a moving train is enticing too.

"Oh." I smile. "I think this could be fun."

She reaches across the bar and pats my arm. "It's long overdue for you to start having fun again. You have the rest of your life ahead of you and I don't want you succumbing to depression because of those fools. I can't lose you too, Henry."

Her eyes swim with tears and I swallow down my bubbling emotion.

"Grandma, I'm not going anywhere. Now where can we find some paper?"

## Fifteen Ways to Kill Adam

I stare at the typed title on the page and grin. After a brainstorming session with Grandma, my body thrummed with a thrill I haven't felt since riding on a rollercoaster with Helen right before she got sick. Grandma has left me to work on my story while she gets dinner ready and my fingers don't hesitate before launching into a frenzy.

Turns out fifteen ways to kill Adam aren't enough and I add eight more ways to my outline. The new title is: **Twenty-Three Ways to Kill Adam**. Each chapter is a short story of how I brutally end his existence. It's twisted, yet a healthy way to manage my hate for this kid.

I've gone through fourteen pages before Grandma peeks her head in my room to call me for dinner. The house smells of chicken and dumplings, my favorite, and my stomach growls.

"How's it coming along?" she questions as she walks over to where I've set up the typewriter on my desk in my room.

I hand her the title page and grin. "This is actually fun, Grandma. I mean, I still hate Adam, but writing about him helps him stay tolerable in my head. What do you think about the title?"

She laughs. "Twenty-three ways, huh? Why not twenty or twenty-five? That's a random number."

"The title is a working title. I'm sure tomorrow he'll piss me off and I'll think of some more ways."

She pats my shoulder and smiles. "Thank you for trying

this, Little Guy. I want you to be free of your past. We'll do whatever it takes. Even if that means killing no good idiots like Adam."

***

### *Twenty-Three Ways to Kill Adam*, Chapter Three— Vagina Face:

ADAM'S EYES WIDEN IN FEAR. *His insults and jokes can't help him out of the pickle he's gotten himself into this time. Where are his friends when he needs them? The one he calls Vagina Face prowls toward him waving his hunting knife at the foolish boy.*

*"Please," he begs, "I'm sorry."*

*Vagina Face laughs when Adam pisses his pants. "Too late for apologies."*

*Adam attempts to run but stumbles over his own feet and falls hard onto his knees and elbows. His attacker doesn't waste any time pouncing on him and plunging the wicked knife deep into his back alongside his spine. Adam's breath is stolen from him and all reality is torn from his grip as Vagina Face punctures his lung with how deep he stabbed him. He's helpless to move as the knife is then dragged in a downward motion, severing veins, ligaments, muscles and skin along the way.*

*Vagina Face wants to show him how it feels to have his life flash before his eyes. What it feels like to hurt like he does both on the inside and out.*

***

"What do you think?" I ask, sweat beading on my upper

lip. I'm nervous to show Grandma my book but at the same time, I want her to be proud of me.

She slips her bifocals on and holds out the typewritten paper in front of her as she reads the first three chapters.

"Wow," she praises finally, and I let out a rush of relieved breath. "You've really painted a picture for me there, Hank."

I beam at her and my fingers twitch to write some more. "You think so? I thought by making myself a character too and writing in third person, it would really give the story a spooky element."

She chuckles. "It's spooky alright. I'm not completely sold on your character's name though."

My cheeks blaze and I drop my gaze to the floor. "He calls me that, Grandma."

When I steal a glance at her, she sniffles and her eyes are pooling with unshed tears. "Then you keep it in the story, little guy. Adam deserves what he gets in your book and I hope Vagina Face doesn't go easy on him."

I snort at hearing my grandma say "vagina" and she laughs too.

Plopping down beside her on the sofa, I hug her. "Thank you, Grandma, for being here for me and helping me. Sometimes I feel like my brain is a jumbled mess of fear and hate and sadness. But then," I tell her with a grin, "you hug me and I feel a bit of peace. My mind numbs and I don't live in state of duress."

She drapes an arm around me and squeezes me to her. I inhale the floral scent that I cling so desperately to. Without Grandma, I'm nothing.

"I love you, Little Guy."

### *Twenty-Three Ways to Kill Adam*, Chapter Six— Freak Face:

ADAM WAKES TO A THROBBING *in his skull. Like a thousand elephants are parading around inside the confines of his brain. He's barely able to shake the fog of it in order to figure out where he's at. The last thing he remembers is Freak Face swinging a baseball bat at his head.*

*But what happened afterwards?*

*Did Freak Face take him somewhere?*

*He lets out a groan once he tries to move his arms. Realization that he's bound to a chair washes over him and he begins wiggling in a feeble attempt to free himself.*

*"You're not going anywhere," a voice growls from the shadows.*

*Adam's body succumbs to a chill that he feels all the way down to his soul and for a moment, he's frozen in terror, no longer attempting to escape.*

*"W-w-what are you going to do to me?" he stammers, finally finding his voice.*

*Freak Face laughs but it is hollow and cold. For three weeks, Adam's been teasing the kid that looks like he got his head caught up in the garbage disposal, so it doesn't take rocket science to understand why he's here with him.*

*"Adam," Freak Face grumbles, "you've made my life a fucking nightmare. Do you have any clue how much it hurts to lose your entire family and nearly your own life in the process only to have stupid fucks at your school rub it in your face*

*each day that you no longer have anything to live for?"*

Adam's guilt slides through his veins, thick and black with remorse. He never really thought about what Freak Face was feeling. Truth is, he doesn't even know what happened to the damaged boy, only what spread through the rumor mill at school.

Adam wants to apologize to Freak Face—to tell him he's sorry for the suffering he endured in his past and at the hand of Adam and his friends. The apology is on the tip of his tongue, ready to ring into the air before them.

But his words fail him the moment Freak Face steps from the shadows. The long blade in Freak Face's hand glints from the lone lightbulb above them. It's wicked huge and looks sharp enough to cut through bone.

A sick thought forms in Adam's brain. *Will he try and cut through my bones?*

"F-F-Freak Face, don't," he stammers, his voice coming out in sobs.

But Freak Face doesn't falter. In fact, he charges for him. Adam slams his eyes closed to avoid facing whatever it is Freak Face plans on doing to him.

"Say ahh," he grunts and Adam cries out when the boy pries open his mouth.

"Noooo!" His plea, although a garbled one, echoes off the walls of the room. Freak Face ignores him and pinches his tongue between his finger and thumb, yanking it out of his mouth as far as it will go.

"You'll never say another bad thing about me or my family," Freak Face hisses in a satisfied tone.

Without warning, Freak Face begins sawing at the edge of

Adam's tongue with the blade that isn't as sharp as he originally imagined. Blinding white pain shatters through him and a wave of dizziness washes over him, bringing him nearly to the point of unconsciousness. An unearthly wail bursts from Adam but the monster before him is unrelenting in his task of cutting out his tongue.

Even though the pain is searing and the worst thing he's ever been through, he prays it will soon be over. Surely the doctors can sew his tongue back on.

A tugging and then a final rip alerts Adam to the fact that his tongue is no longer attached. Hot blood gushes from his mouth and down his chin like an erupting volcano. The room spins as he succumbs to shock. He barely notices when Freak Face tosses the tip of his tongue into his lap or that he's moved back into the shadows.

It isn't until he reappears that Adam really begins to panic.

"Ahhh," he cries out in a way he hopes sounds like begging.

Freak Face laughs, this time he sounds lighter and free. Adam can't help but realize he pushed the boy to this place. If only he could turn back time...

A ripping sound makes Adam blink away his daze only to see Freak Face approaching with a long strip of silver Duct tape.

Is he going to try and reattach his tongue with it? Adam can't help but be hopeful as blood runs rapidly from him. The room spins again and between that and the pain, he thinks he might vomit.

Freak Face slams Adams jaw closed with the palm of his hand and then proceeds to affix the tape over his mouth.

No!

*Adam squirms and wails but to no avail. Blood fills his mouth quickly and he swallows in an effort not to suffocate. Bile meets the blood in his throat and they both burst from his nose in a deadly, explosive combination.*

*The room darkens as Adam realizes he's near the end.*

*If only he'd have left Freak Face alone.*

*If only he'd have become his friend instead of his enemy.*

*If only he'd have kept his damn mouth shut.*

*Now Freak Face has the last laugh because Adam's mouth is indeed shut and without a tongue, he'll never say an unkind word again.*

*"Bye, Adam."*

*Freak Face grabs hold of his shoulders and pushes him back in the chair he's ruthlessly bound to. The back of his head hits the concrete floor with a sickening crunch that nearly knocks him out.*

*But that isn't what worries Adam.*

*No.*

*What worries him is the blood that's pooling and filling every orifice in his head. He can't swallow it all and it has nowhere to go. The blackness eats away the diminishing remnants of light from the single lightbulb above him until he's gone forever.*

# CHAPTER

## The Present

The banging in my head won't fucking stop. Sick memories of my father and Helen's terrified face haunt me even as I crack open my eyes. Sunlight pours in through the window and I curse myself for not having covered it last night before passing out. I'm staying at the Sunny Fucking Inn all right.

*Bang! Bang! Bang!*

I realize that the banging isn't in my head but on the door of my room and I grumble. It's too damn early for visitors. When it won't stop, I finally shove a foot out from under the covers in an attempt to get up. The chilly air in the room has me dragging my foot back under the covers. Leesa always complains that I like it way too cold to which I always leave the air at a temperature that's comfortable to her. However, when I'm traveling alone, I have full control and like to make it cold as shit.

*Bang! Bang! Bang!*

I can hear a female bitching on the other side of the door and for a moment, I cringe, worrying Linda has shown up. The last thing I need is an early-ass, impromptu meeting with my agent.

The banging stops and I grunt in relief. I've barely closed my eyes when I hear tapping on the window. Grumbling, I roll over and yank the covers off my head to see who's on the other side of the window so I can tell them to go the fuck away.

An angel.

Helen?

Love explodes from within the confines of my chest.

The sun comes from around her silhouette and her dark hair hangs in waves in front of her. She's a perfect vision.

"Let me in, old man!"

I blink away my sleepy daze to realize its Alex, not Helen. Disappointment creeps its way throughout me but I quickly squash it down. I want to see Alex though. She's my only link to my sister.

"Hold on!" I exclaim as I slip out of the bed. My boxers are sporting morning wood because I need to take a piss, so I head to the bathroom to take care of it. The pee, not my erection. On the way, I unlock the door to my room and disappear.

As I pee, I hear her keys jangle as she sets them down

on the desk or dresser. Plastic bags rustle while she unloads something. After I flush, I wash my hands and face so I appear somewhat presentable, bypassing a comb for my unruly hair, and scrub away the morning breath with my toothbrush. By the time, I open the door to the bathroom, the sounds have stopped and the smell of bacon invades my senses.

"Morning, sleepy head," Alex chirps, her back turned to me. She's scooping gravy from a bowl all over a biscuit so I take the time to check out her appearance this morning. Her hair is in waves, like maybe she let it air dry, and falls midway down her back. Today, she's wearing a sleeveless sundress that falls just above her knees, much more modest than the shorts from yesterday. Helen would approve of this dress.

"You look nice," I tell her as I hunt for my discarded jeans.

She turns from the biscuits and her eyes widen as her gaze flits over my frame. Helen saw me in boxers all the time—she was my sister after all.

"What'd you bring me?" I question as I grab up my jeans and pull them up my legs.

"Bacon, biscuits and gravy, pancakes," she rambles, her voice tight. "It's cold as shit in here."

Not bothering with the buttons on my jeans, I saunter over to her. She gasps and her cheeks turn red when I reach past her to snatch a piece of bacon.

"Thanks," I praise as I inhale the meat, ignoring her complaint about my room temperature. "Couldn't have waited until later?"

Her eyes never leave mine as she watches me eat. "No," she sasses, "don't you have a deadline or something? You can't sleep your day away."

I grunt in annoyance as I steal the plate she prepared and walk back over to the bed. "I stayed up late writing. I'm tired."

She laughs. "Boo-fucking-hoo. You promised me breakfast, so here I am."

I climb onto the bed and settle the Styrofoam in my lap and begin gobbling up the breakfast. "I'm not a morning person," I mumble through my food.

"You think?" she teases. "Seriously, how does your wife put up with your morning attitude?"

Dragging my gaze from my food, I regard her. She's sat down in the desk chair and is sipping on some orange juice, watching me with curious eyes. I see that she's sneaking peaks at the scar on my chest near my shoulder. Maybe I should have put on a shirt.

"She loves me and is used to me I guess," I tell her and polish off my food.

When I stand to dump the empty containers in the trash can, she stands too, setting her glass on the desk. Once I've thrown it away, she strides over to me, her dress sashaying around her. An angel.

"Did this happen then too?" she questions as she enters my personal space, mere inches from my bare chest.

Looking down at her, I drink up the concern that's written all over her face—a face I want to touch—to see if she's real.

"Mmmhmm," I rumble.

She raises a hand and tentatively touches the white, raised flesh. Another jolt of electricity races down my spine. It's as if she really is Helen. My brain has trouble comprehending what to do with her.

Helen was an affectionate girl—always hugging and touching me. It used to annoy me when she'd drape her legs across my lap on the couch while watching television or when she'd chase after me trying to hug me. But when she got sick, I gave her the gift that she so blatantly craved.

And then we were inseparable. There were many times Mom would enter the room and see Helen curled around me to which she would beam and say, "You two used to do this when you were little."

"I want to know your story," Alex says in a whisper, her finger still tracing the lines.

I reach up and cover the top of her hand with mine, pressing her palm to my chest. My eyes close and a contented sigh escapes me. "I want to know your story too."

She whines at my words and I pop my eyes back open to stare down at her. The bottom lip that she favors when nervous has been sucked between her teeth as she chews on it. Helen was always that way, so obvious with her emotions.

"Does it have something to do with Ian?" I demand, the anger infecting my words without my being able to control it.

Tears pool in her eyes and she starts to tear away from me but I don't want her to go so I keep the grip on her wrist. When she realizes I'm not letting go, relief flashes over her features and she lets me pull her back to me. It feels right, so I envelop her in a hug. The need to inhale her is overwhelming, so as I slip my arms around her back to hold her flush against me, I give in to my desire and sniff her.

The shampoo isn't one I recognize but I decide I love it. It's intoxicating and takes residence in my lungs. I hold my breath to keep it in a little longer.

"He's a bad man," she sniffles against my chest. She wraps her arms around my waist and squeezes me back.

I knew the moment I laid eyes on that greasy mother-fucker that he was a bad man. Alex's confession doesn't surprise me in the slightest. What surprises me is the need to beat the living shit out of him for whatever it is he's done to her.

"What did he do to you?"

She lifts her chin and rests it on my chest so that we're staring at one another. Her blue eyes are watery and red around the edges. This immediately reminds me of my sister that night and it's a sucker punch to the gut.

"What didn't he do?" she laughs without humor and slips her hand back up to the scar on my chest. "What happened to you? Who hurt you?"

My eyes fall closed once again as her hand roams further up my body along my neck and then to my cheek. Just like in the police station, I'm captivated by her touch.

"My father," I admit with a sigh and peek an eye open at her.

Her lip trembles. "I'm so sorry."

I want to tell her it's okay even though it's not. That I'm normal despite my past because I'm not.

"It's fine," I lie, and avoid her gaze.

She sighs and stands on her tip-toes, pressing a soft kiss

to my scarred cheek. "It's not fine, Henry. If we're going to be friends, you need to let me know your feelings."

Friends.

Not siblings.

The knife of reality cuts deep.

"It's a long story," I murmur, already craving more of her.

She frowns and pulls away from me. The loss of her touch causes me to double over and a wave of dizziness washes over me.

"Henry, are you okay?" she demands.

"Yeah, I'm just tired is all," I lie and stumble over to bed.

Burying myself under the covers, I evade her inquiries. Alex messes with my head and now I wish I'd told Leesa about her. I want to discuss with my wife what it is about Alex that completely seizes my heart and brain. Leesa always knows what to do.

"You can't hide from me," she complains and surprises me when she slides into the bed with me. This should feel wrong considering I'm a married man but it's not like that with Alex. She's practically my sister.

Before I lose my nerve, I slip a hand around her waist and haul her to me. I need to touch her like I need to breathe. With her scent invading me under the covers, I want to bathe in it—to stain my soul with it.

She whimpers and her body is tense as I bring her back flush against my chest. Her breaths come out in a flurry as I slide my hand over her belly and hold her in place.

"I need to touch you," I say in the slightest whisper. "I need to hold you."

Her body relaxes and soon her fingers trace letters and

patterns over the back of my hand that's splayed across her middle. It soothes me down to my very essence and my eyes grow heavy. We remain in comfortable silence, me inhaling her with every breath and her stroking my hand, for what could be hours before she finally speaks.

"In high school, I interned at Town Hall. Being the sheriff's daughter, certain things were expected of me, like following in my mother's footsteps," she begins. "But I never wanted to be a cop. I was more interested in the way our government worked. So, when I was a senior in high school and an opportunity to intern with the mayor became available, I jumped at the chance knowing it would look stellar on my college applications."

I sense the story will take a dark direction and I want to comfort her. My daughter Callie likes it when I play with her hair, so I begin stroking Alex's long locks as she tells her story.

"Ian was incredible. He was smart and a suave businessman. The town adored him and soon, so did I. It didn't take long for me to become infatuated with him. He would say things to me that no other boy from school had ever said. His words made me feel like a woman."

Anger is boiling from within me and I realize I've quit my petting of her and my hand is gripping her shoulder. I let out a rush of breath and force myself to go back to stroking her despite the fact that my hand trembles with the urge to throttle Ian.

"One day, long after everyone had gone home, he kissed me in his office. I was head over heels for him and would have done anything for him at that point. So when he bent me over his desk and took my virginity with my permission, I thought I was in love. It hurt and I was inexperienced but I craved more from him."

She pauses and sighs. "Every evening, he would fuck me over his desk. I wanted to marry him and have all of his babies. It was delusional."

Her body is taut with the stress of the words, so I pull her hair away from her neck and kiss the flesh there to calm her. "Ian took advantage of a very naïve girl," I growl and go back to stroking her hair.

She wriggles her ass against me and for a second my dick responds against my wishes. I quickly remind myself that this isn't Leesa, but instead a woman that could be my sister, and my dick softens.

"Mom must have realized something was up with me and she used her investigative skills to determine that he and I were having sex," she whimpers, "and, Henry, I've never seen her so pissed. I thought she was going to kill Ian. But I begged her not to. Told her I was in love with him and if she interfered I would run away and she'd never see me again."

I press my lips to her shoulder again to urge her to go on.

"One day, I realized I had missed my period. I should have been horrified that my future hung in the balance of a pregnancy test but instead, I was elated. I wanted more than anything to have Ian's baby. College dreams were a thing of the past as fantasies of being a mom and wife took over. When I finally took a test and discovered it was positive, I cried."

Her body quivers as she succumbs to sobs.

"Come here," I coo and turn her to face me. Pulling her against me, I hold her while she cries into my chest. Her tears soak down into my soul and I thrum to kill fucking Ian.

After a bit, she calms down and begins the tracing of her finger over my abdomen as she'd done with my hand earlier, but this time it has a different effect on me. Sick thoughts that don't make me any better than Ian enter my brain and I quickly force them back into the dark confines of my mind.

"Then what happened?" I question, my voice hoarse.

Her fingers pause and I groan because I don't want her to stop.

"I drove straight to his office and interrupted a meeting with the city council—told him it was an emergency. He, at first seemed concerned, as he dragged me back into his office and closed the door. His lips were all over me, comforting me, as I cried happy tears."

Another sob.

"But when I told him I was pregnant, he flipped out. Henry, for a minute there, I thought he was going to kill me."

I jackknife up in bed and she slides away from me. Bloody fucking red blurs my vision and I want to hurt him more than I ever wanted to hurt Adam from my past. This time, typing it out on paper won't suffice. Crushing his nose with my fist seems more fitting.

"Henry, don't."

Alex's words are calm and reassuring—*placating, so much like Helen's would be*—that I relax and lie back down on my back.

"What a fucking asshole," I growl and hug her back to

me.

"That's not the worst of it," she sighs, the sadness in her voice thick as syrup.

I force tranquil thoughts into my head so she can finish her story. I focus on the way her finger tickles as it trails around my belly button, how it lingers near the unbuttoned area of my jeans but continues back in a circle. I focus on the way my body pulsates with energy from her touch.

"He threatened me. Told me if I didn't get an abortion, he'd smear mine and my mom's name through the mud. I was scared and still held on to a tiny shred of hope that we could still be together despite the blip in our relationship. So when he made the appointment with the abortion clinic, I willingly rode with him and let them take away a part of me that will haunt me forever. Afterwards, he dropped me off at home…discarded me like trash. When I came clean to my mother, she was livid. Unfortunately, Ian could afford better attorneys and denied every bit of it. I was made out to be some whiny brat with a crush on a city official and my story was soon swept under the rug," she shudders and lets out a choked sob, "I hate him, Henry."

"What about your father? Where was he when your mom refused to help you?" I demand.

She lets out a harsh laugh. "That asshole is both Ian's and his father's attorney. My daddio pays my mom off," she trembles, "Whenever she needs something from him, he throws money in her face just so long as he doesn't have to associate with his illegitimate daughter. When all this blew up with Ian and she threatened him, my father paid her off for good—my college, a car, her house—because keeping a client is clearly more valuable than the wellbeing of his daughter. He told Mom my future was more important than ruining Ian's. She took the money and sent my ass off to college without even questioning what the fallout would be. This town is fucked, Henry."

I roll back toward her so we're facing one another. My palm finds her cheek and I cradle it. This poor woman. Just like Helen, life was having fun making her its punching bag.

We remain silent while I drink in every freckle on her flesh. I devour the same expression Helen used to bestow upon me—an expression that said she only needed me to be happy despite the crumbling world around her.

She whimpers again when I bring my lips to her forehead and press a kiss there. Her hot breath tickles my neck and I once again feel the lines being blurred as another involuntary thrill courses through me straight down south.

Embarrassment burns through me like a hot, raging fire when my dick thickens to a semi hard-on and presses into her.

"I'm here now and that fucker won't mess with you," I promise in an attempt to draw her attention away from my cock pressing into her.

"Thank you." Her voice is a husky murmur that only serves to fuck with my dick even more.

"I'm tired as hell," I grumble and roll her back to her other side, away from me, and then pull her back up against my chest again. Her hot breaths on my neck were going to make me do regrettable things so a position change was much needed.

I curl my arm around her taut belly again and she settles back into stroking the back of my hand. Soon, my dick softens and I let out a relieved breath into her hair. I don't want her thinking I'm some kind of horny sicko. I'm not at all interested in her physically—she looks like my sister for fucking crying out loud. But my craving to touch her is intense and it feels so damn good when she reciprocates as it soothes bleeding holes in my heart that even Leesa, despite everything she has given me, can't seem to repair.

Soon, I hear Alex's breaths even out and I drift off with her scent invading my soul and thoughts of her sweet face infecting every crevice of my mind.

# CHAPTER 11

I wake up to a phone ringing—a ringtone I don't recognize. It becomes easy to ignore though when I get a gulpful of the sweetest scent I've come to recently love.

Helen.

Well, Alex.

Her leg is thrown across my middle and the bare, inside part of her thigh is resting on the lower part of my belly. The fingers of one hand are tangled in her hair while the other have her wrist caught in a death grip. It's as if I thought she was going to disappear on me while I slept.

"Alex," I grumble out, my voice gravelly from sleep. "Someone's calling you."

She moans as she awakes and it only serves to arouse me, much to my dismay.

"Alex," I try again as I release her wrist and run my fingers down her ribs, slightly tickling her so she'll wake up.

"Stop," she whines. Her thigh slides over my cock and my mind goes black with pleasure. My body pulsates to thrust against her leg like some horny fucking dog.

This is wrong.

Fuck. Fuck. Fuck.

*Think of Grandma. Think of Leesa. Think of any god-damned thing besides the way her bare thigh rubs against your dick through your jeans.*

Everything about this is twisted and I exhale in a rush, hoping to rid myself of my erection in the process.

Growing some balls, I grab onto her knee and push her the rest of the way off me, ignoring the jolt of gratification at the way her body felt touching the most sensitive part of me.

"That's my mom's ring tone," she gripes. I cringe realizing that she's awake and has just witnessed my erection.

"Alex, I'm sorry," I hiss and run a frustrated hand through my hair. "Your leg was there and—"

She sits up and runs her thumb over my lips, shutting me up. Her dark hair is a mess and I can't fucking believe how much she looks like Helen right now, peering down at me with compassionate, glowing blue eyes.

"You're a man and a man's body reacts when his dick is touched. I know you weren't disrespecting me if that's what you're worried about."

I let out a breath I'd been holding. "Thank you, Alex."

She climbs out of the bed and my body immediately chills at her loss. I watch her straighten out her dress that now has wrinkles all over it, as she locates her phone on the desk. While she checks her phone, I slip out of bed and stalk toward the bathroom, careful to keep my raging hard-on out of view.

Locking the bathroom door behind me, I walk over to the toilet and yank my offending appendage out so I can take a piss. But I don't need to piss, not really. What I need is…

I pull on it with one long stroke and my eyes roll back. My attempts to visualize Leesa are futile because I can hear Alex's loud voice on the other side of the door. Blue eyes are all I can think about as I yank on my cock, punishing it for twisting my already fucked-up head.

Pleasure is coursing through me as I tease myself with a much needed release when she knocks on the bathroom door. I jerk my hand away from the part of me that's brutally throbbing in protest.

"Yeah?" I question in a breathless manner. Guilt is stabbing me as I realize that I was whacking off to someone who wasn't Leesa. And furthermore, someone who looks like my sister.

What the fuck is wrong with me?

"That was Mom. Something happened to Dottie and she was checking on me. She asked if I had seen you, Henry." Her voice drops low, "But I lied and told her no."

I push my cock back into my jeans and fasten them. As I wash my hands, I catch a glimpse of my reflection. A fucking horror story stares back and what's worse is the inside is even more disgusting.

Tearing my gaze away from the mirror before I smash it to bits, I unlock the door and swing it open. Alex regards me with crossed arms and a worried look.

"Why is your mom looking for me?" I question as I stalk

over to the closet where I hung up my shirts and yank one from the hanger.

Alex's eyes skim over my chest before she answers me. "I don't know but I said I'd let her know when I saw you for breakfast. But then she asked me to cancel our breakfast."

This time, my phone rings, and the guilt is back. Leesa.

"I need to take this," I grunt as I pull the shirt over my head and stuff my arms through the openings.

Alex begins collecting her keys and purse from the desk while I answer.

"Hello?" I ask, my breath ragged.

"Hey baby," Leesa's sultry voice rings out. "How are you doing? Did you get anymore writing done?"

I scrub my scarred, scruffy cheek with my palm and steal a glance at Alex before answering. "I've been doing some character profiling."

Not a lie.

Alex raises an amused brow at me.

"Hmm," Leesa hums into the phone. "I'm coming to see you."

My stomach bottoms out and I want to throw up. As much as I miss the fuck out of my wife, things are a mess in my head right now. "I, uh," I mutter but don't have anything else to say.

Alex mouths, "I'll see you later," and slips out the door without another word. With her exit, the life in me is sucked out with her.

"Leesa," I groan, hating what I'm about to tell her, but I need her help.

"What's up, baby?"

I stroll over to the window and see Alex climb up into the driver's seat of her mother's Tahoe. She dons her oversized sunglasses and applies some lip gloss before hightailing it out of the parking lot.

"I met someone…" I trail off.

"Oh, a good character for your book?" she questions, her voice tight. "I saw your excerpt on Facebook."

I'm still staring out the window and scratching my jawline as I try to figure out how to tell her this. There's no easy way.

"I met a woman who looks like Helen."

Something clatters in the background and Leesa's breath causes the line to go raspy. "Hank." There's a concerned twinge to the way she says my name.

"Yesterday, the car that I nearly hit, was this girl—this, er, woman. Anyway, I got out to help her and I was fucking stunned as hell to see my sister looking back at me."

She is silent for a moment, digesting my words. "She's not your sister, baby."

"Yeah," I grumble, pushing thoughts of how my cock responded to her back into the depths of my mind. "But, she looks just like her and even acts a lot like her. And her laugh…"

I close my eyes and envision Alex's pink lips tugging into an amused grin.

"Jesus, Leesa, she's exactly like my sister."

"So what then? You helped her and drove to Blue Hill?"

With a grunt, I stride over to the desk chair and plop down. "I gave her a ride. We talked. Her mom is the sheriff."

This gets an overwrought reaction from my wife. "What?

131

Hank, why do I get the feeling there's more to this? And I don't think it's a good idea for you to be hanging out with some sixteen-year-old girl that's the daughter of the sheriff while you're supposed to be working."

She's frustrated with me.

"Baby," I sigh and roll my finger across the pad of my laptop so it will turn on. "She's not sixteen, she's eighteen."

"I see," she clips out in a tone that makes me thinks she's jealous. "Hank, promise me you'll stay away from her until I get there. My parents will be back from Aruba tonight and I'll drop the kids off with them so I can leave out in the morning to come see you."

The idea of having her here with me is both comforting and the cause of great anxiety. If she's here, I can take my mind off of Alex. But, if she's here, I can't very well see Alex and that stresses me the fuck out because I'm already twitching to see her again.

A knock on the door startles me and a relieved grin spreads over my face. "Someone's here," I tell her as I stand. "I need to go but I'll call you after I get some writing done."

The knock is louder this time and I stride toward the door.

"I love you," Leesa says. "Please just listen to what I said. You know I am supportive of your therapy and coping but I feel like this girl isn't therapeutic, but damaging instead. Stay away from her and I'll talk to you soon."

I tell her what she wants to hear and hang up so I can answer the door to who I hope is Alex. But when I twist the knob and pull open the door, a different angel stands in my doorway.

"Mr. McElroy," Holly greets, her voice dripping with venom. Okay, so a very pissed off angel.

I'm once again affected by the fact that this woman looks like the older version of my sister.

"Come in," I blurt out and then do a cursory sweep over the room to make sure Alex hasn't left anything damning.

She follows me into the room and I see her eyes drag over my things as she does an internal cataloguing of everything. "Look, I'm going to cut to the chase here."

I saunter past her and sit down on the bed, motioning for her to sit at the desk. "Then by all means, please do."

Her lips purse together in an angry line as she sits. "Henry, Dorothy Cosgrove was murdered last night."

The name means nothing to me.

"Sorry to hear that," I state. "Were you close to her?"

Her nostrils flare in sudden anger at my uninterested tone. "Yes, in fact, you met Dottie just yesterday at the station. Kind of convenient that she shows up dead after seeing you."

I scowl. "I didn't speak two words to the woman so I don't really understand why you're here telling me this."

"Well," she continues, "she was killed from having her head bashed into the floor of her front porch. Does that sound familiar?"

I gape at her. "Like in my book?"

Her face turns bright red with anger. "Yes, like in your book. Where were you last night between the hours of two and four in the morning?" she demands.

"Asleep. I was asleep," I blurt out.

She stands from the desk chair and walks over to the

trash can. "Was Alex here this morning?"

Fuck. "Um, I um," I stammer.

Her face is furious when she snaps her head to look at me. "What does some sick, married fuck want with an eighteen-year-old girl he just met yesterday?" she snarls.

I clench my jaw and wince in pain. Every now and again, I forget that half the teeth in my mouth are fake and are precariously attached to my body. Clenching hurts.

"Did you come here to accuse me of all this bullshit because right now, all you have are theories and not proof? I wrote that piece and posted to Facebook just after midnight. That allowed plenty of time for someone to murder Dottie. Why aren't you checking into Ian?" I poke. "That prick was at the station yesterday too."

At the mention of his name, she becomes rigid with fury. "I've interrogated him as well."

"And?" I query.

She sets her jaw and drops her gaze to her feet. "He's been cleared." Her tone is blunt and she sounds unhappy from the statement.

"Sounds like that happens a lot with him," I mutter under my breath. "What about that freaky fuck that was snapping pictures of me yesterday afternoon? Clive something or other. Alex saw him too. Have you talked to him?"

Why the hell do I have to do the sheriff's job for her?

Holly glares at me but for a brief moment, I see doubt. Her gaze softens and she once again looks like Helen. I try not to fuck with her anymore by staring blatantly at her and affix my gaze elsewhere.

"Can you tell me more about him?" she questions in a

defeated tone, clearly unable to tie me to the crime.

"Uh, let's see, he was about my height. A little on the un-fit side. Dark, messy hair like mine but unwashed looking." I reveal what I remember. "Dirty fingernails."

She nods and we both turn our attention to the door when someone knocks.

*Fuck! Fuck! Fuck!*

If Alex shows up while her mom is interrogating the hell out of me, I'm going to be in deep shit.

Holly narrows her eyes at me and storms over to the door. When she opens it and another officer stands on the other side, I exhale loudly in relief, which earns me a suspicious glare from her.

"Find anything, Joey?"

The man shakes his head at her and I drag my eyes over his appearance. A shadow of scruff dots his cheeks and his eyes are red-rimmed. His unkempt hair and disheveled appearance makes me wonder if he even slept last night. I remember Leesa telling me the deputy was a drunk.

"Nothing," he grumbles. "Author boy here drives a black, four-door sedan. Dottie's neighbor, Sharleen, claimed to have seen a white, two-door sedan come through there a couple of times yesterday. Since they live on a dead end, she thought it was suspicious."

Fucking finally. Maybe they'll leave me the hell alone now.

"If you two will excuse me, I have work to do," I say in a dismissive tone as I rise from the bed and stalk over to the door.

"Joey, go to the car," Holly mutters.

Once he's out of earshot, she walks over to me until she's just inches from me. "I don't know who you are but when you show up and someone dies, I get suspicious. I'm also not stupid and know you were with my daughter this morning." She waves her hand toward the trashcan full of food to-go containers—enough for two people. "So help me, if you touch a hair on her head, I'll put a bullet in your skull without thinking twice."

Her threat saturates through to my bones because I know for a fact I will touch her daughter again. And I hope soon.

"We've made friends. She's a nice woman. If she wants to remain my friend, I don't know that there's really anything you can do to stop her," I say with a hint of smugness. "Besides, maybe you should be going after that stupid fuck-up of a mayor instead. Is your job more important than your daughter? Where were you and this proverbial bullet when he was fucking her while under age and impregnating her?"

The slap comes out of nowhere and my jaw smarts in pain from the force of it.

"He's untouchable," she spits out, "and don't think I don't imagine every single night what it would be like to give that bastard what he deserves."

I rub my cheek and pin her with a serious stare. "Holly, I would never hurt Alex," I explain. *She looks like my goddamned sister, for crying out loud.* "But, I can guarantee you that if that man ever hurts her, he'll have me to answer to. And unlike you, I'm not afraid of him."

Her eyes fill with hot, angry tears—*so Helen*—and she storms out of my room, slamming the door behind her.

With a shake of my head, I plop down at my desk and ignore the hundreds of unread messages and emails, especially from that of my agent, and begin writing. Soon, reality is stolen away as I am dragged into the fictional world I've created.

# CHAPTER

W riters block.

Fucking devil.

And the reason why I'm in this godforsaken town to begin with.

Leaning back in the desk chair, I frown at the words on my screen—the blinking cursor mocking me every half second. My brain is all over the place, certainly not focused on my work. All I can seem to think about is her.

Alex.

Leesa knows. She always knows. I hadn't wanted to reveal my secret about Alex, but my wife took a vow long ago to take care of me for better, for worse, for richer, for poorer, in *sickness* or in health, to love and to cherish till death do us part.

My wife takes her obligations to the sanctity of our marriage very seriously. I'd be lying if I said this was my first meltdown in life. In actuality, there have been many times I've lost my footing on the edge and sunk down into the deep end of life.

But my love…

She fishes me out every time. Her love and strength holds me up when I no longer have the mental capacity to do it myself.

And she's on her way—will be here tomorrow.

A thundering in my heart soothes the parts of me that are cracked and wilting.

But, this is also why I can't fucking focus on *Blue Hill Blood*.

With an annoyed sigh, I stand and locate my wallet and keys. It's well into the afternoon, not too early for a drink. Stuffing my wallet into my back pocket, I stride out of my room and lock up behind me.

The drive to The Pelican bar Leesa told me about that appears to be open isn't but ten minutes or so from the inn. As I pull into a nearly empty lot, only a few cars lining the front row, I decide this will do just fine and park.

A nondescript building with a spectacular view of the bay stands as a beacon not for ships but for drunks and it calls to them. Despite the boring edifice with a plain, uneven sign hanging above the door boasting of the name, this place no doubt has heard its fair share of alcohol-laden tales.

I climb out of my car and cursing from a few cars down alerts my attention. Narrowing my eyes, I see a tall man with linebacker shoulders leaned into the window of a car on the driver's side. Their argument piques my attention, sparking some of my creative juices, so I prowl around the cars to be nosy.

"Goddammit, Brenda," a deep voice snarls. "How many times have I told you that when I give you a hundred dollars for groceries, you're supposed to buy fucking groceries? Not scented lotion. Not make-up. Not shitty-ass vitamins that don't do a damn thing."

A sob.

I can't make out what she's saying back to him, so I slink around the car for a better listen. From my vantage point, in front of the vehicle one spot over, I can see the woman. Her mascara is running down her cheeks which are bright red from crying and by the way she's breathing so heavily, it sounds like she may hyperventilate.

"I don't care if those pills help with your hot flashes. You're the one that went off and hit menopause. Not my problem. You wasting my money is a huge problem!"

She wails again, her voice wobbling with a plea.

The ape of a man shocks me when he reaches in the car and pops her upside her nose with the back of his hand. Anger explodes within me. I would never fucking hit my wife. Before I know it, I've charged over to him and have yanked him away from the car.

"What the f—" he starts but I push him hard into the gravel, ignoring the screams of the woman in the car.

The man's eyes darken with rage and he climbs back to his feet, swaying slightly. Nothing but a damn drunk beating on his woman.

"Leave the lady alone," I snap and square my shoulders, preparing to hit him in *his* nose—see how he likes it.

"It is none of your damn business, prissy asshole. Are you wearing fucking makeup?" he growls, "Don't you know we don't want none of your pansy-ass kind here? Go back to California or wherever the hell it is you take it up the ass!"

Anger explodes from within me. All I see is Adam. The taunts. The ridicule. Teasing me for my pink, mottled flesh.

With this idiot, I don't think. I don't bottle it up to write for later like all those years ago.

No.

I'm going to kill him.

Charging forward, I rear back my fist and by the time I reach him, I slam my fist against his cheek. Searing pain detonates in my hand as my bones connect with his. His grunt is his only response as he stumbles backwards and eventually falls on his ass. The woman from the car shoves open the car door and runs to her abuser while I gape at her.

"Billy! Oh, my baby, are you alright?" she cries as she squats beside him.

Billy? The bar. The name. This asshole must be Holly's brother.

He's dazed and his head rolls a little off to one side. I want to knock it completely off. The fool makes no moves to stand but instead allows his spineless wife to fuss and carry on about him. If that were my Leesa, she'd have given me a matching bruise on the other side.

The thought of her calms me and the red evaporates from my vision.

"What in the hell is going on out here?" a familiar voice barks out as they exit the bar.

I snap my head and am thankful to see the deputy, Joey,

I think his name was.

"This man was roughing up his woman," I explain, my chest still heaving from exertion. "I stepped in and he got belligerent so I knocked his ass on the ground."

Joey rounds the car, wearing a white T-shirt and his navy police slacks, and surveys the scene before him. When he fucking winks at Brenda, I remember I'm not in normal society—I'm in a goddamned small town where they don't do shit the right way. I mean, the mayor was fucking an underage girl, got her pregnant, and nobody did a thing. He didn't even get a slap on his wrist.

The rage rears its ugly head once again.

Joey has the sense to realize the impending storm because he leaps into action. "Brenda, sweetheart, why don't you take Billy home? He's clearly had a long day. I'll tell Judy to cover his shift—she was just complaining about needing the extra money," he orders in a friendly tone. "And you, Mr. McElroy, let me buy you a drink, buddy."

Buddy.

I'm not his fucking buddy.

I want to tell him as much but he disarms me with a genuine smile and waves me toward the bar. Wisely, I snap into action and stride through two cars on the other side of where Brenda is helping a still dazed Billy to his feet.

Joey opens up the dark, tinted glass door—the only window into the place—and slaps me in a jovial manner on the shoulder as I enter. As soon as I step through the threshold, I'm assaulted by the smell of cigarette smoke. It burns my sensitive throat with every breath I take and my eyes water. I'm tempted to just leave but when my eyes finally adjust and

I survey the small pub, I realize I'm in a writer's playground.

Several, what I'm assuming are regulars, considering the time of day, dot the barstools, leaning into their drinks with their backs hunched. A sad, soft country song belts out its sorrows from a jukebox behind the sole pool table in the bar. Nobody's playing pool, but a big fellow with a beard sits in a barstool near it, possessively gripping a pool stick in one hand and the waist of an aging woman in far too few articles of clothing, in the other.

"Come, meet Judy," Joey says from behind me and he takes off toward the bar where a young woman with bleached blond hair and tits hanging out of her tank top swipes it clean with a rag.

I unglue my feet from the wood floor and take unrushed steps over to them, eye-balling everyone in the place, cataloguing their features, their sadness, and their pitifulness.

The words "altercation" and "this guy" are whispered before I get there, causing me to bristle.

"So, you think you can cover Billy's shift?" he questions as he plops down onto a bar stool.

Her gaze flickers over to mine as I sit beside him and disgust flashes over her features. But, probably remembering her job depends on tips, she chases the nasty look away and plasters on a saccharine smile.

"Of course, Joey. I'd do anything for Billy. You know that."

Realization washes over me. By the way she fondly spoke of that asshole and by the way she leans over the bar, baring her cleavage, this woman has probably fucked them both at some point.

"Thanks, doll," he praises. "I'll have another Jack and Coke. My friend here would like?"

He tosses me an expectant look. My eyes skim over his dulled from liquor brown eyes, red from drinking nose, and half-cocked lazy grin.

"Do you have wine?" I question, preparing myself for ridicule.

They both laugh and Judy starts making drinks. "Funny guy. What brings you here?"

I groan but watch her ass jiggle in her short black shorts. One glance Joey's way tells me he's doing the same. Our reasons are different though. He'd probably like to bend her over whereas, I wonder how Eli would handle someone like her—with her fake smiles and fake blonde hair.

"Work."

She looks over her shoulder at me and laughs. "Vague much?"

Joey chuckles back, his eyes never leaving her ass. "He's an author. His next book takes place in our town. Ol' Henry here is a *New York Times* bestseller and one of his books is in production for a movie. He's big time."

Judy turns and sets down a Jack and Coke in front of each of us. I frown but grip it with my long fingers anyway.

"Wow, movie man. You write scary stuff? Like Stephen King?" she questions, this time resting her elbows on the bar in front of me, giving me prime view of her saggy tits.

"Something like that but more like James Patterson," I tell her as I drop my gaze into the glass.

Jack Daniels, or hard liquor of any kind, is never a good idea with my conditions. For one, the hard liquor burns the fuck out of my throat. But then, it eventually sets to numbing things rather quickly. Leesa hates when I drink the stuff.

Bringing the glass to my lips, I sniff the liquid and decide one drink won't kill me. I sip gingerly and my eyes water at the intense pain that assaults me when I swallow. Two sets of eyes are on me as I choke down the drink.

"You weren't kidding about the wine, were you babe?" Judy laughs and Joey joins in.

"This fellow's from New York City," Joey says in an exaggerated tone.

They're having fun at my expense.

"New Hampshire," I bite out with a little more anger than I intended.

Both of them seem to be enjoying my presence and they burst out into amused laughter. Joey slaps my shoulder, nearly causing me to spill my drink all down my chin.

"I told Holly you weren't a killer. People like you are usually victims," he says with humor, but a threat weaving its way through his teasing words.

Another patron comes through the door and Judy turns her attention to him. I drag my gaze over to Joey and see that all jokes are gone. He's glaring at me.

"You better watch your ass in Blue Hill, Henry. This town is close and we all help each other. Billy is my best friend and the brother of my partner and our sheriff, Holly. We protect our own."

I narrow my gaze at the jerk as he chugs down the rest of his drink.

"Like you protected Alex?" I demand under my breath.

His eyes flick around to make sure nobody is listening to

our exchange and he leans closer to me—close enough that I can smell the liquor on his breath through the clouds of stale smoke in this joint.

"What do you know about Alex?"

Leaning away from his stench, I take a bigger gulp of the amber liquid and enjoy the fact that it doesn't burn as badly this time.

"I know that your mayor fucked up big time and you idiots didn't do anything about it."

His face darkens with fury. "Don't say another word about that shit. It's been dealt with."

I laugh without humor and pin him with a menacing glare. "By sweeping it under the fucking rug? That's how you dealt with it? Just like you dealt with that wife beater outside?"

He stands so suddenly that I think he might try to kick my ass right here in the bar. I don't let him intimidate me and slowly drink the Jack and Coke which is quickly giving me liquid courage.

"Mr. McElroy, is that you?"

Joey and I turn to regard the voice. That weirdo Clive from yesterday slides into the seat beside me. "You promised me a drink—to pick your brain—but I imagined it would be coffee not liquor. It's all good," he says with a grin, "Miss, I'll have a Shirley Temple."

My lips quirk up into a smile and I decide I'm happy for the reprieve.

"Judy, put my drinks on my tab. This guy can pay for his own shit. Lunch break is over. I have to get back to the station," Joey barks out and saunters out of the bar without so much as a glance backwards.

I've pissed him off.

Good.

"I can't believe he's going back to serve and protect drunker than a skunk," I muse aloud.

Clive gapes out the glass door window. "I, uh, wow."

Judy, not at all impressed with the two of us, now wears a frown that ages her ten years. She drops another Jack and Coke down, this time in front of Clive, and storms off to help other patrons.

Clive stares down in confusion into his glass. "I ordered a Shirley Temple."

I shake my now empty glass at him. "I ordered wine. Apparently all they sell in this dump is Jack and Coke."

He seems perturbed by the action and I can't help but commiserate. At least I have someone, besides Alex, in this town that likes me.

"So, what do you want to know?" I probe as he gingerly sips the drink.

"Ew, this is sick." He shoves it my way but his face lights up at my question. "Oh, God. Like everything. When you wrote *Jacksonville Blood* back in the nineties, did you know you were going to publish? It was harshly written in comparison to your other novels. Almost like journal entries."

I think back to when I was in college. Those were some rough times as well, until I met Leesa. I'd gone to Jacksonville, Mississippi with my grandma for a family reunion. The people were scummy and rude, but it made for a perfect breeding ground for my book. Several family members, cousins twice removed, would nosily ask about what happened that night.

Grandma, ever the hero, would always put them right in their place and tell them to mind their own business. It sucked being a grown man yet still needing Grandma's protection from the big bad universe. But, without her protection from the mocking world, I'm not sure I could have survived back then.

"Well, it was my first book. Of course it wasn't as smoothly written as the rest. It was the birth of the Kill Town series and it was a messy one. I think each book gets better and better," I say, slightly in defense to my work.

His nose is snarled up in disgust as I, now rather easily, drink down my second glass. "I wasn't saying it was bad. Just different. Okay, new question. Last night, you posted on Facebook a new teaser. Now, all over the local news is the story of how an old woman was brutally murdered. Seems coincidental."

He's watching my face for a reaction—some sort of indication that I was the one responsible. I narrow my eyes at him. "What are you insinuating?"

My like for the guy is gone as he not-so-blatantly accuses me of murder.

"I'm not insinuating anything. It just seems coincidental that the woman had her head bashed in on the wood planks of her front porch, just like in the story."

I drain my glass and slam it down before regarding him with suspicion. "Wood planks? That porch wasn't described in my story and the police never said anything about that."

His cheeks redden and he glances away. "Um, so what was the first piece you ever wrote?" he questions, changing the subject so fast I nearly get whiplash.

My mind is still reeling at how he has such a vital piece of information. I'll have to find out where he's staying so I can pass on the information for Holly to go investigate. I don't trust this guy who's so easily inserted himself into my life.

Judy, out of nowhere, sets two more drinks in front of us. This time, there's a cherry in his drink. What a smartass.

I meet her gaze and send her a threatening look that says, *Keep it up.* She has the sense to scurry off to do more work. Clive pushes his glass over to me, not before stealing the cherry first though.

"*Twenty-three Ways to Kill Adam,*" I say as I take a swig of the liquor that warms me from the inside. Since I skipped lunch while writing, I'm beginning to feel the effects of the liquor and my vision blurs.

"How did I not know about this? I've studied so much about you and your work but this is news to me," he says in astonishment.

I rattle the ice in my nearly empty glass and take a swallow before answering. "I never published it. It's sacred to me and close to my heart."

Clive pouts at my answer and glances at my now empty glass. "Throw me a bone, man. I'm your biggest fan. I swear I won't tell a soul. What was it about?"

I snort with laughter. "The title *is* the synopsis."

He frowns.

"Fine, okay," I chuckle, feeling loose from the alcohol. "Adam used to tease the hell out of me. I wrote it as a form of therapy. I'm sure I could get sued for that shit if it ever got out. That's our secret."

His bone.

Clive's features light up in a joyous manner and I decide I kind of like him gushing over me. So, I throw him another bone.

"What's your email? I'll send you an excerpt."

"W-what?" he stammers. "Are you serious? Oh my God!"

My laughter booms through the quiet bar as I revel in his love for my work. While he fishes in his pocket for something to write on, I down the next glass as well. If Leesa were here, she'd be having a shit fit.

I clumsily yank my phone from my pocket and attempt to text her. The numbers blur and I frown at the realization of how drunk I am.

"Do you want me to type something for you?" Clive asks.

He seems concerned, so I hand over my phone. "Tell Leesa I love her."

His hands greedily take the phone from me and he sets to flying through a text for me. It seems longer than it should but I'm thankful that it will at least not seem that I'm drunk.

"Another drink?" Judy asks in an abrupt tone.

Now there are two Judy tramps.

"Huh? No. Ugh, in fact, I may need to call a cab," I groan as I slide off the stool.

My body is heavy and my knees are weak. They buckle and I flail my arms to grab something to keep from falling. Clive grips my arm with surprising strength and holds me up. He drops the phone into my back pocket and slaps some cash onto the bar.

"I'll take you back to Sunny Inn."

# CHAPTER

A pounding on the door drags me out of my drunken fog and it takes a moment to realize I'm passed out face down on my bed. I grumble and roll out of the bed toward the source of my throbbing headache.

"What?" I snarl as I open the door.

It's now dark outside but the sun is standing in my doorway.

"You're a grumpy-ass old man, you know that?" Alex teases. Her red, white, and blue painted nails are clutched onto her hips and one side is cocked out. This evening, she's wearing a loose, pink tank top that hangs low on her chest, and I have to force myself to look at her face. She grins at me and I lose myself in that smile of hers. So radiant.

"You're annoying. You know that?" I rib back.

I groan when she stretches out her arms and steps against

me. My arms immediately wrap around her thin body and hers around mine. She's warm and smells too good. I'm sucked into the haze that is her and I don't want to let go.

"You stink."

I laugh at her blunt words. "Did you come here to tell me I stink?"

She pulls away and I let out a ragged sigh from the loss. "Yeah, and to see if you were hungry."

Nothing sounds good at the moment, except the shower. *And her.*

"I can eat, I guess."

She giggles and swats my arm. "Shower and I'll go pick up some hot and ready pizza."

Before I can answer, she bounds down the covered walkway toward the parking lot. Stepping out, I watch her as she leaves. She's wearing those same shorts from yesterday and her ass bounces with each step she takes. I wonder why she changed out of her dress.

Memories from this morning infect my brain and I remember Leesa's words.

*Stay away from her. She's not Helen.*

And the more time I spend with Alex, the more I realize that she's *not* Helen. But, it doesn't change the fact that I want to touch her and for her to touch me. She has the same healing power that Leesa has—something deep in my soul craves her.

When she's out of sight, I shut the door but slide the metal latch so she can come back in. The room sways a bit as I turn a little too quickly and I come to terms with the fact that I'm still kind of buzzed. Along the way to the bathroom,

I shed my clothes but stop halfway when I notice a sticky note stuck to my laptop screen.

**_I only read the page you had open and boy was it tempting to go back to read the rest but I refrained because I didn't want to take advantage of you. Happy writing, Clive._**

I rip off his note and crumple it in my fist. While I was thankful for his ride, this shit pisses me off. He had no right to read one goddamned sentence. Tossing it to the ground, I strip the rest of the way and make my way into the bathroom.

I'm not sure how long I've stayed under the steam of the spray stewing over Clive but eventually the bathroom door swings open and clangs against the wall, startling me.

"Jesus, Scarface. What are you doing in there? If you're whacking off, you're taking forever. I'd have had you coming in five minutes. Now get out here already before it gets cold," Alex laughs and slams the door behind her.

All thoughts of Clive dissipate because now she's filled my head with something else. Dirty, raunchy thoughts infect my mind and my dick thickens before me.

_My God, this woman fucks with my head._

I force her out of my head and rinse off. I give myself a few minutes to exit the shower and dry off. By the time I'm finished in the bathroom my dick has relaxed. I don't bother with my wet mop and wrap a towel low around my waist so I can search for something to wear.

When I pull open the door, I realize I'm in trouble again. Alex is sitting cross-legged in the middle of the bed eating a slice of pizza. Her eyes lift to me standing in the doorway and I stand frozen as she skims her gaze along my bare chest to where my towel is hung on my hips.

*This girl.*

She looks just like Helen, yet she's inherently different.

I want to spend time with her—to cuddle with her—but then something sick and sinister knifes its way through my veins. Something that I quickly shove to the recesses of my mind.

"Close your eyes," I grunt out my demand as I saunter over to my suitcase where I know I packed some pajama pants. My stomach grumbles loud enough to send Alex into a fit of giggles.

"You're like a kid," she laughs. "I think if I weren't here to help you, you'd have starved already."

I shake my head and tug out the pants. Dropping my towel, I step into the bottoms and drag them up my waist. Once they're in place, I look over my shoulder to see her watching me with a satisfied smile on her lips.

"I told you to close your eyes. And I would survive," I argue. I stride over to the desk and lift the pizza box. Delectable scents waft out from the box and my stomach whines again. Once I select a big piece of pepperoni, I pull it out and spend a good minute stretching the gooey cheese just to free it.

I lean up against the desk and watch her as I eat. She doesn't take her time and inhales the pizza as if it may be her last slice ever. When she starts licking her fingers clean, I have to turn away from her.

"Why do you like hanging out with me?" I question in a thick, husky voice.

She laughs from behind me and I hear the bed squeak

as she climbs off. Soon, her still wet fingers trail up my spine as she reaches around me to grab another slice. Her breasts graze the outer part of my arm and my cock twitches.

*I don't want her.*

But a part of me knows better.

"You're funny. Smart. Different. And kind of cute," she flirts.

Rolling my eyes, I turn to regard her. "Funny, hell yes. Smart, the smartest. Different, you have no idea. But cute? Even kind of? Fuck off." I flash her a teasing grin and she blushes.

"More than kind of," she admits in a soft voice and once again drops her gaze to my bare chest.

I swallow and narrow my eyes at her. "I'm twenty years older than you, Alex. It would be obvious to anyone why I'd want to hang out with a sassy, beautiful college chick, even though those aren't my reasons. Well, maybe the sassy part. But you? It makes no sense. You don't know anything about my work or anything about who I am. For all you know, I'm a psychopath."

Her lips curve up into a cute smile. "I like older men. They seem to understand the old soul within me. I just clicked with you. I'm not sure how to explain it. And you are cute, old man. Especially without a shirt."

I frown at the dangerous path we're going down. Feeling guilty, I glance around the room hunting for my phone, anything to avoid her flirtatious grin.

"I'm married. Plus…" I trail off. *You look like my sister.* "It just isn't right for us to hang out. My wife will be here in the morning. Maybe you should go."

The words sicken me as they roll off my tongue and the pizza roils in my stomach. When I steal a look at her, she's still staring at my chest but her thoughts are introspective. The pout on her lips fucking kills me.

"We're just friends, Henry," she finally says in defeat. "Don't make me leave."

She's no longer looking at my chest like she wants to lick it. Instead, I see the same sadness Helen used to carry around with her. It fucking guts me.

"God, come here," I order with a growl and tug her over to me. When she begins to cry, I stroke her hair and let her tears soak the skin of my chest. "Shhh."

Her sobs quieten down eventually and I pull away to look at her. "What was all that about? I know you aren't all up in arms about not seeing me, having only known me for two days. What is it, Alex?"

Shame washes over her features and she diverts her watery blue eyes back to my chest.

"I ran into Ian again."

Rage surges through my veins. "What happened?"

She laughs out a hollow, bitter laugh. "What does it matter? Ian can say whatever the fuck he wants in this town. He runs this place. I don't even know why I came back for the dumb fair this weekend. Stupid. I'm not over him or the loss of the baby."

Her truth surprises me and I quake with an animalistic need to protect her. Much like I would protect Helen, or Leesa, or my girls. No man like Ian should be allowed to walk this Earth.

"Want me to kill him?"

This time her giggle is real and the smile brightens up the room. "No need for that, but sometimes I wish he would find someone else to harass and leave me alone."

We stand in silence and eat for a few more minutes until she speaks up again.

"Besides being cute and sassy, why do you tolerate being around me when you should be working?" she questions and saunters over to her purse.

My eyes skim down her bare legs and I blurt out the truth. "You look like my sister, Helen."

She stops and turns to stare at me. "That's weird."

With a groan I scrub my scarred, furry cheek. "She's dead."

Her lips pout again and I can't take the pitiful look so I drag my gaze to my feet.

"Henry, that's even weirder."

I sigh. "I know. I just miss her so damn much, you know? We were affectionate and close. Cancer had a hit out for her life but Dad robbed the lethal bitch of the chance. My sister was their victim at only sixteen."

Tears well in her eyes and as they spill over, she hastily swipes them away. "Oh."

Oh.

All she has to say is fucking *oh*.

I guess it does sound a bit warped.

"I'm sorry, Alex. If you want to leave…" I trail off but she bends over and begins digging in her purse. Her ass hangs out and I have to look away.

"I don't want to leave you idiot. That makes me feel closer to you, knowing that I remind you of her. It also confuses me," she says when she lifts back up and turns to me. I watch, completely mesmerized, as she chews on her bottom lip while deep in thought.

"Why does it confuse you?"

She hides something behind her back and bounces back over to me. "I just thought, you know, that you liked me. Physically." Her cheeks redden the slightest bit and she bites her lip in an almost bashful way.

"I'm married. Leesa is my everything."

Alex ponders my words. "Not everything. She's not Helen." Her words are grim and they find their way deep into the dark corners of my soul. "Now, which hand?"

Her sudden change of subject has me reeling. "Uh, that one." I point to her left hand and she laughs when she produces a fifth of whisky. Blue eyes sparkle with mischief and I can't help but grin at her.

"I don't drink that stuff," I argue, a tinge of whininess in my voice. "Besides, how did you buy liquor if you're not twenty-one yet?"

She laughs. "Poe hooked me up. Oh, and nice try. I smelled Jack on you earlier. You're not fooling me. Do you want to see what's in the other hand? It's a present for you."

I nod and hold out my hand, unsure what to expect.

When she pulls her other hand from behind her back, the room spins. Reality shifts and my mind flip-flops from past to present. I'm confused.

"Surely you know what this is, old man," she laughs, shoving it toward me. "It's a Rubik's cube."

I snap my eyes closed and shake the misperception from my head. "I don't understand."

"Weren't you born like in the seventies?" she questions, the playfulness fading as she no doubt questions her choice of gift. "Besides, your profile picture on Facebook is a Rubik's cube. For some reason I thought you might like it…"

Dragging my eyes back open, I'm still stunned by the sight of her standing there looking every bit like Helen.

"I need a drink," I rasp out and steal the whisky from her grip.

She frowns when I unscrew the cap and take a long pull from the liquor.

"Henry, I'm sorry. I didn't know it would upset you."

Once again, big fat crocodile tears in her eyes do me in. I press my eyes closed and sip from the bottle, slower this time. The burn in my throat is painful but the ache in my heart is excruciating.

Taking the bottle with me, I crawl into the bed and prop up the pillows. Like old times. Alex watches me with a careful look and waits for me to say something. With a sigh, I pat the bed beside me.

Her smile is small but she walks over to the side of the bed I'm sitting on and hands me the cube.

"What color?" I question as I take it from her.

*Never blue.*

*Green, always green.*

*Green, always green.*

*Green, always green.*

*And then red.*

"Blue."

My heart freezes in my chest and the smile on my lips is immediate. "Really? Blue?" I say in disbelief. She nods and I feel almost high from that one word. "Get comfy, Alex. I'm about to show you my mad skills," I tell her with a smug grin.

The uncomfortable air has dissipated and she smiles back, once again the free bird I first met.

"Okay, but I'm stealing a shirt," she says and bounds over to the closet. "Close your eyes."

Her words mock me from earlier and I disobey. Taking another long pull on the alcohol, I watch with sick pleasure as she turns her back to me and peels off the pink tank revealing a black bra underneath. My fingers twitch to drag the tips along her flesh there—to see if her skin will raise with goosebumps.

"I want to touch you," I murmur, not entirely sure that she even hears me.

She shimmies out of her shorts and the matching black thong barely covering her hypnotizes me. Her small ass jiggles as she works to find the openings of my T-shirt. The material is soon over her head and slides over her skin, robbing me of the images I'd like to see more of.

She crawls onto the bed beside me and steals the liquor. "Damn, it's a good thing I brought two bottles. You downed this thing."

My skin heats at her words and I cringe realizing I've been drinking too much. Again. In the same day. Leesa needs to hurry and get here. Things are starting to wobble out of control.

"Blue," I grumble and begin rapidly twisting and turning the cube. It takes longer than it did when I was a kid, but soon I'm able to hand it over to her which earns me a squeal of excitement.

"That's so freaking cool," she gushes. "Must have taken *years* of practice."

Her dig on my age makes me want to punish her—the way I'd punish Helen. "Take it back," I tease with a growl as I dig my fingers in a playful manner into her ribs.

She screams out laughing, clearly ticklish as hell, and I have to struggle in my inebriated state to hold her down. Soon, I have both her hands pinned above her head while she lies flat on the bed underneath my straddled legs. My victim.

"S-s-stop!" she howls as she wiggles.

I don't stop tickling until her face is red from laughter and tears are streaming down.

"Ready to take it back?" I taunt, dragging my fingertip along the area that drives her wild.

Ever the sassy-ass woman that she is, she shakes her head no. My finger pauses its journey and I cock an eyebrow at her. "Are you sure? Because I could go all night."

Her eyelids flutter and she squirms beneath me. "You could go all night, huh?"

Once again, she forces thoughts into my head that aren't right. Yet, my cock hardens in response.

*Where is Leesa when I need her?*

My grip must have loosened on her wrists because she frees one and strokes my thigh. It doesn't do anything to alleviate my hard-on.

"I want to tell you a secret," she whispers. "Come here."

Dropping to one elbow, I turn my good ear to her mouth. Her hot breath tickles me and my mind slips into a place it doesn't get to go often. The light begins to dim and darkness rushes past every door and thought in my head. Happy memories are snuffed out as the demons run rapidly by, wreaking havoc along the way. Anger and bitterness rear their ugly heads. Hate for my father batters my soul and leaves me defenseless. Bandages that Leesa painstakingly affixed are ripped off without further thought.

"I want you to touch me too," she murmurs, answering my statement from earlier.

Turning to stare at her, I see that she has freckles, lots of them. The blue in her eyes is almost green. And her hair is redder than I originally thought. Her lips aren't as thin as Helen's. She's different.

*Not Helen.*

*Alex. Alex. Alex.*

A temptress in disguise of an angel.

Her fingers slide up my neck and she tugs me to her. Our lips graze each other's and an electric jolt zaps through me causing what little light is left in me to flicker. It is completely smothered the moment I close my eyes and kiss her and thick, black, darkness takes over.

Tongues.

Open mouths.

Moans.

I want her.

*All of her.*

# CHAPTER 14

Another moan, not a sound I ever heard from my sister, echoes in the room. She slides her legs out from beneath me one by one and allows me to settle my painfully hard cock against the heat of her that I can feel through her scrap of panties and my pajama pants.

"This isn't right," I mumble against her lips as I grind into her, eliciting a sound that I want to hear more of from her.

*God, I need Leesa here.*

"I'm not Helen," Alex murmurs as she scratches her fingernails down my shoulders.

*Not Helen.*

*Alex. Alex. Alex.*

But not Leesa either.

"Leesa," I groan, the ache in my chest stealing my breath.

"Shhh. She doesn't have to know, Henry. Just us."

My eyes roll back when she reaches between us and frees my cock from my pants.

"I'm going to tell her," I hiss and thrust against her hand that's squeezing my dick. "She'll fix this. She'll fix me."

Alex runs her thumb over the tip and I nearly come from the touch. "No, Henry. Please. Let's let this be our secret."

"I want to fuck you—my sister!" I snarl and pop my eyes open to glare at her.

Her hooded eyes meet mine. "I'm not your sister, baby. And nobody but you is stopping us."

She pulls her panties to the side and teases her entrance with my dick. Wet and ready.

"She'll fix this," I groan, praying for strength.

But I'm never strong enough. Leesa's the strong one.

I slam my eyes closed and wade through the black hole in my head that is sucking all signs of life and humanity with each passing second. Surely I can find that one bulb. That one sparkle that can see me through this time. Leesa always promised me I wouldn't have to do this alone—that marriage was about the other carrying the weaker one when they could no longer carry on themselves.

Easing my way into Alex, inch by inch, I hate myself for being weak. Hate myself for being the sick one—the one that always needs carrying. *I need my wife.*

"Yes," Alex gasps when I've shoved myself in to the hilt.

Her body is tight and grips my cock almost painfully. I begin thrusting slow at first and then as I see the woman that resembles my sister moaning out my name in passion, I become nauseous. Fucking nauseous.

And angry.

"Fuck you for making me want this," I snarl and slam my hand over her throat.

Her eyes widen in shock but she grips my wrist in a way that indicates trust. It guts me. For a moment, I feel very much like my favorite character Eli, and I wonder what would happen if I were to not release my grip.

*Would she die?*

*Could Leesa fix that too?*

Of course she could.

But I'm strong. I can control myself. Leesa will be proud.

Alex slips her other hand between us and massages her clit as I pound into her, my grip never waning.

She's purple. And beautiful.

"An angel," I hiss as my nuts begin to draw up into my body, my climax near. "I love you, Helen."

Alex tries to shake her head but my hand around her throat immobilizes her. When her eyes flutter and her massaging slows, I relax my grip. She looks dead.

Like Helen.

*No. No. No.*

"Alex," I cry out and bring my lips to her plump, bloated ones. "I'm so sorry. I'm so sorry."

Over and over again I chant my apologies until her eyes begin to flutter back open. A smile traces her lips and I slam my mouth to hers. I want to fix it—her. Kiss away all her pain.

"Do it again, Henry," she rasps out. "Choke me. Hurt me. Fuck me."

I groan but soon am thrusting hard inside of her. My

hand slides back over her throat but I keep my mouth on hers so I can gauge the breaths she takes.

"You're not Helen," I say aloud to remind us both.

"No, baby," she gasps. "Don't kill me. Take me there but not over the edge."

I suck her lip between my teeth and grip her hard enough that she claws at my shoulder. Pressing harder against her windpipe, I hope to snuff out her breath. Her life. Helen is dead. Why does she get to live over her? It makes no sense.

"Shit," I groan when my orgasm splinters through me.

I mark her from the inside.

My hot seed splashes every part of her tight heat and runs back out the moment my dick begins to soften.

Stars skitter across my vison and weakness takes over. The grip on her throat relaxes and I collapse on top of her. While still inside of her, I listen for signs of life. Did I fuck up too bad? Did I cross the line?

*I need Leesa.*

A small gasp alerts me to the fact that Alex is still alive and kicking. She's weaker than I am and lies there limp and useless.

I'll fix her.

Fix her like Leesa fixes me.

"So good," I praise as I trail kisses along her lips and down her neck. "You're too good to me, Alex."

She shivers as I kiss down her collar bone and between her breasts. Hope isn't lost when she threads her fingers in my hair. I tongue her belly button and taste her all the way down to her bare pussy.

*Leesa keeps a small thatch of hair for me. That's the way*

*I like it.*

Spreading her open for me, I suck the part of her that throbs and pulsates, despite having almost been choked to death. Nipping and sucking and licking for seconds or perhaps hours is all it takes before she's screaming my name in ecstasy.

When she's come down from her high, I hold her.

Then I bathe her.

I feed her cold pizza.

I bring her the second bottle of liquor.

She lets me hold her some more.

And as my eyes drift closed, I can't help but think that Leesa would be so proud.

*I fixed it.*

<hr />

I'm tired. So fucking tired but I can't get the thoughts from earlier out of my head. Alex breathes softly with sleep beneath me and I take a minute to stare at her. I press a quick kiss to her lips and slip out of bed. It's sometime in the middle of the night, but I need to clear my head. I fumble around the dark until I'm dressed and snatch my keys from the desk before heading out.

The September air is still warm and I know I'll need another shower after this. Trotting over to my car, I get in and try to determine where it is I'll drive to. I'm still a bit tipsy but my vision isn't blurred or anything so I set out. The clock on the dash says one fourteen so I consider heading to The Pelican. But seeing Judy or Joey again might make me fucking crazy so instead I just drive.

My drive ended up being therapeutic. And when I park in front of the Sunny Inn, I decide that I need to write. My creative juices are flowing and I'm desperate to get more of this story down.

I all but jog back to the room and breathe a sigh of relief that Alex is still stretched out in my bed, alive, and sleeping. After a quick shower to wash away the heat of the night, I settle in at the desk and begin tapping away.

---

*She's alive.*

*For now.*

*And while Candace recovers from the last dose of torture in his basement, Eli decides he needs a stiff drink.*

*He pulls up to a decaying bar, one he'd rather not step a spoiled foot into, but knows that he must keep a low profile. The place is empty. All but one, white, Crown Vic sits in the parking lot.*

*Empty is good.*

*Eli climbs out of the car and rolls his neck around on his shoulders. It's been grueling work for him, testing the limits of her life day in and day out. He's had his little science project in his basement for a week now. And he hasn't yet grown bored of her.*

*The bitch still moans like a whore when he fucks her.*

*Eli swallows down the desire to drive back home and choke the shit out of her. It's way more fun when he draws it out. However, he's craving a hit to kill and soon.*

*"Be right with you," a female says as he enters the dingy bar.*

*A bleached blonde is talking animatedly to a man sitting on a barstool. They laugh together and he decides he hates their laughs. What he loves, though, is the anonymity this bar brings. He can have a drink and not get noticed or bothered.*

*Sliding onto a stool at the far end of the bar, he waits for the bartender to take his order. But after he's been waiting for at least five minutes, he finally looks down to see them shamelessly flirting. Anger blooms in his chest. His hands fist out in front of him on the bar. All he wants is a goddamned drink.*

*Eli sends her a scathing look and eventually she rolls her eyes at the man she's been flirting with. With a not-so-casual point in his direction, she lets the man know she has to help Eli. When she finally makes it over to him, he barks out his order.*

*"Dirty martini." His tone is sharp.*

*She laughs at him and he bristles with fury. How dare she act like he's a nuisance? Someone ought to teach this bitch a lesson.*

*"Sure thing, city boy. I'll get right on that," she says in a sarcastic tone and saunters off toward the bottles.*

*He bites his lip and watches her ass as she walks away. Her flabby ass needs more coverage. Those tight, black shorts let it all hang out and he's fucking disgusted. At least Candace in the basement has a nice body and supple lips that he likes turning purple.*

*The thought of Candace warms him and he feels a smile playing at his lips. He misses her. Actually misses the twat. Not that he's delusional into thinking they could be girlfriend and boyfriend or some shit like that. More like…he misses fucking her while he chokes her to the brink of death. He loves when her eyes become bloodshot and eventually lifeless. It gives him a hard-on just thinking about it.*

*Perhaps he'll reward her with some food later. He honestly can't remember the last time she ate and he doesn't think she can live off of his sperm alone. Feeding her is definitely a priority when he gets home.*

*"Redneck martini in a dirty glass," the blonde bitch laughs as she sets down an iceless glass of an amber liquid in front of him.*

*"What the hell is this?" he snarls in disgust, his nostrils flaring at the ridiculous drink.*

*"City boy, we don't carry your fruity drinks here. In this town, you drink like a man," she says and nods her head toward the man who is now glaring at Eli.*

*"And men drink Jack and Coke," he growls at Eli.*

*The. Fucking. Nerve.*

*With eyes on the blonde hag, Eli drains the abomination and has to choke the shit down. And instead of slamming the glass on the countertop like most normal people would, Eli stands and hurls it at her face. He's not normal after all. The moment the glass connects with her nose, she screams in pain and crumples to the floor.*

*"What the fuck?" the man barks out and reaches for something on his belt. He sways as he withdraws a gun. "Hands in the air. I'm placing you under arrest!"*

*Eli doesn't give the man a chance to steady his shaking hands and charges for him, running low. Seconds later, his head connects with the man's belly and he tackles him to the ground. Eli, being younger and more fit, easily wrestles the gun from the man. He wants to shove the gun into his mouth and shoot him, painting the shitty floor with his blood, but he doesn't.*

*No, Eli craves to feed his earlier need. The one he hasn't fulfilled with Candace because she's just too much fun to toy with.*

*Tonight, these two shit-stains are paying the ultimate price for how they treated Eli as if he were the filth.*

*He can hardly contain his excitement as he yanks the gun away and stands up. The bitch still wails from the floor on the other side of the bar and the man before him is blurting out a string of curse words.*

*He could just shoot them both. Make it look like a murder suicide.*

*Too easy. Not much fun.*

*A million different ways to murder these two brainless idiots flit through his mind. Unfortunately, the blonde bimbo robs him of his thoughts when he hears her speaking to 911.*

*"Y-y-yes, he hit me! Come quick!"*

*Rage explodes from within him and he aims the gun at the cop. The pull of the trigger is a quick one and the bullet hits the cop in the throat. Eli pauses for a blissful moment to watch the blood surge from the hole in his neck. When the man falls on his back with a sick thud, the blood spurts at first and then bubbles from the chunk that was torn from him. The man's eyes lose their clarity with each passing second and he bleeds out in a quick flash of a moment.*

*Eli hates that he couldn't spend more time enjoying his death.*

*Unfortunately, he has another problem to deal with.*

*Careful not to step in the blood, he sidesteps the body and* stalks around the bar. The blonde is crouched, hissing into the phone, blood running from her nose.

She looks sort of pretty with wild, frantic eyes and a swollen fucking nose. Storming over to her, he yanks the phone from her and turns it off.

"Don't hurt me! Leave me alone!" she shrieks.

Her shrieks are exhilarating. He wants to hear them all night long but there isn't time for that. He'll have to go back and make Candace shriek instead.

Swinging the gun across her temple, he watches in satisfaction when she falls over onto some stacked glasses in a crate under the bar. They clatter and she moans. He aims the gun and fires the rest of the rounds at her ugly face.

When she stops twitching, he finds the glass he drank from that broke her nose but somehow remained intact and picks it up. Using a cloth from the counter, he thoroughly cleans her phone and the gun. Striding back over to the dead cop, Eli carefully pries open his hand and wraps his fingers around the weapon.

Snatching up his souvenir glass from the countertop, he struts out of the bar and cleans the handles of the door on the way out.

He misses Candace and can't wait to see how she likes his new glass.

Will her nose make the same popping nose when he throws it at her?

# CHAPTER 15

I awake to the sound of my phone going fucking crazy. What in the ever-loving hell is going on? Grumbling and squinting at the morning sunshine that beams in through the window, I slip out from under Alex and stumble toward the source.

*Linda. My annoying agent.*

"What?" I snap, my head throbbing as I try to ignore what happened last night with Alex.

"Oh, sugar, cut the grumpy routine. You're really making the publishers happy with your teasers. Activity is insane. Insane I tell you, on both Twitter and Facebook!" she gushes. "The longer excerpt you posted last night was enough to send the social media community into an uproar. Your rank on *Adair Village Blood* has improved and you're back in the top ten again, Hank!"

Her bubbly attitude grates on my nerves and I want to hang up on her.

"Okay. That's great, Linda," I grumble and steal a glance at Alex. In this light, her neck is exposed and an ugly purple bruise is visible. *Shit.*

"Anyway, I just wanted to call and tell you to keep up the good work. Talk soon!"

I hang up and notice that I've missed several calls and texts from Leesa. My heart aches from missing her. She can't get here soon enough.

"Who was that?" Alex rasps from the bed.

I chance another look at her and remorse washes over me. A good night's sleep has helped clear my head and I can't help but feel guilty at what I've done to her.

Crawling my naked ass back into bed with her, I pull her into my arms.

"Alex, I'm sorry you ever got involved with me," I sigh. "I have issues."

She turns her face to look up at mine. The sass is back and she arches an eyebrow at me. "Henry, you gave me the most intense night of my life. What happened in here last night was special."

I close my eyes and wonder how Leesa will fix this one. This time is different.

"You should leave," I growl, hoping the sharp tone of my voice scares her away from me.

It doesn't scare her and I realize this the moment her small hand closes around my limp cock. Of course it jolts from her touch and I lean back against the pillows closing my eyes.

"Go Alex. Before it's too late."

I groan when the sheets slip down my chest and her hot breath tickles my sensitive flesh as her mouth lowers on my now hardening cock.

"Alex," I say through clenched teeth. "Oh, God."

The beautiful woman has her way with me. And I allow it. I lose myself in memories of my story. How Eli handled the cop and the bartender. How Candace remains alive in his basement.

Soon, I'm coming in Alex's mouth with a grunt and she swallows me down like I'm her favorite drink.

"Let's run away," she purrs as she curls her naked body around mine.

Not an option.

"Hmm," I say in response. I'm biding my time. It shouldn't be long.

"I could make you happy, Henry. We could make love. You could hurt me. The two of us get on so well. It's perfect," she says with a sigh and I can't help but wonder if she had the same delusions with Ian.

"I'm married, Alex. You're an amazing girl. What we've done is not right though. Leesa is coming and she won't be pleased. My wife is my world."

She straddles me and her mouth finds mine. In between kisses she murmurs, "I don't understand. You're letting me do these things to you, yet you talk as if she were to walk through that door right now, you'd drop me like a bad habit. Do I not satisfy you? Do you not feel this, Henry?"

I yank her to me and kiss her hard as she slides herself over my length. The woman fucks me like there's no tomorrow and I can't keep a thought straight in my head.

"I feel you. God, I feel you."

"Good," she moans. "Don't leave me. Don't push me away."

Her tight heat clenches around my dick and I explode with my orgasm within her. "Shit!"

Alex shudders and screams my name out in ecstasy. My climax pumps into her until I have nothing left to give.

When we've both relaxed, I hold her to me, relishing in our last moments together. Soon, she'll be gone. Soon, Leesa will fix this.

She's just begun to doze against my chest when I hear a click on my door followed by it swinging open.

Leesa.

Leesa.

Leesa!

"Oh, Hank."

"Leesa."

Alex, still on my cock, sits up and stares over her shoulder in shock. My wife, my beautiful angel, stands in the doorway. Her messy hair is piled up on top of her head and her face is free of makeup. She's the most gorgeous thing I have ever seen.

"You. Shower, now," she says in the same firm tone she uses on the kids. "Alex, is it?"

Alex turns to me with wild, teary eyes and I shrug my shoulders at her. "She'll fix it."

She scrambles off of me and I get a glimpse of her white ass as she climbs off the bed. "Fix what, Henry? There's nothing to fix. We fucked. Two adults. *Fucking*," she hisses at my wife.

Leesa's lips purse into a firm line as she closes the door behind her and locks it. "Listen, little girl, you've gone and messed with something you had no right messing with. Not only did you apparently fuck my husband, but you opened up a goddamned can of worms. Now get in the shower and wash my husband from your body before I drag you in there and do it myself."

Alex shoots me a horrified look but I turn away.

She bursts into tears but wisely heeds Leesa's command and storms into the bathroom. The door slams behind her and we soon hear the shower start.

Leesa turns her attention in my direction and steps toward me.

"I thought you were doing better." The sadness in her voice niggles at my heart and I ache inside.

"I was fine," I murmur. "Until I stopped to help her."

She sits down and pats my leg. "I know, baby."

I want to kiss her. I want to touch her. I want to fuck my wife.

"I'm so sorry, Leesa. She's my Helen," I try to explain.

Leesa frowns. "Hank, I know. But don't you worry, we'll get through this together."

I sigh in relief at her reassurance and lean back against the pillows. My dark world seems lighter and freer now that my angel has arrived.

"I had some great pie at this diner the other day. We should go there for lunch today," I tell her as I slide out of bed. "Poe might hook us up with a freebie."

I find some jeans and pull them on. Once I button them

up, I regard my wife. Tears well in her eyes but she holds her chin high. Falling to my knees in front of her beside the bed, I wrap my arms around her waist and bury my face between her legs. She's wearing jeans but I catch a whiff of her perfume and I groan in relief.

*She's here.*

"I missed you so much," I sigh and playfully bite her thigh.

Her smile is evident through her voice. She threads her fingers in my hair and says, "I missed you too, Hank. I'm sorry I couldn't come fast enough. The kids miss you."

I push her back onto the bed and shove her T-shirt up. Nipping at the flesh of her belly that's marred with scars from having our children, I groan in happiness. I feel content with the familiarity of this. My Leesa is home.

"I miss them so fucking badly. The fair is Saturday. You should have Dave and Barb bring them up. They'd have such a blast."

She moans when I push her shirt up over her full breasts and nibble the flesh that spills over the top of her bra.

"Hank," she gasps. "I love you. Make love to me, baby."

My dick is raw from fucking *what's her name* but I'd do anything for Leesa. "Yes."

"After your shower," she murmurs. "After your shower, I want you, baby."

I groan. My dick is a fucking statue but she's right. I want to be clean and untainted for her.

"Leesa." I look up at her with a serious gaze. "I love you. More than life itself. Thank you for always knowing what to do."

Her unshed tears finally spill over her cheeks. "Never again, Hank. I promise. I won't ever let this happen again."

Her vow sinks its way into my soul and I rejoice. I trust her promise.

"Thank you, Leesa. It will always be you. You know that."

She nods and a beautiful smile graces her perfect lips. "I do know this, baby. And that's why I work so hard for us. For you. You're worth it. Do you hear me, my love? Worth. It. I'll wade through the bullshit and find you every time. Every time. Let's get her out of here, shower, make love, and then have pie."

Perfection.

My wife is absolute perfection.

"Of course, angel."

The shower shuts off and Leesa lifts up on her elbows. "Hank, I need to take care of this."

I groan, not wanting to leave my place bowed at her feet worshiping the woman who protects me. "I know."

Pulling away from her, I stand and help her to her feet. She stands on her toes and pecks me on the cheek before striding over to the bathroom door. The door swings open and Alex meets her gaze in a petulant fashion with one sassy brow raised in slight defiance.

"Excuse me," she hisses through her clenched teeth at my wife.

Leesa steps to the side and points at Alex's discarded clothes from last night. "Get dressed. And, I need you to take this."

Alex and I both stare in confusion as Leesa retrieves a pill from her pocket.

"What? I'm not taking that," Alex snaps as she pulls on her clothes.

I frown at her and shake my head. "Just do as she says, Alex."

Her eyes find mine and they flicker with hurt at my easy betrayal of her over my wife.

"What is it?" Alex questions but refuses to raise her hand to accept the pill.

Leesa sighs in frustration. "It's a morning after pill. Just take it. I know how Hank gets and I can bet every cent I have that you had unprotected sex with him. And I pray you don't have any STDs."

Alex glares at her. "I've only slept with one other man and the day he forced me to have an abortion, I learned through tests taken there that I am free of diseases. What kind of sicko family are you two?"

I drop my gaze to my feet.

Leesa handles the question with ease. "A sicko family that sticks together until the end. Through sickness and through health. You, sweetie, are just an illusion and a distraction."

Sparing a glance at Alex, I see her lip trembling. I feel sorry for her. She didn't know. She could never know.

"You're a spineless asshole, Henry," Alex spits out as she snatches the pill from Leesa.

She tosses it into her mouth and makes a dramatic show of swallowing and then opening her mouth to show my wife. Leesa nods her approval and pulls a wad of cash from her other pocket.

"Here," she thrusts it Alex's way. "Take this and forget you ever met my husband. I'm sorry, but it's better this way."

Alex slaps the money out of her hand and struts past her to her purse that's on the floor. She jerks it up and throws me one last look. "I don't want your money. I'm not a whore. What we had, no matter how short or wrong, was real. Goodbye, Henry. Remember me, the way I look like *her*, the next time you're fucking your old lady."

Leesa gasps and Alex turns on her heel, bolting out the door as quickly as possible.

"I think that went well," Leesa says.

I walk over to her and wrap my arms around her. "I'm so sorry."

She buries her face in my chest. "Baby, I made you a promise a long time ago. Don't you remember that night?"

That night is the first time I felt loved completely and unconditionally. Sure, my family loved me, but with Leesa, it was always different. With Leesa, she loved all of me—even the ugly parts.

I kiss the top of her head and lose myself to the memory.

*"Hank, let me in!" Leesa shrieks from the other side of my dorm room door.*

*Her tone alarms me and I climb off the bed. Not bothering finding a pair of pants, I rush over to the door and fling it open. Leesa, always a fucking knockout, eyes my naked appearance and her lip quivers.*

*"Are you cheating on me?" she hisses, the tears running down her cheeks with no signs of stopping.*

*I follow her gaze to look at the woman in my bed.*

Helen.

"I found her," I whisper in a conspiratorial tone. "She's supposed to be dead, but I found her."

It truly is amazing. One minute, I'm walking to my next class. The next thing I know, I'm running into her. Helen.

"Who?" Leesa sobs. She's so radiant tonight. Her dark hair is pulled into a sleek, neat ponytail. I want to cut the rubber band free and grip her hair as I plunge into my girlfriend. This woman is so fucking gorgeous and I can't ever get enough of touching her.

"Helen," I tell her simply.

She chews on her lip and her sad eyes meet mine. "Hank," she says in a soft tone. "Remember, Helen died."

The happiness of finding Helen is overshadowed by dark memories. Truth of what happened to my sister. Hate for my father rushes through me.

"Then who's that?" I question with a tremor in my voice.

She purses her lips together and lifts her chin. Pushing past me, she strides toward the bed where the Helen lookalike lies immobile, thanks to the pill I dropped into her drink. I admire Leesa's ass in her tight jeans. Last night, when we were both a little drunk, she let me put it everywhere. When I put it in her ass for the first time, she screamed and I came within seconds. I knew then I'd marry her.

"Hank, I'm going to fix this. Come on, help me pick her up."

That night, Leesa *did* fix it. Just like always. Then, we came back to my dorm room and we made love. Things were different after that and it wasn't long before I proposed. She never hesitated in her response.

What Leesa and I have is true love.

She's the strong one and me the weak.

When I fall, she picks me back up and never once complains.

"Let's have another baby," I murmur into her hair as I grab a handful of her ass.

Her giggle soothes my soul that flickers between darkness and light. With Leesa, the light is always there.

"I'm too old," she pouts.

Sliding my hands into her hair, I tug it down so I can see her face.

Sadness graces her features but she attempts to push it away with a playful smile.

"You're not forty yet, baby," I growl against her lips. "The girls would love to have another sibling."

She stands on her toes and brushes her lips against mine. "Okay, yes, Hank. Let's do it."

# CHAPTER

I'm dragging my wife to the bathroom when someone pounds at the door.

"I'll get it," Leesa says in a firm tone, no doubt thinking it might be Alex.

She breaks away from me and hurries to the door. When she opens it, we're both surprised to see Holly and another policewoman by her side.

"Mr. McElroy," Holly snarls, through her tears, "can you tell us where you were between the hours of one and three in the morning?"

I steal a glance at Leesa and her face blanches white.

"I, uh, was sleeping. Here," I blurt out.

Holly pushes past my wife into my room and stalks over to me. Her fury is palpable and I'm stunned by her rage. I don't have time to even flinch when she backhands me hard across my cheek. "You bastard!" she hisses. "You killed my partner!"

I'm still gaping at her, now with my palm to my stinging cheek, when the other policewoman yanks her away from me.

"Holly, calm down. We're here to question him. Not accuse him," she tells her.

Leesa shoots me a panicked look and I frown at her.

"Why would you think I killed your partner?" I demand in an incredulous tone. "I was here all night. Writing. I even posted a new teaser on Facebook. You can check my computer."

Holly's eyes simmer down and she blinks away her tears. "Well, it's kind of funny that you roll into town and bodies start piling up. I'm not stupid, Henry. Now, if you don't have a solid alibi that says you were anywhere but The Pelican where my partner and the bartender were slaughtered, then I'm placing you under arrest."

"I-I-I…" I trail off.

"He was with me, Mom. I spent the night with him. We made love."

I jerk my head to see Alex standing in the doorway.

"What?" Holly hisses at her.

Alex sneaks a glance in my direction. Her tearstained cheeks tug at my heart and I'm mesmerized by her trembling lip. Only hours ago I had that lip around—

"Mother. We had sex. But apparently he prefers his wife over me," she sniffles.

Holly snaps her head back toward me and this time when she charges me, I'm ready for her. Easily, I seize her biceps and twist her around so that her back is to my chest. She's sweating and I pick up the salty scent the moment I have her in my arms.

The other policewoman is fumbling to pull her gun from her holster and I realize this is escalating way too fast.

"I didn't kill your partner. And, I'm sorry about Alex," I whisper against her hair.

She squirms and shouts out obscenities but I grip her tighter.

"I think you all need to leave," Leesa barks. "If you need to talk to my husband, then we'll come to the station and talk to another officer. Apparently you're too close to this case."

Realization must hit Holly because she relaxes in my arms. The other policewoman has her hand on her gun but never removed it. I can see the panic on her face. The wild, darting eyes. Quivering lip. She's young and doesn't know how to handle her boss that's just flipped her shit.

"Fine. Come to the station and make an official statement," she hisses and jerks free of my grasp. Stalking back over to Alex, Holly shoots a venomous gaze at me. "And I want you gone. Get out of my town before I shoot your ass and drag you into the bay."

Leesa takes a step toward her. "Should I mention that little threat in our statement when we come to the station?"

Holly's face reddens. She's furious.

"I didn't think so. Take your bullshit elsewhere. We'll stay until my husband completes his job. And if you come in here again without a warrant or reasonable cause to arrest Hank, then I'll step over your jurisdiction and get the Feds involved. So, back the fuck off."

Holly snatches Alex's wrist and hauls her out the door. Alex shoots another sad look my way and I twitch to go to her. To hug her and make it all better. She can't help who I am.

Leesa storms over to the door once they're gone and slams it shut. "Don't, Hank. Stop thinking about her. She doesn't fit in our equation. You know it's always been complicated for us."

My shoulders sag but I sigh in relief when she hugs me. Her head tilts back and she exposes her pale neck to me. It reminds me that Alex's bruises were gone. She must have been putting makeup on them in the car when Holly showed up.

"You should be pissed at me, baby. I'm toxic for you," I grumble, hating the words as I say them. "Do you ever think of leaving me? Marrying a good man."

Her eyes darken and she glares at me. "Never. You are my husband and my love. Get those thoughts out of your head right now. That girl has twisted you up—everything we've been working on—she's fucked it up in two days. Get her out of your head, baby. I'm here now. Every step of the way. Mom and Dad said they'll keep the kids as long as they need to. I'll take care of you while you write and then we'll leave this ridiculous town. No more depressing talk, okay?"

I nod and steal a kiss. Her full lips are always swollen and needy. Some nights I spend hours nibbling and sucking on them. And what they can do to my cock. It's sinful.

"I see that you're done talking." She laughs the moment my hard-on presses into her belly. "And we'll do just that after our shower."

We made love and cuddled in bed for hours until our bellies began to grumble in protest. I needed to write but couldn't really do that while starving. Now, we're pulling into the diner where Poe works at.

"This is where I ran into that guy," I tell her as I park the car.

Leesa, her cheeks still rosy from the two orgasms I gave her, flits her eyes over to me. "What guy?"

I scrub my cheeks with my palms and sigh. "He cornered me saying he was a huge fan and shit. When he saw I was eating with Alex, he started asking about you which only served to piss me off. I should have told you about her sooner, but I didn't want to just yet."

She frowns at my words. "Hank, you know you're supposed to tell me everything."

Shame courses through my veins. She's right. For the first time in our entire marriage, I withheld my finding "Helen" and tried to fix it all alone. That just blew up in my fucking face. Never again.

"I'm so sorry, Leesa."

She flashes a smile at me that brightens lingering darkness from within me. "Honey, I'm still here."

Her words wash over me and I grin back. "Thank you. Anyway, Clive is his name, turned out to be sort of okay. I ran into him at the bar and—"

"The Pelican?" she interrupts. Hope radiates over her features, her pink cheeks turn even pinker.

"Yeah," I tell her with a little excitement, understanding what she's thinking without her even having to say a word. "I was pissed because the cop and the bartender were being assholes. Anyway, he showed up all star-struck and I decided I really liked the guy. He even texted you for me when I was too shitfaced to do it on my own."

Her eyes widen. "Ahhh, I see. That makes sense now."

My brows furrow in confusion. "What makes sense now?"

"Your text."

Anger rises in my chest as I worry about what that idiot sent to her. "What'd it say? I never went back and looked."

She pulls her phone from her purse and hands it to me. "Read it."

I swipe open her phone and skip past her most recent text. Pulling up my name just below, I glare at the screen.

**Me: Dearest Leesa.My sexy wife.I love you. Each night when we're apart, I dream of tasting every inch of you. Please tell me what YOU dream of tasting…**

My knuckles turn white as I grip the phone.

"Was he trying to fucking sext with you?" I snarl. I'm going to punch the asshole in his Adam's apple the next time I see him.

"Don't worry, baby," she murmurs, "I had a feeling it wasn't you. You never say stuff like that through text. I just ignored it."

I grumble and go back to the list of texts on her phone. The one before mine says Eric.

"Who the fuck is Eric?" I growl.

Her eyes widen and her cheeks blaze. "Nobody. Give me

my phone and let's go eat."

I don't like the way she reaches for it, dead set on not letting me read what her and fucking Eric had to say. Snatching her hand with my free one, I thread my fingers with hers and hold it tightly against my thigh while I read what she and Eric have been up to.

> **Leesa: It's happening again. Sorry, for not calling. I know you're busy and I'm packing to leave.**
>
> **Eric: Is he on anything?**
>
> **Leesa: No. He won't take what he's supposed to—says it interferes with his "process."**
>
> **Eric: Can you make him?**
>
> **Leesa: Possibly. That's why I'm leaving.**
>
> **Eric: I'll call in something stronger. It'll be waiting for you on your way out of town.**
>
> **Leesa: Thanks so much, Eric. You've been incredible through this.**
>
> **Eric: Of course, dear. You know I'd do anything for you.**

Their conversation ends with her sending him a smiley face and him sending her a heart.

"What the hell is going on here?" I demand and read through it again to make it try and make sense. It's like they're talking in goddamned code.

"Baby..." She starts to tremble. "It's not what you think."

I jerk my hand out of hers and my entire body quakes with the urge to hit something. If only stupid Clive were here...

"Then what is it, Leesa?"

She panics and dives a hand into her purse. When she

unearths it, she's holding a pill bottle. I take it from her wobbly hand and read that it's an antipsychotic medication prescribed to me.

"Dr. Lassiter?" I murmur as I read the bottle. "Why do you text with him?"

I'm still hung up on the fact that they text like they're best fucking friends.

"Ever since," she whimpers, "last time… I called him after the last time. Told him about your episodes and how you wouldn't help yourself. He said that as a friend he wanted to help. So now, I just tell him how you're doing and he gives me suggestions or new prescriptions."

My mind replays the last time we went to see him. Tall, muscular guy, not much older than me. Greying hair and bright green eyes. Now I remember those green eyes strayed to Leesa far too many times. Those green eyes lingered on her lips as she spoke. Everything in me screams to gouge out those green eyes with a spoon.

"Are you fucking him?" I snap.

She lets out a choked sound. "What? No! Heavens no, Hank. *I* would never do that to you."

Her words have their intended effect and my heart shatters. *She* wouldn't, but *I* would.

"Is that even legal? He turns into your fucking chum and treats me on the side without my knowing? What the hell, Leesa? I don't even pay attention to the prescriptions you pick up for me. I trust you."

"Stop, Hank. He could get into a lot of trouble for that but he's doing it to help us. This is the only way that's been working. Every time we would see doctors, you said they were all quacks. You actually liked this one."

I do punch something this time. The steering wheel. "That's before I knew he was fucking my wife!"

She yelps and buries her face in her hands. "I didn't fuck him, Hank. Jesus, will you calm down?"

Her back quakes with sobs and, despite my anger, I reach out to reassure her. Splaying a palm over her back, I rub her in a gentle manner.

"I just want to help you," she murmurs through her tears. "That's all I've ever wanted to do."

I stare at the pill bottle in my hand. The pills do fuck with my writing mojo which is why I don't take them, especially when on a deadline. "I'll take these the moment I finish this story. And then," I promise, before my tone turns cold, "I'm getting a new doctor. I'll be more open to what they have to say but we're not going back to that sneaky-ass motherfucker."

Her shoulders hunch in dejection. "Okay, thank you."

She finally lifts up and I lean toward her. "I just get jealous, Leesa. You can't see it but that conversation is nothing but a way for him to get his dick in your pants. You're mine and some asshole doctor isn't taking you away from me."

Slipping my fingers into her hair, I tug her to me. She moans the moment my lips cover hers. So sweet. I kiss her softly at first but as my possessiveness over my wife rears its ugly head, I deepen the kiss, most likely bruising her lips in the process.

"I love you," I groan when I finally stop for air.

Her chest heaves and both of her hands find my cheeks. "I love you. *Only* you, Hank. Always has been and always will be."

Again, her words knife me.

I certainly can't say the same.

Doors rattle in my head with memories I'd rather not think about. The need to latch on to anything that reminds me of Helen has always crippled me with an all-consuming obsession. An obsession that has threatened both my marriage and my sanity on many occasions.

"She looks like Helen," I whisper against her lips in defense.

Her breath hitches and she chokes back another sob. "I know, Hank."

Pulling away from her, I use my thumbs to swipe away her tears. She's so beautiful with her red face and now messy hair. Each time she sniffles or her lip trembles, I want to haul her into my lap. It isn't often that I'm the strong one and she needs me to hold her. But when it happens, I'm always ready.

"Stay right there," I tell her as I climb out of the car.

Running around the back of the car, I make my way to her door and open it. Offering my hand to her, I flash her a rogue grin.

"My lady."

She smiles as she slips a long, bare leg out of the car and accepts my hand. After our shower, she changed into a pair of khaki shorts. And even though they're much longer than Alex's and hide everything my wife has to offer, I still think they're sexy.

"Thank you," she giggles as I pull her out of the car.

Once I shut the door, I push her against the car and kiss her hard enough to steal her breath. My hands roam her delectable body without a care that everyone in the diner is probably getting a show. But the moment my hand slips between her legs, Leesa playfully pushes me away.

"Not here, handsome."

Her tears are gone and she's all smiles again—just the way I love her.

In a reluctant manner, I pull away from her and seal her hand with mine. Together, we walk into the dumpy diner that has amazing pie. This place is hopping with customers and we have to wait about ten minutes before they seat us. Once we've ordered, I admire my wife from across the table.

"Were the girls excited to spend some time with their grandparents?" I question as I sip on the water our waiter dropped off.

Her eyes glitter with pride, like they always do when talking about our girls. "Oh yes. Daddy was going to take Callie fishing on the pond today. Mom and Whitney had a date for pedicures. My parents missed them."

I smile at her and we enjoy a nice late lunch together flirting and talking about our kids. I've missed my wife and the distraction she is from the pain that bubbles and festers inside my head. When Leesa's here, it all fades into black. It's background noise. She's a beautiful song that I can't help but get stuck inside my head.

The squeal of tires in the parking lot causes both Leesa and I to look out the window. An old Camaro, probably as old as Whitney, slams into a parking space. A second later the door swings open and that lanky guy, Poe, pops out of the car.

He's pissed.

A cigarette dangles precariously between his lips as he storms toward the entrance of the diner. With each step, his too-short black Soundgarden T-shirt rises and shows the waistband of his boxers poking out of his slightly sagging pants. His wild, dark hair ruffles in the wind as he stalks this way.

As he nears the entrance and spies me in a booth by the window, he flings his cigarette and fists his hands at his sides, picking up his pace. The second he pushes through the door and the cow bell jangles, letting us know of his presence, he explodes.

"You pervert motherfucker!" he roars as he charges for me.

"What?"

It's all I get before he reaches into the booth and grabs a handful of my shirt. Even though he's kind of skinny, his adrenaline must be fueling him because he drags me out and pushes me to the floor. Leesa, along with many other patrons and diner staff, babble and shriek as I hurry to my feet in preparation to defend myself.

"I love her and you—you—you use her and toss her out like fucking trash!" he spits out and swings his fist at me.

Prepared for him this time, I step out of the way and clock him in the jaw.

"Mind your own business," I snap as Poe stumbles away from me, howling in pain.

"She is my goddamned business!" he snarls back but keeps his distance.

"Take it outside, boys. I'm calling the police," a husky female voice says from behind the counter.

Leesa scoots out of the booth and tosses a wad of cash onto the table. "Come on, Hank. We're leaving. Now."

Poe stalks after us and the moment we're outside he starts screaming again but this time keeping his physical proximity farther away.

"How could you use her like that? She's fucking fragile as shit, man, and you probably ruined her!"

"Sir, you should probably go home. We're leaving and he won't—"

"Are you his wife?" Poe interrupts Leesa with a sneer. "Did you know he fucked the woman I love? Where the hell were you?"

Leesa huffs in anger and points a finger at him. "Yes, I know, asshole. Maybe you should be comforting her rather than harassing my husband. He wasn't the only one in that bed."

Poe's features darken and I swear to God if he says another thing to my wife, I'm going to deck him right here in this parking lot.

"That's enough, buddy," a familiar voice says from behind me.

I chance a glance over my shoulder to see Clive striding to stand between us.

Poe attempts to charge at me again, but Clive stops him and holds him back. "Mr. McElroy, maybe you and the missus should leave. I'll handle this."

Leesa doesn't wait for me to agree and drags me back toward the car. Once we're settled inside and she's driving away from the diner, she looks over and shakes her head.

"Did you make enemies with everyone in this town?"

she questions in a faux annoyed tone. I know better than to think she's mad at me. She knows this is exactly what I need for a good story.

"Not on purpose. But, I have my next scene all lined up," I chuckle.

She threads her fingers with mine and we hold hands the whole way back while I plot aloud where my story is going next.

# CHAPTER 17

"They made fun of me. And you know how I feel about that," Eli snaps, causing Candace to jump. His eyes skim over her appearance and he smiles. She's naked and hangs from the rafters in the basement. Her long legs quiver either from the chill of the concrete that her toes barely touch or from her fear of Eli. Either way, Eli likes it.

"You should have seen her face," he chuckles in a dark tone. "There was nothing left of it by the time I got done with her."

A tear rolls down Candace's cheek and she bites down on the cloth that gags her. The only time Eli removes it is when he wants to shove something else in there. She's learned her lesson about hurting him. He's ingrained that lesson into her head over and over again. Now, she doesn't dare try to hurt him or fight back. The bitch takes it all like a fucking champ.

*"Are you hungry?" he asks in a soft tone.*

*Her eyes widen in surprise. Truth is, he's developing a tender spot in his heart for her. If he can control himself, he'd like to keep her in this basement for weeks or months. Years even. His cock stiffens at the thought of having her at his disposal whenever he wants while he wreaks havoc out in the world.*

*"I brought you some chips," he tells her. "I'm going to cut you down and let you eat. Don't try anything stupid or I'll slit your throat in a heartbeat."*

*She whimpers but nods emphatically.*

*"Good girl," he praises.*

*He unsheathes his big knife that he stole from the old man's basement. It's his favorite and it slices so perfectly. Candace knows this. His eyes flit to her belly where she's no longer bandaged up. She'll forever have the word "bitch" carved into her stomach. He doesn't want her to ever forget.*

*As Eli approaches her, his nostrils flare in disgust. She pisses and shits on herself all day and he's the fucker that ends up having to clean it all up when he gets home. This pet of his is worse than a puppy.*

*He hacks away at the rope and frees the dirty woman. She's weak and crumples to the floor, cracking her head against the concrete.*

*It reminds him of the day Marla paid for her sins against him. The way her skull popped when it hit the concrete just outside his bedroom window. It's a sound that warms and satisfies him.*

*"Well, shit," he grumbles and kneels beside her.*

*She's breathing but her gash on her head has reopened. He lets out a string of curse words but sets to redressing her wounds. The woman doesn't wake up so he binds her wrists behind her and then ties them to her ankles.*

*"I'll be back. I'm going to pick us up something special to eat," he tells her even though she is knocked out and can't hear him.*

*On the way to pick up dinner, Eli decides that Candace needs a bath and he doesn't want to be the one to do it. Maybe he'll find someone to help him. Once he gets their take-out from a hole-in-the-wall diner and is loading it in the car, a Camaro speeds into the parking lot. A goofy-ass guy built like a stick man steps out and adjusts an apron on his hips, clearly late for his shift.*

*"Hey," Eli calls out, seizing an opportunity. "Want to make four hundred bucks?"*

*The guy stops and regards Eli with a nasty smirk. "I'm no homo, man."*

*Eli rolls his eyes. "I don't want you for sex. I need help lifting an engine in my basement to sell to this guy on Craigslist. I'll make eight hundred bucks on the deal. I'm willing to give you half just to get it out of my basement," he lies with ease. "He'll be there soon and said he doesn't want to wait around."*

*The guy seems unsure but the lure of more than he'll probably make all week working at the diner works.*

*"You live around here?" he questions.*

*Eli nods. "A few streets past the post office. I can run you over there really quick and bring you back. That beauty looks like quite a gas guzzler," he states, pointing at the Camaro. "We'll be back in twenty minutes, tops. You'll be a little late for your shift but not too late to get you fired."*

*The guy eventually concedes and strides over to Eli's car. Both men climb into the car and ride in silence over to his house. It might seem awkward, but Eli is comfortable in silence. Apparently this guy is too.*

*"What's your name?" Eli finally asks, eager to be able to call him something.*

*"Bo. Yours?"*

*"Patrick."*

*They pull into the driveway and Eli hopes that Bo doesn't know the old man who now resides in one of the freezers downstairs. Eli makes sure to grab his take-out from the backseat before heading inside. When he risks a glance at the guy following him, he doesn't suspect any knowledge to whom used to live here prior to Eli.*

*"Excuse the mess. The housekeeper is still working on it. I bought the house from a hoarder. It was as-is. Still trying to get order around here."*

*Bo grunts and follows Eli to the door to the basement.*

*"It's in here," Eli says as he opens the door and ushers him inside.*

*Bo, in an unsuspecting manner, walks in front of him and trots down the stairs. He's completely oblivious to what has been living the last couple of weeks down there.*

*"She's just over there," Eli assures Bo the moment they reach the landing at the bottom.*

*Bo turns to see Candace on the floor and stares for what seems like several long seconds.*

*"What the hell? Is this some sort of joke?" he demands and twists around to face Eli.*

But Eli was ready for him and unsheathes his big knife that still has Candace's blood caked on it. "Does this look like a joke?" he questions, waving the knife at the guy.

Bo stumbles backwards a bit and his gaze flits between Eli and his pet.

"I need you to wash her. She stinks something awful," Eli says with a yawn as he walks over to a nearby freezer, setting the food on top.

Bo gapes at him as if Eli is a certifiable nut. Bo is the nut for accepting a ride from a stranger and then following him into his basement.

"I didn't stutter. The sink's over there. Everything you'll need is on the counter by the sink. She's too weak to stand so you're going to need to fill a bucket."

Bo twitches and for a moment Eli thinks the man may charge at him. That would be a fatal mistake.

"Wash the bitch now or I'll cut your cock off and feed it to her. She hasn't eaten much while under my care and might enjoy a little meat."

Bo, clearly a fucking pussy, shudders at his words and scrambles into action. He steps over Candace's now moaning body and heads over to the sink.

"Make sure the water's warm for her," Eli orders.

Bo mutters something under his breath. What the fuck does it matter or some shit like that. It matters because Eli says it matters. If he wants her to have warm water, then Bo better give her warm water if he still wants his dick to remain intact.

Eli digs around in the bag until he finds the burger he ordered for Candace. He pulls a chunk off and walks over to her *while Bo is filling the bucket.*

*"Eat this if you want to live," Eli tells her in a flat tone.*

*Her eyes flutter open and she flashes him a thankful smile. My God, he missed that smile. What he loves most about her smile is making it go the fuck away. He slices the rope between her wrists and ankles, to which she sighs in relief to be freed. When she raises a dirty hand to accept the meat though, Eli swats it away. He pushes the meat into her mouth and watches her as she chews hungrily.*

*"Was that good? Do you want some more?" he questions, a playful tone in his voice.*

*She nods and attempts to sit up. He doesn't want to touch her so he watches as she sits up at a snail's pace. Her eyes are sunk down into her skull and he wonders how close she was to dying had he not fed her. She tries another smile on her cracked lips. The smile makes Eli hard because he knows how beautiful she can be when he wipes it the fuck off her face.*

*"Such a good girl," he praises.*

*Bo eventually finishes with the bucket and takes a step toward Candace.*

*"Ma'am, are you okay?" he questions in a whisper.*

*Eli walks back over to the food and tears off another piece of the burger. Candace follows him with hungry eyes and ignores Bo.*

*"She's fine. Now bathe her. Every inch of her. I want her smelling good enough for me to eat off her goddamn tits if I want."*

*Bo kneels beside her and sets to wringing out a rag from the bucket. The moment the rag touches her skin, she whimpers.*

"Is it too cold?" Eli snarls at her, ready to bash Bo in the fucking head if it is.

She shakes her head and parts her dry lips open.

"Too hot?"

"It's nice," she rasps out.

Bo takes that as permission and begins thoroughly scrubbing her as if she's his pet. The way he lovingly washes every bit of her in such a tender way, makes Eli jealous. He wonders if Bo wants to fuck her. By the way the rag lingers on her breasts, he thinks that he does. When Bo strays away from between her legs, Eli storms over to them making them both flinch.

"Clean her pussy. She's no longer bleeding from her period but she stinks something awful. I don't want to smell it anymore. Spread her open and wash all of her," Eli instructs with a hiss.

Bo groans but raises a brow at Candace as to ask for permission. She steals a glance at Eli—good girl—and he nods. Leaning back on her elbows, she spreads her knees apart. As he begins washing her between her legs, she lets out a whimper. Eli has fed her nothing but pain and sex. And like the trained little pet she is, she lets out a moan.

Eli knows this moan and likes it. When he glances at Bo, he sees the idiot is massaging her clit like some pervert.

"You want to fuck her, don't you," Eli smiles, recognizing another deviant soul.

Bo's cheeks blotch red and he ignores Eli. He makes no moves to stop "washing" her there though. She writhes against his touch like a needy whore.

"I'm feeling generous, Bo. Would you like to fuck that clean pussy?" Eli questions. "I mean, you cleaned it, after all.

*No one will know."*

*Bo glances up at Eli with a bewildered look. "R-r-really?"*

*Anger bubbles in Eli's chest but he wants to see if Bo will really do it.*

*"Really. She likes it rough," Eli confides.*

*Bo's eyes darken and he sets his jaw. "Okay."*

*Candace sends him a confused look and Eli wiggles the cheeseburger at her. Understanding that if she's a good girl and does as she's told, she'll get fed, Candace opens herself up more to Bo.*

*Something inside of Bo snaps and he begins tearing at his belt. Pretty soon he's pulled out his impressive dick—much more impressive than Eli's—and slaps her pussy with it.*

*"You want this?" he demands in a tone that must feel aggressive to him but really makes him sound like a fucking fool.*

*Eli chews on his lip to hide his smirk. Stupid motherfucker is nothing compared to Eli. FUCKING NOTHING.*

*"Yes, please," she begs, her eyes never leaving the burger piece between Eli's fingers.*

*Bo pushes into her and groans. "Shit, this feels good."*

*"Do you want him to hurt you Candace?" Eli questions.*

*Without hesitation, she nods and smiles.*

*Eli's pretty sure Bo almost came from the mere thought of hurting the woman.*

*"How?"*

*With a roll of his eyes, Eli shrugs his shoulders. "I don't give a fuck how. Just do it."*

*Bo, as he thrusts hard into the woman, rears his arm back and slaps her across the face. Her smile is wiped off her face and tears spring in her eyes.*

*Eli sees red.*

*He stole her smile. HIS smile.*

*Snatching up the knife, Eli storms over to where Bo fucks her like a madman and reaches around him. With one quick movement, he slices Bo across the front of his throat. Blood bursts from him and sprays the woman, dirtying her right back up. Bo's fingers clutch at his throat but it's a lost cause and he crumples on top of Candace.*

*His blood soaks her skin and pools around her.*

*But is she upset?*

*No, she's smiling again.*

*Her mouth is parted, waiting for that cheeseburger.*

*"Good girl," Eli praises and kneels beside her. Shoving another bite into her mouth, she moans with greed. Once she has gobbled it down, he pushes his finger back into her mouth and lets her suck the grease from it. She sucks his finger much like she sucks his dick. Like a hungry whore.*

*Popping his finger back out of her mouth, he sits back on his haunches and gives Bo a push. The corpse rolls off of her with a thud against the concrete.*

*Candace, with blood smeared on her white tits, is quite stunning. Her nickname, bitch, carved into her belly completes the look. But what makes her truly a vision is her smile.*

*A smile he can't wait to steal over and over again.*

*Her smile isn't Bo's to take.*

*It's all Eli's.*

*"Do you want the rest of the cheeseburger?"*

*She nods with happy tears in her eyes.*

*Eli, not at all afraid of her overpowering him, tosses her* the knife. "*Bring me his dick and you can have your burger.*"

*Candace scrambles over to the knife and the wild glint in her eyes makes her look positively horrifying.*

*She doesn't pause but snatches up the knife and crawls over to Bo. A few uncoordinated saws later and she frees the no longer impressive member. On shaky legs, she stands and wobbles over to Eli. He braces himself wondering if she'll try and hurt him. But when she drops both the knife and the dick on the freezer beside him, he knows better. Her dulled eyes find his and she waits with surprising patience for her reward.*

*"On your knees," he barks.*

*She falls to them and stares up at him, gracing him with a smile that he'll take away later. His hand finds her matted hair and he strokes her much like a man would his favorite dog. The bitch leans in to his touch and closes her eyes.*

*"Good girl," he says, pride in his voice. Morsel by morsel, he feeds his pet and she rewards him much later when she lets him fuck her doggie style in the ass.*

⋯⋯⋯⋯▪▪▪▪▪▪⋯⋯⋯⋯

"What's going to happen?" Leesa questions, her hands on my shoulders as she reads my laptop screen.

I lean back in the chair and reach my arms around her neck. She dips down and kisses my lips.

"You'll have to wait and see," I tease her.

She playfully slaps my chest and pouts. "Fine. We'll just have to write a little story of our own."

When she releases me and saunters over to the bed, peeling clothes off along the way, I hurry and copy a section about Bo getting his throat slit and paste it into Facebook.

Once I'm finished, I chase after her and we spend most of the night trying to make another baby.

# CHAPTER 10

## The Past

Anxiety twists my stomach into knots as I watch my fiancée thumb through my notebooks. Her dark eyebrows are pinched together and I wonder if this is all too much. Will she send me packing for good? We've already been through so much but I want to reveal this part of myself to her.

"That's a lot of notes on how to kill Adam," she says followed by a humorless laugh.

I swallow down my unease and attempt to take the notebook from her. She leans back onto the couch cushion and pulls it just out of my reach. "Stop," she whines, "I'm reading."

Groaning, I sit back and trace lines with my fingertips along her bare legs that are draped across my lap. This woman has the sexiest legs I've ever been near enough to touch.

"Are you wearing panties?" I question in an attempt to distract her.

Undeterred, she flips a page in the notebook and ignores me.

I slip my hand between her legs under her khaki skirt and push my way between her thighs, forcing them to part for me. With a drag of my fingertip along her slit, I nearly grunt aloud when my finger meets a cotton resistance. Teasing her with my finger, I grin in satisfaction when her panties begin to grow wet for me.

I glance up at her to gauge her mood but her face is hidden behind the notebook. My cock is eager and ready to be inside of her if I can ever make her stop reading. She's already been through three this afternoon and has read into the deepest, darkest parts of my mind.

"Are you ready to run for the hills?" I ask, my voice husky.

She lets out a whimper, to which I smile in a smug fashion as I push her panties to the side and probe her entrance with my index finger. A moan escapes her as I slip it inside of her.

"Is the story more interesting than this?"

The notebook falls to the floor, giving me my answer.

---

I lay stretched out on my bed and stroke her hair thinking about all we've gone through in our two years of dating.

When she lost the baby, not long after we first got together, something fused my soul to hers. Knowing we lost something that was an equal part of her as it was of me, was both heartbreaking and eye-opening. It made me realize that, sure, we may have been young and unprepared for that baby, but I wanted to spend the rest of my life with her. There was plenty of time to get pregnant and get married, not that I wanted to wait long for either.

"What are you thinking about?" I question and draw her closer to me. I need to feel her heartbeat.

She sighs and curls herself around my naked body. "I think you should publish, Hank."

I'm already shaking my head before the words leave her mouth. "What? No. There's no way in hell I'm letting Adam read about all the ways I'd love to hack him into tiny pieces."

We both chuckle and I can't help but wonder where he ended up. He's probably some college superstar football player or some shit, smiling and giving other motherfuckers a hard time.

"No, I'm not talking about any of your diary entries or Adam stories. I'm talking about something new. You're really good at this, baby. Even your early stuff when you were in your teens is well written."

My mind lingers on the story I recently started writing after finding inspiration at the family reunion Grandma and I went to.

"Well, I kind of had this story that I've been working on called *Jacksonville Blood*," I begin.

"Tell me about it."

For the next half our, I explain to her every detail of my

story and my main character named Eli. By the time I finish, she's sitting up in the bed with wide, eager eyes. My eyes drop to her bare tits that jiggle each time she talks.

"This story is great. Finish it and I'll help you mail it out to publishers. I just know you can go far with this, Hank. You're too talented not to. Besides, I think you'd make a much better writer than a teacher."

I mull over her words. Teaching never was my passion but I'd somehow hoped to take a stand between bullies and victims in a way my teachers were never really able to. However, the idea of standing in front of thirty kids each day, putting my scars on display would cause my anxiety to go through the roof. Whenever I have to give a presentation in school, I almost always attempt to talk my teachers into an alternative way to grade me.

"There's no money in books. You know that, babe," I tell her with a small fight, but already imagining a future as a writer.

"It doesn't matter. I'll be here with you and we'll do it together.

Six weeks.

Six long weeks I've stared at my manuscript. Leesa tries to help. But my characters are being difficult. She even goes with me to people watch at the mall. Still though, nothing helps. Needing a break, I stand from my desk in a huff. I'd call my fiancée to see if she wants to go have coffee and then fuck but I know she's at the library working on a paper.

Grabbing my keys along the way, I leave my dorm and

head toward my car. Maybe if I have a drink or two, I'll feel in the mood to write some more. Six weeks with no more than a thousand words is killing my self-esteem.

I drive past the bar near campus that most of the college kids go to and instead head for a dumpy one just outside of town. When Leesa and I leave some weekends to go to her parents, we pass by it and motorcycles usually line the parking spots just outside of the front door.

It takes me a good twenty minutes but soon I'm parked beside said bikes and strutting inside. The moment I enter, I'm assaulted by smoke and my nostrils flare in protest. Ignoring them, I stride over to the bar and order a glass of chardonnay. Most bars laugh at me when I order wine, but with this one being so close to some upper-class neighborhoods, despite it being a biker bar, it seems to cater to both scenes because the grungy man with a greying beard brings me one without lifting a burly eyebrow.

It's in a water spotted glass, but beggars can't be choosers.

Pulling out a handheld notebook, I begin taking notes. The pungent smell and the way it claws at my lungs. The smoothness of the mahogany bar against my forearms. The dim lights that make me squint through the smoke haze.

Since my characters are all being sons of bitches and not talking to me, at least I can improve on my descriptive scene writing. I'm deep in thought, scribbling down notes and on my third glass of wine when I catch whiff of a new scent. This one is sweeter and it draws my attention away from my notebook.

A young woman with long, dark hair sits on the stool

beside me and flashes me the most harmless of smiles. Innocent yet provocative. It instantly makes me think of Eli. I've yet to fully develop him and understand his entire backstory but the moment I see this woman, it begins weaving a rapid tale.

"Hi," she says, batting her eyelashes at me in a flirtatious manner. I know I'm not the best looking guy because of my scars and mangled ear so my first thought is that she must be a prostitute.

"Hi," I grumble back but my eyes never leaving her green ones. She purses her lips together in a way she must deem as sexy and leans forward, giving me a glimpse of her tits that are hanging out of her V-neck tank.

Her tits are nothing compared to Leesa's which I love marking with my teeth.

"Wanna have some fun?" she questions and wriggles her chest at me.

Not really.

But something about her claws at the inside of my brain. It's like I need to know more about her. For Eli.

"What do you call fun?" I ask with a half-smile.

Her eyes widen in delight over the notion that I've seemed to have taken her bait.

"You could come to the bathroom and I could show you. I have some coke and there's enough to share," she purrs, resting her palm on my jean-clad thigh.

I'm nodding before I can talk myself out of what a bad idea this is. I need to learn more about her though and perhaps the privacy of the bathroom would help.

She slides off the stool and wobbles a bit in her too-high

heels. The woman is young, maybe Leesa's age and looks good in her short black skirt that reveals her long, toned legs. It's sad that she can't find a decent man to take care of her and is instead turning tricks for cash. She leads the way down a dark hallway and I follow her into the bathroom at the end of the hall.

I'm nearly blinded by the bright bathroom light the moment she pushes inside. The sounds of the jukebox are muffled once in the tiny bathroom. She locks the door behind me as I check out the room. Small. Toilet in one corner. Sink in the other. A long bench along the wall.

"Let's do a line first and then we can party," she murmurs and winks at me.

In the revealing light, I can see her black eyeliner is smudged and her hair is a bit greasy. She's not at all as pretty or put together as I originally thought.

"How do you party?" I question as she digs shit out of her purse.

"Strip shows are five dollars. Blow jobs are twenty. If you want to fuck me in here, that's forty. Somewhere else, like your car or behind the bar will cost you more. I don't do anal but if you become a regular customer and treat me right, I would consider it for an additional cost."

I gape at her as she wipes down the ledge above the sink and begins pouring her drugs up there. It seems unsanitary and bizarre but she works efficiently at chopping and shaping the substance into two neat rows, as if she does this often. Using a small, cut-off straw, she snorts one line of the white powder up and follows it with a delightful squeal.

"Shit, that's some good stuff," she chirps and hands the

straw to me.

Walking over to the drugs, I frown when I realize the other line is waiting, this time for me.

"I've never done this before," I tell her honestly.

Flashing me a grin, she wobbles over to me. "How much money do you have?"

"A hundred and twenty dollars."

"Mmm," she practically moans. "Take the hit and I will give you the best night of your life."

What I really want is to get back to my car so I can hurry and write down my newest ideas for Eli. A woman named Marla that looks like the cleaned up version of this lady before me has begun to formulate in my mind. This new character development will push the story that has sat idle for weeks. I'm fucking elated.

"Maybe I should go. I'm a writer and I really need to work."

Her eyes widen. "A writer? Did you know that some of the best writers wrote while high or drunk?"

I nod and my curiosity finally wins out. Before I change my mind, I stalk over to the mirror and snort the line. The instant it hits my system, I flip the fuck out.

Fire.

Raging fire is burning my goddamned throat!

"Fuck!" I roar and rip at the hair on my head. "It burns!"

She starts laughing behind me as if this is normal behavior for a first timer. All it does is fuel my anger. When I turn to see her taking her shirt off, I'm livid. Who does she think she is? She probably gave me drugs laced with something.

The moment she frees herself from her shirt and her

bare tits bounce as she wobbles, I decide I need to get away from her. She is reaching for me when I lose my shit. With one hard shove, I push her away from me. My skin crawls and my head is about to explode from the shit she gave me.

The woman stumbles backwards and falls. Everything happens in slow motion. Her fall. The crack of her head on the dirty, tiled floor. A pool of blood around her head that grows in radius with each passing second.

"Ma'am, are you okay?" I question, my voice husky.

Her wide-opened eyes remain dull and unblinking. I stare at her for a few moments before I get a sick idea.

I need to document everything about her. The way her skin feels. How the blood looks. Everything. In haste, I jot down several notes in my notebook and tuck it back into my pocket when I finish. Locking the door behind me and turning off the light, I leave her in there. The bar has many patrons so nobody notices when I pay my tab and thank the bartender or when I leave.

The entire drive back to campus, I'm so fucking high. It could be from the drugs or from the girl's death. Either way it's exhilarating. I can't wait to tell Leesa.

When I get back to my dorm room, she's sprawled out on my bed studying, looking sexy as hell in a short denim skirt. I toss my keys on my dresser and stride over to my desk.

"Well, hello to you too," she complains when I don't acknowledge her and set to scribbling in my bigger notebook.

The words flow.

And flow.

And don't stop fucking flowing until a migraine seizes

my every thought.

"Shit," I hiss in defeat and rest my forehead on my desk.

"Come to bed, baby," Leesa's sleepy voice mutters behind me.

I lift my head up and squint against the light on my desk. It's dark outside and she's turned off all the lights. A cold slice of pizza sits untouched on a plate at the corner of the desk, nauseating me with its pungent stench.

"What time is it? How long did I work for?" I groan as I stand, stretching my aching body in the process.

"It's after three in the morning, Hank," she says in a whisper. "You've been at it for nearly twelve hours."

Despite my raging headache, I'm fucking pleased as hell knowing that I wrote so much. It was all because of her. Eli's Marla. The moment I named her as a character in my book, it took off like wildfire.

The drugs gave me the killer migraine afterwards but watching that girl gave me something much better.

She gave me words.

With her death, she breathed life into *Jacksonville Blood*. Her death won't be in vain. She'll forever live on in the pages of this book.

I strip down to my boxers and crawl into bed behind Leesa. Her breathing is soft and rhythmic but I know she isn't fully asleep.

"Baby, I'm sorry if I ignored you. It was the story. I was in its clutches and couldn't stop until I got it out."

She runs her fingers along my forearm under the covers. "You were like a man possessed. I'm not sure you even heard a word I said to you. But, I watched over your shoulder as you wrote. This is unlike anything you've ever written before. It was vibrant and real. What happened to you?"

I grin but wince when my head throbs even more. "Well, I met a hooker and got high."

She tenses but I squeeze her to me in a reassuring way, kissing the back of her head.

"Don't worry. I didn't have sex with her or anything. She was the subject of my character profiling at this bar I went to."

"No wonder it seemed real," she muses. "Did something happen to the girl in real life like Marla in the story when Eli pushed her from the window?"

I beam, ignoring the staggering pain in my head from the action. "I pushed her. She cracked her head open on the tile floor. It really made a popping sound, Leesa. Fucking unreal."

When she starts to sob, it only manages to aggravate my headache. "Shhh," I whisper and hold her tight. "Everything's okay."

Hiccupping through her tears but making no moves to leave my arms, she cries, "Everything is *not* okay, Hank."

# CHAPTER 19

## Present

I wake to a thundering in my head, not unlike those from many years ago, back in college when I tried coke, and my phone going off somewhere in the room. Groaning, I roll over to kiss my wife, only the sheets are cold and she's gone.

What the fuck?

"Leesa?" I bark out, hoping she's in the bathroom.

I'm met with silence. Panic threatens to suffocate me as I scramble around looking for my jeans. She wouldn't leave me. Leesa would never do that to me. But my heart squeezes anyway simply from imagining the possibility. I'm about to go fucking insane when the front door pops open and my radiant wife walks in with arms full of take-out.

"Morning, sweetie. I'd hoped to get back before you woke up. Did you sleep well?" she chirps and starts unloading the food onto the desk.

My heart is still flopping around in my chest like a goddamned fish on the banks of a river.

"Yeah, fine. Was that you calling?" I question as I now hunt for my phone, accepting a kiss and my coffee when I walk past her. The kiss soothes my aching soul and the coffee will bring clarity to my broken mind.

"No, it was probably Linda. She's been trying to reach you but I told her you'd call her back once you woke up. That woman is so damn persistent," she gripes. I watch as she efficiently cuts up a stack of pancakes and pours syrup all over them.

"I'll call her back and see what's up."

Linda answers on the first ring. "My God, Hank! I swear, do I have to move in with you to get a word in with you?" she bitches.

Laughing I ruefully shake my head. "Not on your life. Now what do you want?"

She gets down to business. "That last teaser. Phenomenal. But, why didn't you tell me there have been murders mirroring your book in Blue Hill? Didn't you think that was newsworthy? I mean, it is everywhere. The town's mayor, Ian something or other, has been giving interviews to anyone and everyone. CNN, FOX, NBC, all the networks have their conspiracy theories. The publisher is talking to their attorneys trying to figure out if they should ignore the attention or attempt to silence your writing and save face."

"Save face for what? I didn't do anything wrong except

for write my book," I snap and throw Leesa an exasperated look. Her lips purse together as she regards me with concerned eyes.

"I know that. The publishers know that. But apparently, the public does not know that. A lot of the heat has been placed on Sheriff Norton. Apparently this Ian character really must not like her because he keeps steering the attention toward her, saying, funny how the murders were of two different people *she* worked with. He even went as far as to say perhaps she killed that bartender and her partner because she was jealous of their relationship. It's a clusterfuck of epic proportions, Hank."

I groan in defeat and scrub my palm against my marred cheek in frustration. "So, what? I give up writing something that feeds my family because some idiot cop is killing people in her precinct? The book's almost done for fucking crying out loud."

Linda laughs and it causes me to bristle in irritation. "No. The exact opposite really. While the publisher decides what to do, I say keep writing. You're number one on all lists for *Adair Village Blood*, Hank. Your other books are in the slots underneath. Have you checked your sales lately? Well I have. The controversy is selling your books like crazy. Until the publisher pulls the plug, I say keep doing what you're doing. You may even be able to sneak in one more teaser before it all hits the fan. What do you think?"

I don't want to stop writing and can't help but agree. "I'll keep writing. It's all I can do."

She squeals in delight and I have to pull the phone away from my ear. "Great! Oh, and one more thing. You have to do that speech."

Color drains from my face and the room spins. "What speech?" I seethe.

"The mayor in one of his interviews claimed that the Blue Hill Fair was still on this year, despite the terrible atrocities his town has faced, and that you had previously agreed to give a speech. Now, I'm going to warn you, things could get ugly because of the murders. So, make it short and sweet. Tell them how sorry you are for the loss their town has been through, so that you don't seem like some asshole for refusing to speak to them. I know you'll do a great job. Have Leesa stand up there beside you. Everyone loves Leesa."

I cringe but know this is necessary. "Fine. I'll do the speech. Don't let them pull the plug, Linda. This story is too good not to release."

Another excited squeal; she works on commission from my sales after all.

She wishes me luck and we hang up.

"I'll fill you in on the way to the fair in a couple of hours. I have to write and then we'll go," I tell Leesa.

Dropping her gaze to her food, she nods. She knows the drill.

<hr />

*Candace has really begun to grow on Eli. His desire to dispatch her grows less and less as the desire to hurt her and watch her beg grows more and more.*

*The woman worships him. Unlike Marla. That bitch. Marla treated him as if he were some annoying child. But Candace? Candace does anything and everything he asks of her.*

*It's been another long week since he killed that goober, Bo. She's continued to stay in the basement but he lets her have sponge baths and food more often. And now that the house-keeper has organized and cleaned the entire top floor of the house, Eli thinks it's time to give Candace a present.*

*"Come, pet. I have a gift for you," he tells her in a soft, almost loving tone.*

*She doesn't hesitate to scramble to her unbound feet and scurry over to him. He's noticed that she's been taking special care to clean herself and even asked for a toothbrush and shampoo a couple of days ago.*

*Of course he told her no. He only gives her what he wants to give her.*

*He clasps his hand with her chilled one and guides her to-ward the steps to go upstairs. Her body is still weak and wob-bly so by the second step he worries she'll lose her footing and break her neck. To ward off any accidents, he scoops her slight body into his arms and strides easily up the steps. The moment the warmth from the home envelops them, Candace lets out a small, relieved moan.*

*The light must be too bright in comparison to the dim ones downstairs because she buries her face into his neck to shield her eyes. Pride blossoms in Eli's chest knowing that despite how awful he's been to her, she trusts him to take care of her.*

*"We're here," he tells her and sets her down in a gentle manner onto his bed. "I want you here from now on."*

*It takes her a moment to understand that she'll be sleeping with him versus the cold, cement floor.*

*"Oh, t-t-thank you, Patrick," she sobs. Her lip trembles in a wild manner but a smile, one he doesn't see too often, graces*

*her dry lips.*

*Feeling sure that she'll never tell anyone, that he's suffi-ciently instilled enough fear in her to earn her silence, he de-cides he wants the praise, not some fictional name he created. "My real name is Eli. Now, let's get you showered. I don't want your shitty stink dirtying up my sheets."*

*"Eli," she tries his name out and this time grins. "I like that name much better. It suits you well."*

*He laughs at her and fists his hands at his sides. Her smile is so goddamned cute, he's about to lose control with the need to force it from her face.*

*After a supervised shower of her scrubbing every inch, in-cluding her hair, and an epic tooth brushing event, she finally settles naked into his bed beside him.*

*He expects her fear and her revulsion at the thought of his touch. It's the opposite though. It's as if she craves it. Her fingers explore him in a delicate manner. The defined muscles along his torso. The smattering of hair just below his belly but-ton. His limp cock.*

*He's tired and wants to sleep. Of course he won't until he's secured her.*

*"Lay on your back with an arm there and there." He points to each of the posts on the head of his bed.*

*She nods and does as she's told. Eli climbs out of the bed and retrieves the rope he brought up for this purpose. Like a professional sailor, he trusses her up until her arms are immo-bile. Her chest heaves and he doesn't miss the heated look in her eyes. After all this, she wants him.*

*When she smiles at him, his dick grows hard. Not because she's beautiful but because he wants it fucking gone.*

Climbing over her, he settles himself between her legs and pushes himself into her wet opening. She is turned on right now. Stupid bitch.

"You're a whore," he tells her through his gritted teeth.

She moans and nods, spreading herself more open to him.

"And I want to choke the fuck out of you and come all over your dead goddamned face," he hisses as he thrusts into her.

"Please," she begs.

Another smile.

His strong hand is on her throat in a flash and he's gripping her tight enough to make her gag. Her eyes roll back and her tongue hangs out. The smile is gone. Fucking gone. Just like it should be.

As he pounds into her, he has a thought. What if she became his wife? Bore his child—a child to whom he could teach everything he knows and that could carry on his legacy, once he's long gone. The thought excites him and seconds later, he comes inside of her and releases her neck.

Her breaths come out soft and steady—he's thankful she didn't die. He has plans for her.

His lips find her angry, red neck and he does something out of character. With a soft, gentle brush of his mouth against her flesh, he kisses her.

"I love that you let me do this to you," he mutters against her skin. The hot breath must tickle her because she lets out a moan. And soon, he feels different. Protective even over what's his. He wants to mark her with his seed but he also wants to mark her.

Before long, his dick is hard again and he's thrusting into her slowly, almost in a worshipful way. His lips are on hers and he's kissing her. Candace kisses him back too. Eagerly. Her body tightens and shivers but the moment he slides a hand between them and touches her clit, she orgasms. It's like they were meant to be together.

For the first time since Marla, he doesn't fuck, he makes love.

If Candace will be his and the mother to his child, he needs to take care of her. Fucking Marla had that chance but ruined it the moment she screamed rape. Of course nobody was home that night and he made love to her anyway despite her nonsensical screaming. His mouth on her pussy made her come after he came inside of her. The taste of his semen mixed with her feminine scent was intoxicating. Marla came all over his tongue but was begging for him to let her go. It was hot as hell. All parts of the act.

Until he untied her and she tried to kill him with his lamp. Her threats to ruin him and his father shocked him. The woman had lost her mind. So when she tried to climb out the window to escape him, he shoved her naked, bloody ass the rest of the way.

Nobody ruins Eli Lawrence Firth.

Fucking nobody.

Candace drags Eli back to the present when she hisses.

He shakes his head to rid himself of the lingering hateful Marla fog he was in and releases his grip on her throat. He hadn't realized he was near strangling her once again.

"Shhh, pet. You're mine now. I'm not going to kill you. In fact," he says with a smile, "I've decided that I'm going to get you pregnant. We're going to have a baby."

Candace passes out.

*It's been several months now and Candace glows. Her belly is swollen and each time he sees her, pregnant with his child, he nearly comes in his jeans. Becoming a family man has settled him. He hasn't killed in weeks. He only hurts her some of the time. And unfortunately, he thinks he loves her.*

*Of course he won't ever let her know this.*

*On several occasions, Eli has forgotten to tie her up and in the morning, her body is tangled up with his. He can feel his child kicking through her belly against his ribs.*

*His hate has simmered and something else resides inside of him instead. It reminds him much of his mother and he aches for the sensation.*

*"Do you want a boy or a girl?" she asks from beside him, her finger tracing over his chest.*

*He smiles in the dark bedroom. "A boy, of course."*

*"What happens if we have a girl?"*

*The tension in her voice is thick and he wants to slap her in the fucking face for questioning his motives.*

*"We don't need a girl. We'll just try again."*

*"But… you'll love her too, right?"*

*He laughs. "There won't be anything to love."*

*Her tears wet his chest and he pulls her closer to him. Better for her to understand the truth now rather than be surprised later. They're having a boy. That is what Eli wants and that is what he will get.*

*"Will you take me to the doctor? So we can find out? I promise I won't tell them that…" she trails off.*

*"Tell them what? That you're my captive? You've had plen-*

*ty of opportunities to leave and yet here you are. Each day you let me fuck you over and over while screaming my name. You love me, pet. So what the hell do you think you'll tell these doctors?"*

*"I, uh," she mutters.*

*"You need to shut your mouth before I shut it for you."*

*She nods and snuggles against him.*

*"I'm going to deliver our child. I've been researching and it's pretty standard. You push, I catch. I'll cut the cord and you nurse it. Not much to it. Sure it'll hurt, but you've been through much worse. Haven't you, pet?"*

*A shudder ripples through her and Eli grins. His cock tents the sheets remembering every time he's hurt her much worse. Last week, he whipped her ass with the belt until his arm fucking hurt. Her screams were intense and he ended up coming in his pants before he was done doling out his punishment. Surely childbirth can't be more painful than a good ass whipping.*

*"Will you still keep me after the baby?"*

*He chuckles and shocks both of them when he strokes her hair in a gentle way. "Someone has to take care of it. I take care of you and you take care of it. That's how it should be."*

*"Will you love it?"*

*The ache lingers in his chest. "Of course I will. More than myself."*

*"Do you love me?"*

*"Jesus, what's with the twenty questions? I love what I get to do to you. It's sexy and I don't want to ever stop doing it."*

*Her lips find his chest and her fingers trail south. "So you do love me. You want to stay with me forever?"*

*The thought of having her here always ready for him to do*

with as he pleases warms him. "Yes, I do want you here with me. Always."

"What if someone finds out? What will you do?"

Anger explodes in Eli's chest and he rolls her to where she's beneath him. Her belly between them is huge now.

"How would they ever find out?" he snarls, his hand on her throat. "Are you going to tell someone? Do I not take care of your every fucking need, pet? Your ass is getting fat because I feed you whatever the fuck you want, whenever the fuck you want. When you had a craving for a cheeseburger and strawberry milkshake at dinner, I fucking went and got it for you."

She claws at his wrist trying to get him to release her. But he's too pissed.

"You smell like you stepped out of a goddamned magazine because I buy you expensive shampoos and lotions. I fucking spoil you, pet. And you want to threaten to rip it all away from us?"

His rage is all-consuming. He wants nothing more than to snuff out her life. Right now. But, a kick against his belly through hers reminds him to calm down. With a resigned grunt he releases her and spends the rest of the night kissing her while he makes sweet love to her.

He does love his pet.

She pisses him off but he'd be lost without her. A half of a whole. He'll do whatever it takes to keep them in one piece.

"I love you, pet. Promise me you'll drop these questions and just let us be happy."

"I promise you, Eli."

# CHAPTER 20

My head is still in Eli's story, wondering how it will end. Will he kill Candace or will he find a happy ever after of his own? Leesa has begged me to tell her how it ends but even I don't know that answer. I write and the story guides itself.

"Everyone is looking at us," my wife whines and squeezes my hand as we walk past several booths. The carnies are hollering out enticing calls about how they'll give me a deal so I can "win a prize for the lady". We ignore them and keep walking.

"The carnies?" I ask confused.

She sighs. "No, the people. After Linda called this morning and you wrote, I looked it up. This story is everywhere. Some sites claim you're the murderer. Others follow what Ian is claiming—that Holly did it. This is probably the worst

232

place we could be right now."

I stop and peck her on the cheek before continuing our walk toward the vendors where the scent of smoked turkey legs call to us. "Babe, this is the best place to be. By us not hiding, it shows that we, in fact, have nothing to hide. I'll do the speech and we'll go. It just sucks that because of this, our kids couldn't come out with your parents. I know they would have had fun. Even Whitney, despite her teenage blues."

We both laugh. I spoke to both girls earlier. Whitney, according to Callie, found a boyfriend that lives on the same street as Leesa's parents. She giggled and made fun of catching them kissing. Of course Whitney denied these heinous allegations and said Callie was an annoying pest who followed her everywhere. There's probably truth to both of their stories.

"Oh, there's a table under that tree. Not many people are over there. Grab it up and I'll go get us some food," Leesa exclaims.

I release her hand and trot over to the table before a young couple gets to it and sit down while Leesa heads off in a different direction.

I'm sitting there watching people walk by, when someone sits beside me.

"That didn't take long," I say turning my head.

*Helen.*

*Helen.*

*Helen.*

"Hi Henry," Alex says with a small smile. Her pink lips are slightly swollen and her eyes are red-tinged from crying.

"Are you okay?" I blurt out, my worry for her already

resurfacing.

Shaking her head, she bursts into tears. "No. Did you watch the news? Ian blames my mom for those murders. Internal Affairs is questioning her right now. That asshole just won't fucking stop ruining our lives."

I slide an arm around her, despite every warning bell in my head telling me not to. "I'm sorry. The man is a fucking idiot," I growl.

Her scent invades my lungs as I inhale her. My fingers slide up and down her arm causing goosebumps to rise under them.

"You smell good," I murmur.

Alex dizzies and confuses me. Moments earlier, I was able to distract myself with Eli and Leesa and the news. But now?

Now, all that matters is *her*.

"I miss you," she sobs, her hand finding my thigh. "And now, I can't get ahold of Poe. I think something's happened to him. He was supposed to run the pie throwing booth but he never showed and isn't returning anyone's calls."

She runs circles with her fingers over my khaki shorts and my dick twitches when she gets a little too close to it. Mimicking her action, I reach over and place my hand on her warm thigh just below the hem of her dress.

"I miss you too," I whisper, my lips finding her ear. "I'm sure he's fine. God, I want to touch you."

A rush of breath escapes her when I press a kiss to the shell of her ear.

"Henry, life isn't fair."

I remove my hand from her thigh and cradle her face,

turning her so I can look at her. "I know but it's better this way. Better for you," I murmur before brushing my lips across hers.

She nods and the tears roll down her pretty face. Pulling her in a tight embrace, I hug her until the delicious aroma of a turkey leg invades my senses.

Leesa clears her throat as she sets our food on the table.

"Goodbye, Alex," she snips out.

Alex, clearly startled, scrambles up and away from me. I watch, a frown playing at my lips, as she bounces away from me without so much as a goodbye. Her long, dark hair waves wildly as she runs and her dress lifts with each stride, giving me a glimpse of her pink panties. God, I'm going to fucking miss that girl.

"Hank, that woman is poison to you. Do you understand me? Poison," Leesa clips out. "Look at me."

I drag my gaze away from the enigma that is Alex, who has now disappeared into the crowd and regard my wife. Her hazel-colored eyes blaze with what I know after many years of marriage is protectiveness over me.

"I'm sorry. She does something to me," I grumble in response.

Leesa sighs and pushes my basket of food toward me. "They all do. Alex is no different than Maggie. Or Jeannette. Or Sarah. She is one of *them*, Hank. Put her in that compartment where she belongs inside that head of yours and lock the door. It worries me how she wreaks havoc inside of you mind. Maybe you should take one of your pills. I brought them with me just in case."

I shake my head in a vehement way. "Absolutely not. I'm

so damn close to finishing this book. Another chapter or two and it will be over. As soon as we leave here, we'll head to the inn, I'll write it, and gladly accept the pill from you."

My wife swallows down her emotion and nods. "Fine but I'm not leaving your side. Understand? If you go to the porta-potty, so will I. We can't take any chances. You're too visible here."

We eat in silence as I reminisce about Alex. Her scent lingers, mixing with the turkey leg, and I lick my lips. I miss her. So fucking bad. But Leesa's right. I need to push her out of my head.

"Mr. and Mrs. McElroy, what a pleasant surprise seeing you here," a familiar voice chirps as it approaches our table. I'm snapped out of my Alex fog and see Clive standing at the end of the picnic table. "Have you tried the fried Snickers? I seriously just ate three."

Leesa shoots me a panicked glare and I shake it off. "Clive, you should sit with us."

Her face turns bright red as he plops down beside her. "That teaser you posted, the one with Bo, was amazing," he praises. "It was so detailed. I felt as if I were down in that cold basement. Like I was the one giving her and Bo orders instead of Eli. I'm always so blown away at your ability to draw me into the story."

I beam at him and ignore Leesa's warning stare. She doesn't like this Clive but I think he fits right in when he's not saying inappropriate things to me or my wife. When he's gushing about my stories, I find him quite enjoyable to be around.

"Thanks, Clive."

He babbles on, "And the dick severing was a nice touch. Man, I was shocked but I'm not going to lie, I loved that part. That idiot deserved it and—"

"Wait, what?" Leesa blurts out.

Clive's excitement is washed away as his face blanches. "Uh…"

I sit back and watch their exchange with a smug grin. "You're quite a fan, aren't you?"

"Hank," Leesa warns but I shake my head at her.

Clive nods and drops his gaze to his hands which he's wringing in a nervous manner.

An announcer makes a statement calling for any speakers to head toward the stage and Clive stands in haste. "I should go. I'll be waiting for that excerpt you promised of *Twenty-Three Ways to Kill Adam*."

Standing as well, I reach out and shake his hand. "I'll send it soon, buddy."

He smiles broadly at me and then rushes away from us, soon getting lost in the crowd.

"Hank." Leesa frowns. "He gives me the creeps."

I laugh as we drop our trash into the can and I grab onto her hand after. "He gives me the creeps too. It's kind of nice to meet someone so dedicated though, you know?"

She shakes her head. "No, I don't know. Nor do I care to ever know."

We arrive at the stage and Ian stands on it, handsome as ever, in a pair of cream-colored slacks and orange Polo shirt, making his skin appear tan. This town's mayor is a looker and I notice Leesa's gaze linger for a half a second longer than it should. It makes me burn with hate for the stupid fucker but I'll control myself for Leesa. The press is already all over me, so I'm not about to go to jail for punching the dumb shit on his nose.

"Mr. McElroy," Ian greets with a grin that promises he'll eat me for lunch. "So nice to see you. Everyone is looking forward to hearing what you have to say."

He reaches to shake the hand of my wife and when she gives it to him, he strokes the top of it with his thumb. The idiot probably fucks anything with tits. Well, he's not fucking my wife.

"Please, have a seat over there and I'll introduce you when it's your time," he says, finally letting go of her and strides off toward the microphone.

Leesa shudders. "He's a bad man, Hank."

"I know," I tell her and squeeze her to me. I kiss the top of her head and scan the audience. Of course I don't see *her*. Alex.

"Good afternoon, fine folks of Blue Hill. I'm so happy that you all came out to enjoy our annual fair, despite the terrible tragedies we are facing. Internal Affairs is investigating the homicides along with one of this town's finest. Jealousy can be a bad thing and I can only pray we're all proven wrong about our sheriff."

The crowd babbles at his words and I see several heads nodding in agreement. Fucking asshole.

"Anyway, we have a special guest. *New York Times* bestselling author, Henry McElroy is here today with us. Now, despite the rumors that have run rampant, please allow our talented police force to do their jobs in bringing justice to the real psychopath in this town. Don't place judgments on those around you, especially guests of Blue Hill, without knowing the full story and details of the crimes. I'm sure the police will soon catch the real perpetrator and put them away for a long time. In the meantime, please allow Mr. McElroy to encourage our beautiful community."

Even though the idiot hints that I'm not the murderer, he still pisses me off every time he opens his damn mouth. With a sigh, I strut over to the microphone. Leesa follows me over to it and wraps her arm around my waist in a gesture of support while I speak.

"Good afternoon. I'm incredibly sad that someone has been copying scenes that I concocted in my brain for my book and viciously reenacting them. Now that these murders have been brought to national attention, I have no doubt that the authorities will bring this perpetrator to justice. I ask that if you have any information regarding these deaths that you'll report that information to the police immediately. Thank you all for welcoming me into your town. My wife and I very much enjoy the quaint, welcoming feel of Blue Hill."

A few folks clap but not very many. I'm about to step away from the mic when I hear a commotion behind me. Alex has managed to shove her way past Ian and is charging for me. I am shocked and move away from the microphone, soon understanding it's her intended destination.

"Hi everyone," she barks out through her tears. "Remember me? Sweet little Alex? Your sheriff's daughter? Yep, that's me. I was valedictorian of my high school class. Many of you saw me at town functions and at church with my mom."

Ian starts griping and heads toward us but I square my shoulders, challenging him to touch one goddamned hair on her head. He pauses, hopefully sensing my desire to do bodily harm to him.

"Well, Mom's behind bars. Thanks to that man," she points at Ian. "Did you know that man and I had a torrid love affair when I was seventeen? Did you know that he took my virginity over a desk your city tax dollars paid for? Did you know he forced me to abort our baby?"

Many shocked people begin chattering in the crowd. Meanwhile, Ian shakes his head in denial.

"She's delusional and only trying to protect her mother!" he calls out to the crowd.

Alex shudders with rage and Leesa pats her shoulder in a comforting way.

"Ian, you had sex with a minor. Multiple times. You're a predator against women," Alex screams. "I hate you. You're the one who belongs in jail. Not Mom!"

She charges for him but I pull her to me. "He's not worth it, Alex."

Her body quivers as she sobs in my arms. But just as quickly as she let me hug her, she pulls away and touches my marred cheek. Amid the mounting commotion surrounding us, she holds her gaze to mine before murmuring, "Goodbye, Henry. Don't ever forget me."

The sound of stomping feet behind me alerts us to the presence of security arriving on the scene. Alex tears away from me and clambers down the front of the stage. Everyone watches in awe as she runs away from the mess of accusations she dumped on Ian.

He storms over to the microphone, furious as hell. "You'll have to ignore her. The girl is twisted, just like her mother."

She's not twisted and doesn't deserve to be treated as if she's trash. Not thinking twice, I rear back and punch him on his nose. It pops the second my fist connects and I can't help the satisfaction I feel in knowing I broke it.

"You fool! You fucking fool!" Ian screams at me, his blood soaking his perfectly pressed Polo shirt.

Leesa shrieks behind me but I smile, knowing that idiot got a little of what he deserves. I'm about to drag her out of there when I'm forced to the floor.

"You're under arrest for assault."

---

"They wanted to keep you for questioning for the murders but I told them until they have proof for all that other shit, they would never get the chance," Leesa huffs as we drive back to the inn. I spent the past four hours in an empty cell awaiting bail. I'm tired and hungry as hell. But mostly, I want to finish Eli's story. I'm so close I can almost taste it.

"Do you think Eli should let Candace live?" I ask, my mind lost in the world of my characters.

Leesa lets out an annoyed sigh from beside me. "Really, Hank? Jesus. Get this story down and then we need to go. Understand me? Your kids don't need to see you on the news punching the mayor of this damn town. But guess what? They will because you did it for all the world to see. Why can't you stay in the present with me? I need you to stop obsessing, take your pill, and come home with me."

She's worried.

It all seems to be unravelling.

Our perfect world.

"I will, baby. I promise. I'm so close."

The ride back is a blur and soon, I'm back to where I need to be.

# CHAPTER

# 21

"You're waddling," Eli chuckles as his pet emerges from the bathroom wearing only a towel on her head.

"I'm about to have your baby any day." She pouts, "What do you expect?"

He watches with anticipation as she drops her towel to the floor. Her hair has grown long and he craves to touch her. Somehow, she's managed to stir up his head and inject herself. He doesn't ever want his mind to be free of her.

"Are you getting mouthy with me?" he growls.

She used to flinch but now she only blushes. He knows she's in love with him and desires him every second of every day, especially since becoming pregnant. The woman is insatiable.

"I can be very mouthy," she purrs as she makes her way to him. Her lips, less than a year ago, were cracked and bleeding *from malnourishment and abuse. But now, they're plump and full. And she knows how to use them to his great satisfaction.*

*She's just kneeling before him at the foot of the bed when a shriek pierces the air. Eli jerks up and meets her wide, horrified stare.*

*"What?"*

*"I think my water just broke," she whispers, tears welling in her eyes.*

*Eli's heart patters with excitement. The time has come. His son will soon be here.*

*"Shit, um, get into the bed," he stammers, still in disbelief over what is about to happen.*

*Tears roll down her cheeks while she winces in pain. "We'll ruin our bed. I prepared the second bedroom to deliver the baby. Fresh towels, scissors for the umbilical cord. It's all in there, Eli."*

*He's thankful she had the foresight to prepare the room. He'd noticed that she'd been nesting as the books said she would and had cleaned this house from top to bottom. He'd even let the maid go months ago. His pet makes the perfect wife. They're married in his mind despite having not been able to set foot into a church with her. The moment she missed her first period and showed him the positive pregnancy test, it sealed their fate together.*

*"Shit!" she cries out and doubles over. "This hurts, Eli."*

*Scrambling from the bed, he lifts her now heavy-ass in his arms and strides from the room. Once he steps foot into the second bedroom, he smiles noticing what great pride she took in setting up this delivery room.*

*"We're going to have our son soon, pet," he tells her as he*

sets her down. "Don't you worry about a thing."

She sobs and lets out an otherworldly scream when another contraction seizes her. He leans over her and kisses her lips in a reassuring manner. "My pet, hang in there. I love you and we'll get through this together."

Months ago, he'd have stabbed the motherfucker he's recently become. He's soft. Because of her.

"What if it's a girl?" she mutters so quietly he almost doesn't hear.

Rage ripples through him at her question. She knows the fucking answer. "How many times do I have to tell you?" he seethes. "We'll start over. Just like we talked about. Try again for a boy. I don't want a girl."

She howls out in pain or from the realization of what's to come, he's not sure. He hauls off and slaps the shit out of her to knock some sense into her.

"Stop acting like a stupid bitch. I could gut you right now and take that baby if I chose to. But I, for some goddamn reason, love you and want to share our son with you. So shut the fuck up and push him out."

Her eyes blaze with fury when they meet his and for a moment he's surprised at her brave glare. But she loses the fight and cries out again when another contraction seizes her. He scrambles into motion and drags her to the edge of the bed. When he pushes her knees apart, he stares in shock.

Dark hair.

Eli can see the top of his head.

"Holy shit, baby! You can do this! I can see him!" he exclaims.

He's so proud as she clutches onto her knees and bares

*down pushing with all her might. Her face turns purple, much like when he chokes her, and he becomes hard. The books say the woman isn't safe for sex until six weeks after birth but Eli knows he won't be able to wait six hours, much less six weeks. He'll fuck her whenever he pleases because she's his wife.*

*The head is pushed out of her opening and he can almost see his son's eyes. But she gasps and the baby slides back into her.*

*"Shit," he barks. "Don't stop. You have to keep pushing him out."*

*"I can't," she wails. "It's too hard."*

*"I don't give a fuck. Push this baby out. I'm getting him out one way or another. It would be in your best interest for you to do it."*

*His threat works, even though deep down he knows he won't kill her—not now after everything. She begins to push once again with all her might.*

*Their baby's head breaches her opening and Eli fights tears.*

*Eli never cries, but the baby, even with the white shit all over its face and in its eyes, is the most beautiful thing he's ever laid eyes on.*

*His son.*

*All his.*

*Now, he owns two things in this world. Pet and baby boy.*

*He reaches over and clasps onto her hand. "He's coming. A few more pushes."*

*Her sobs are a thing of the past as determination washes over her. She screams and it's wicked, chilling Eli to his bones. A woman giving birth much resembles something from a nightmare.*

*She's so close but is having trouble with the baby's shoulders. He tries to grip the slippery thing but it's only coming out when her body says it's coming out.*

*"One more push," he urges and pats her knee.*

*Another bone-chilling howl escapes her as she pushes hard. This time, the shoulders slip out and the baby falls into Eli's waiting arms. He's stunned to be staring at this tiny thing that he created. It is beautiful and scary as fuck at the same time.*

*"I want to hold him," she sobs, her arms outstretched.*

*With shaky hands, he sets him on her belly as he searches for the scissors to cut the cord. She tugs the blanket toward her and covers him to keep him warm.*

*"There, there, son," she purrs as she pops him on the back. At first Eli bristles with anger thinking she's hurt him but the moment he cries out, sounding much like a dying cat, he breathes a sigh of relief. Apparently motherly instincts are truly a thing of existence. She knew just what to do.*

*"I'm going to get him to nurse," she tells him and guides their baby's mouth to her huge tit.*

*Eli watches in awe as he latches on. "Pet, this is amazing. He's ours."*

*Tears well in her eyes and she nods. "This baby will grow and develop. Feel things. See things. Experience things. This baby will lead a full, healthy life."*

*He scrunches his brows together in confusion. "Of course he will."*

*Snatching up the scissors from the table at the end of the bed, he makes his way around to the side of the bed where he* can better access their son's cord. When he tugs the blanket away to reveal his naked flesh, Eli widens his eyes in shock.

"Where's his penis?"

He's so stunned and quite frankly devastated at what has to be done that he doesn't expect his pet's next move. From under the pillow, she jerks out the same knife he used to cut her nickname into her belly and plunges it into his neck.

Searing pain blinds him and he stumbles away from her.

A million thoughts blast through him.

She wanted to know where the bleach was to clean the tub. He absently told her it was in the basement and when she reemerged carrying the jug, he didn't question it. But the stupid fuck left that goddamned knife down there. A knife that she easily sneaked back upstairs and apparently hid. Waiting for this moment.

Candace never loved Eli.

She was only biding her time.

Eli falls to the floor with an oof and tries unsuccessfully to remove the knife. More blood than he expects pours from him which means she had to have nicked an artery.

Her venomous gaze meets his as she nurses their daughter. He blinks at her but darkness is quickly stealing him away from his family.

"You stupid man," she hisses. "Why don't you die already?"

His pet's words mock the same words he said to her nearly a year ago that night when she tried to escape and ended up becoming his prisoner instead.

"P-p-pet," he gurgles out.

She strokes their daughter's hair and glares over at him. "I was never your fucking pet. I was your goddamned captive.

*Not anymore, Eli. I'm free and our daughter will live. So fucking die already."*

*His daughter is the last thing he sees before he drifts off.*

*He would never have been able to kill that baby.*

*But Pet didn't know that.*

---

# Blue Hill Blood Epilogue

## Candace

BEING A SINGLE MOTHER IS *a challenge. Every night when Ellie, named affectionately after her father, cries with colic, Candace bravely takes care of her. She's patient as she holds her and kisses her baby's soft flesh while whispering promises of a safe, bright future.*

*Wrangling Eli's corpse down into the basement was difficult, especially only hours after giving birth. But Candace is a strong woman both inside and out. Besides, gravity took care of the rest when she kicked him down that first step. As soon as she heals, she and Ellie are leaving this hell hole she's called home for almost a year. Her daughter will never have to face the man that abused her mother. The man that took what he wanted and tortured her until she was on the brink of death.*

*Her daughter will be free. Much like Candace now will be.*

*"Tomorrow, we'll leave," she assures her daughter. Ellie coos and Candace's black, broken heart warms.*

*She hates to admit she'll miss Eli. After all they'd been through together, she did feel loved by him. Had he just been*

249

*Patrick from the coffee shop and been good to her, they could have all of this without the terror in between. Eli ruined it the moment he tried to kill her the first time.*

*Candace always knew she would get away. Hope coursed through her even during the darkest of times. She was a smart girl, after all, and planned and waited patiently. When the opportunity arose and it was time to protect her baby girl, Candace, much like a momma bear, killed to defend what was hers.*

*Eli may have abused her but he did give her a gift. It was the least he could do considering all he put her through.*

*Tomorrow, they're leaving him and the past behind.*

*Tomorrow, they will start anew.*

*Candace knows that if she made it this far, the rest will be a cake walk.*

*And for the first time in forever, she smiles.*

*Nobody steals her smile this time.*

*THE END*

I stare at the two words on my screen. Two words that not only end a book but my entire life's legacy. My fingers itch to hit the backspace bar. To erase it all and let Eli kill Candace and her baby. Then, I could write another book. The terror, as well as the paychecks, could continue.

But it's time to move on.

Before I change my mind, I email it to Linda and my editor, sealing the deal.

"I love you, Hank." Leesa kisses the top of my head, apparently proud of the ending that she watched me write over my shoulder, littering my shirt with her chewed fingernail bits all the while.

I sigh and hold out my hand. She presses the pill into my palm and kisses me once more.

"I love you too, baby," I assure her and swallow down the medication that will soon chase away my demons. Medicine that turns colorful parts of my head into black and white sections that are easy to define. No grey.

Leaning back in my chair, I let the calming waves of the medication surge through me. Dark thoughts dissipate as light enters the space. I allow myself one memory of Helen before I slam that door for who knows how long.

*"Doctor?" my sister questions as she holds my Rubik's cube.*

*I glance over at her and shadows cause the bags under her eyes to seem darker. It causes a chill to run down my spine. Lately, she's seemed weaker—less mentally there. I hate it.*

*"No. I hate doctors," I grumble. "Maybe a teacher?"*

*She laughs and the sound obliterates my anger as it weaves itself into my soul. I reach over and take the cube from her.*

*"What color?" I ask, even though I already know her answer. My fingers begin twisting, already knowing the path to get there.*

*"Green."*

*She may or may not have said that aloud. But it's always her answer so it doesn't matter. I twist and turn until I change it to what she always requests.*

*"I'll always be with you, Hank. Even when you can't remember what I look like, I'll be there." She rolls onto her side and pokes me in the chest. "There. Don't you forget it either."*

*Her morbid words sicken me and I look away from her probing eyes.*

*"I'd rather just see you every day instead." My complaint is always the same.*

*She snuggles up beside me and hugs me across my middle. One day I won't be able to touch her or talk to her. One day I'll be all alone. Inhaling her scent that reeks of impending death, I memorize her. I let her take up residence in my lungs and live there forever.*

*"I won't ever forget you, Helen. I'll always do whatever it takes to remember you. And if I ever find your doppelgänger, then I'm making her my best friend," I tease and tickle her ribs.*

*She squeals with laughter and I let that sound thread its way into my heart. I don't tickle her anymore, knowing she doesn't have the strength for it, and instead hug her to me.*

A pound on the door startles me from my memory and Leesa breaks away to answer the door. On the other side, two men in suits flashing FBI badges stand with grim faces and two more local officers flank them.

"Henry Eliot McElroy, you're under arrest for the murders of Dorothy Cosgrove, Joseph Matlock, Judith Meyers, and Poe Alexander, whose dismembered body we discovered this afternoon in the bay. We're also seizing your laptop. You're going down, cop killer."

I stand, now fully stolen by the drug-induced haze, and hold my arms forward. Leesa chatters on about suing them and they have the wrong guy but I willingly let them cuff me. My thoughts linger on Helen as she fades into the recesses of my mind. I try to think about Eli and Candace as the man reads me my Miranda rights but I can't recall what happened.

The rush of the medication seems like too much after not having taken it for so long and my lunch from the fair grumbles in my belly. If they would stop jerking me around so much, I wouldn't feel so nauseous.

As soon as we make it out the door and down the corridor toward the parking lots, flashes go off around us. People, I'm guessing reporters, begin shouting out questions and accusations. It's all too much. Bile rises in my throat and I empty my stomach.

"Motherfucker," one of the men holding my bicep complains. "That shit is all over my slacks."

They have to practically drag me to the black sedan as the world spins and tilts around me. As soon as they deposit me into the backseat, I flop to my side and pass out.

# CHAPTER 22

Leesa

Post-traumatic stress disorder.

Depersonalization disorder.

Borderline personality disorder.

Multiple focused paraphilias.

I remember sitting with Hank's psychiatrist not long after we had married—needing to put a name to his conditions—and being stunned into silence when the doctor rattled off the list.

This man, with more disorders than I knew what to do with, was my husband.

The one I committed my entire life to.

My whole heart to.

And despite the many prescriptions and therapies that

promised to fix him, there was only one way.

*Me.*

With Hank, I was always the solution. The numbing remedy. The cure.

But sometimes, despite my constant intervening in every single aspect of his life, even I wasn't able to stop when his mind flipped its switch and went rogue.

When his mind would fight against me, its most valiant ally, I'd lose him. He'd mentally break and it was always so hard bringing him back. Just like now.

But I will fix him.

Every time, *I* fix him.

<hr />

"No, Mother, he's not guilty," I sigh in frustration into the phone. "They still don't have proof aside from what he's written in his novel. The only straw they have, which they keep desperately holding on to, is that there are witnesses to the altercation between Poe and Hank. Other than that, a jury will rip the prosecution apart."

She rambles on and fills me in on the girls. I listen in an absent manner as I pace around my hotel room. The room at the inn has been secured by the authorities for their investigation so I had to book another place.

"Okay, thanks for everything. I love you," I tell her and hang up.

Tossing the phone onto the table, I stride over to the window and wait. He'll be here soon—the answer to this mess.

When I spy a white sedan pulling into the parking lot,

panic rises in my chest. Can I do this? Can I do what needs to be done to free my husband?

A calm washes over me.

Of course I can.

I always do.

The first time he lost his damn mind, I did what had to be done to free him from the steely clutches of his wicked mind.

* * *

*The mysterious man has taken me to bed for weeks now, worshipping my body with his hot breath on my flesh and tongue in any crevice he can reach. When I first met him, I wasn't originally attracted to him but as we spoke, I felt myself hurtling toward his heart with breakneck speed. Hank was different than any other man I'd been involved with. He was real and passionate, almost obsessive in wanting me.*

*"You look like her," he hisses and his long fingers slide around my throat. The man has brought me to many epic orgasms as he's choked me. It's dirty yet addicting. He does it in such a loving way though that I trust he'll never truly hurt me. And always, afterwards, he apologizes. Truth is though, I love it. I'm too shy to admit it but when his fingers slip up my chest, I always break out into a sweat with anticipation.*

*"Who?"*

*He's mentioned a "her" before but never indicated who she was.*

*"Helen," he snarls in a way that sends a chill skittering down my spine.*

*Something is different. Normally, our encounters are sex-*

ual. This time, it feels cold. He forces his way inside of me and I cry out. Despite not being fully wet and ready, I still enjoy the way he feels inside of me. Hank has broken me for any other man. He may not love me yet but I already love him.

"Who is Helen?" I mutter as his grip tightens. Stars dance across my vision until he decides to loosen his hold.

"My sister."

My blood grows ice cold and rushes through my veins. His dead sister. He thinks I look like his dead sister yet he makes love to me multiple times a day. Scratching at his wrist, I try to break free of his hold.

"This isn't right," he snaps, his grip once again too tight. "Blue eyes, just like hers. You look like her and I'm fucking you. I'm fucking my sister!"

I squirm and wiggle as I fade in and out of consciousness. He's going to kill me this time.

This man will end my life.

"S-t-t-top. I'm not her," I sob when he briefly relaxes his hand.

"Shit," he gasps, "Leesa, I'm sorry."

His lips are all over mine the moment he lets my throat go. When I met his grandma last weekend, she warned me that he'd been through a lot and that it would be difficult to love him. I thought she was just a bitch. Now, I know what she means.

"Hank." I slide my fingers into his hair. "I'm not her. I'm Leesa."

He nods and proceeds to kiss my neck while I stare at the picture of him and his sister on his nightstand. Hank watches Helen in the photo as she smiles for the camera. Her hair is *shoulder-length, straight and inky black. Sad, brown eyes peer back at me from the picture.*

*I look nothing like her.*

*She is slender and tall. I'm short and have curves.*

*My eyes are hazel, not blue. Hers are brown, not blue.*

*My hair is wavy and chocolate-colored.*

*This man is delusional.*

*"I'm so sorry, Leesa," he murmurs into my ear. "I love you."*

*His words pierce my heart with realization. This man needs help. Help maybe I could give. We get along great, have amazing sex, and he loves me. I love him too.*

*I can fix him. I can fix this.*

*Soon he's fucking me like there's no tomorrow and I'm climaxing hard. There has to be a way to get through this. Hank is a good man.*

*My thoughts are stolen though the moment his hand is back on my throat.*

*"How can you look like her? This isn't fair! Why do you get to live but she died?"*

*The complete one-eighty confuses me and I'm once again scrambling to save myself. I claw at his grip but he's too strong. Will it always be like this? Until the time he doesn't let go?*

*I must have passed out because I awake to him crying on my chest. My fingers find his hair and I stroke him in a tender manner. His soul has broken wide open and it's in this room, haunting us both.*

*"I still love you, Hank. No matter what."*

*He sits up and regards me with red, teary eyes. "I'll kill you one day. You have to know this."*

*I shake my head at him and blurt out something that I*

*know will have a huge impact.* "You won't be killing just me. You'll kill our child too."

*The transformation is surreal. His tortured soul drains into a place inside of himself where he hides away his pain and in its place joy radiates from him.*

"You're pregnant?"

*I accept his kiss.* "We're pregnant."

*It's just one small lie but it saves my life for another day.*

A quiet rap on the door jerks me from my thoughts and I swallow down my sadness. It was rough when a few weeks later I told him I'd lost the baby. He was too smart to lie so blatantly to. Once he went from wanting to kill me to wanting to be my husband instead, things went smoother. The "death" of our baby was eye-opening for him and we grew stronger for it. It wasn't until many years later that I realized what an epic mistake I'd made. After several unsuccessful attempts at getting pregnant, we went to a specialist. When I opened the results only to discover he was sterile, my life flashed again before my eyes.

I had to fix it.

Just like I'm fixing it now.

I flip the lock and open the door. That creep Clive smiles at me.

"About time. My husband needs me and you were taking forever," I huff.

He enters the room and locks the door behind him. A shudder rips through me but I swallow down my fear and lift my chin.

I'm fixing things.

"Hank adores you," I lie. "You know that right?"

Clive's eyes widen as I skim over his appearance. He's much younger than me and not at all fit like my husband but the resemblance is there. Dark hair. Same deep, twisted soul hiding behind his eyes.

"He's the most amazing man in the entire world. Now that he's gone to jail, I'll never get the excerpt he promised me."

I sigh and prepare myself to negotiate. "He's not the only amazing man," I purr and take a step toward him. "Anyone ever tell you how much you look like him?"

He gulps loud enough for me to hear the moment I grip onto his T-shirt. I press my tits against his chest and can feel his hard-on against my belly.

"Uh, Mrs. McElroy, what are you doing? I thought we were going to talk," he rushes out in a nervous chatter.

"I had an idea," I tell him as my hands roam his body. "I could give you *Twenty-Three Ways to Kill Adam*."

He breaks away to stare at me with wide, incredulous eyes. I swear the idea of being given the book gets his cock harder than a woman touching him.

"Are you serious? Why would you do that?"

I smile at him and lick my lips. His eyes drop down to them and hunger flashes over his features. I may be pushing forty but I'm not dead yet.

"I want something in return. Two somethings in fact."

He nods, stupid man, before knowing what it is I want.

"First of all, I want you to fuck me. No condom. Please tell me you're clean."

His eyes bug out of his head and his jaw drops open. "Are you trying to get back at him for Alex? I don't know. Mr. McElroy is a good guy. I'm not sure I could do that to him."

I giggle and stand on my toes to brush a kiss on his lips. His breath reeks of an infected tooth and I want to barf on him.

"Oh silly, Hank and I do this sort of thing all the time. Why do you think I wasn't mad when I found out about Alex? Don't you want to fuck me?"

He clenches his eyes closed. With the way his pathetic cock pokes into me, I know my answer.

"Yes, but…" he trails off.

"But what?"

His face blazes crimson and he seems unwilling to spit out his words. "I'm a v-v-virgin."

I smile at him. "That's perfect, Clive."

He groans when I start to peel his shirt from his body. I catch a whiff of his body odor and my stomach roils. It takes everything in me to focus on why I'm doing this.

I'm fixing it for Hank.

"Mmm," I faux moan. "I want you so bad."

He struggles with his belt buckle while I step away to strip out of my own clothes. Once I'm naked, I crawl onto the bed and spread my legs for him.

"I brought his manuscript with me. His original type-written pages from when he was fifteen years old," I tell him, dangling the carrot that he desperately wants.

When things get out of control for Hank, I always bring *Twenty-Three Ways to Kill Adam* with me—to remind him that there are better ways to handle the demons inside his head like he once did long ago when Adam teased him relentlessly.

Clive's dick flops around as he climbs onto the bed, looking very much like a kid in a candy store. He even licks his lips, although, I'm pretty sure it has more to do with the manuscript than it does me.

"Fuck me, handsome," I instruct.

He settles between my legs and with clumsy fingers he attempts to guide his dick inside of me. When he fumbles and slips it toward my ass twice, I finally take over and guide him into myself.

"Oh, shit. Fucking shit," he grunts the moment he pushes all the way into me.

I close my eyes and think about my husband. I think about his hands all over me, worshipping and loving me as Clive delivers a series of quick thrusts into me.

"Yes, I'm coming," I lie and clench my pussy.

"Oh God!"

He starts to pull out but I dig my heels into his ass and hold him inside of me. His cock explodes with his orgasm, filling me with his hot seed.

His labored breathing fills the room. "I'm sorry I came so quick. It's just…" he trails off.

I reopen my eyes and smile at him. "It was perfect, Clive. Now, stay inside of me for a bit and tuck that pillow beneath me so I'll be more comfortable."

He reaches over, ever a loyal subject, and slides it under me. His stinky, sweaty body settles over mine but at least his come is no longer running out of me. I hold him like this for a long while, entertaining him with stories of Hank. When he grows hard again, I let him fuck me once more. It can't hurt the cause.

"I can't believe I had sex with *The* Mrs. McElroy," he mutters in disbelief.

Smiling at him, I pat his arm. "Twice. You're a naughty man."

"I'm so excited to read that book. Your husband is my idol. I look forward to everything he puts out. This book, *Blue Hill Blood*, has been surreal."

I stroke his greasy hair and peer at him. "So you know the real Hank, huh?"

His cheeks redden and he nods. "Yeah."

"It's as if he morphs into another person," I say, sadness eating at my words.

He gulps. "I was shocked when I watched him kill that old woman. But I couldn't stop staring. I had to touch her after he left. Make sure it wasn't a dream," he says conspiratorially, as if he's sharing a secret with me.

"It wasn't a dream, Clive. It's how he writes. I do my best to keep him out of trouble but this time, trouble found him."

He nods and his eyes glass over, no doubt reliving the horrible murders inflicted by my husband. Yet after a short moment of silence, a small smile traces his lips and with it brings clarity. His gaze slithers over mine and his brows furrow.

"I want to fuck you again," he tells me, his dick growing from limp to hard.

The idea of having sex with him again makes me want to throw up. He's sick and twisted and dirty. But I know what needs to be done. I quirk my lips up into what I hope is a sultry smile and let out an eager moan.

"Did it turn you on seeing their bodies?" I probe and spread myself open for him.

"Yes. It excited me, yes," he groans as he drives into me. His thrusts are punishing and I crave to push him away from me. It isn't over quick like I wish. He's able to last longer and longer each time.

My mind begs to crawl into some dark place but I force myself to be present. To focus on this man that I so desperately need.

I wait until he comes once more and has relaxed on my chest before bringing on the waterworks. "Oh, Clive."

He jerks his face up in concern to look at me. "What is it Mrs. McElroy?"

A sob erupts from me. "My entire life is ruined. Hank will go to jail. His children will be without a father. He'll never be able to write again."

He rapidly blinks at me and runs a thumb over my cheek. His fingers stink—probably because he likes touching dead old ladies for fun—and I hold my breath.

"What are you saying?"

"I'm saying, he's ruined," I cry out in defeat. "I wish there was a way. Some way to help him. I wish someone who understands how important his work is to this world could find a way to fix it."

Clive's features darken and for once he looks like a man. I fucked the virgin boy into submission. Time to step up, Clive. A million thoughts must claw through his brain and for a moment, I watch them all cross over his features.

*Do it, Clive.*

You know you want to.

Do it for Hank.

Eventually, his eyes find mine and his features are resolute. I drag my gaze over his mottled flesh and am thankful he resembles my husband. Their hair is so similar and their eyes—same unhinged glint in them. Reaching for him, I then drag my fingertips along his flesh.

*Do it, Clive.*

Be a fucking man.

My thumb drags over his lips, begging him to speak the words that we both know need to be said to make everything right in the world.

My world.

Hank's world.

Grow a pair and step up, Clive.

"What if he didn't take the fall?" he queries aloud.

I gasp in faux shock.

It has the intended effect because his face contorts into a hard but decided look. "What if someone who knew every detail of the crimes took the blame instead?"

Thank God.

Clive *is* a man.

I could kiss him and this time I wouldn't be faking any emotion.

"I'd probably suck that man's dick and give him whatever he wanted," I laugh but I put every blazing, thankful emotion I have into my expression.

He stares at me, now fully understanding his role, and flashes me a smile. "I could be that man, Mrs. McElroy."

Tears spill over and I shake my head. "Oh, Clive. I would

never ask that of you."

Yet, I *am* asking that of you. Loud as fucking day. Read between the lines, Clive. Take the bait, Clive. Save my husband, Clive.

"Show it to me. *Twenty-Three Ways to Kill Adam*," he says in a gruff tone as he finally climbs off of me. His heat rushes from me and I pray it was enough.

I slide off the bed after him and ignore his come as it runs down my thighs. Dropping to my knees where my suitcase is, I unzip the outer compartment and pull out the bound manuscript.

"Promise me you'll never publish this or show it to anyone," I say in a firm tone.

He nods and snatches it from my hand like a greedy child stealing the last cookie. After he devours several pages, he flicks his gaze over to me.

"I'll do it. Give me tonight, with you," he says, lifting his chin in a brave manner, "and this manuscript. Tomorrow, I'll turn myself in."

Real tears spill down my cheeks. "You're willing to go to prison for Hank?"

He nods. "I feel so close to him and you now. We're like family. Family steps up where they're needed. My aunt is old and will die soon. I have nothing to live for on this Earth. But Mr. McElroy? He has you and the girls. And Eli. He can't lose all of that."

I bite my lip and withhold the fact that Eli dies in this book.

"You're the hero in this story, Clive."

He beams at me.

Crawling toward him, I give him my promise.

I fixed it.

# CHAPTER 23

Leesa

Last night is getting wiped from my memory forever. I did heinous and unforgivable things in the name of love. Hank will never know but it seals my being able to bring him home with me. And that's all that matters.

This morning, I took my time washing that man's stink from me. The only thing that matters is whether or not he was able to get me pregnant. Only time will tell. But if Hank wants a baby, then he's getting a baby.

Just like last time.

When I discovered he was sterile, I cried the entire afternoon. He thought I was emotional from my period. I never showed him the results and later told him we were both physically able to have children. It took a long time to build up the courage but eventually, I called my friend Austin from college. He was a good friend to me and had enough similar qualities to Hank. At first, he told me I was nuts for suggesting such an idea. But after much begging and a signed, legal document by his attorney that stated he wouldn't be responsible for the child, I had sex with him.

And after a few weeks of trying and a positive pregnancy test later, I had a baby for Hank.

It was harder though with Callie. By then, Austin was married with a kid of his own on the way. He refused to cheat on his wife Carla but he did ejaculate into a cup and insert the turkey baster inside of me. It was very clinical and there was nothing sexual about the way I became pregnant with her.

This time, I would have asked him again, except two years ago, Carla had him get a vasectomy. At the time, I worried about having any more children. Thankfully, Hank had said we were through until the night before last.

If he ever discovers his children aren't his, I shudder to think what he would do.

Clive left a few hours ago and promised me he would first secure a few of his "treasures," as he called the manuscript I gave him, before he headed to the station. I'm getting antsy and can't wait any longer. I miss my husband.

I'm about to climb out of my car after I pull into a parking spot at the police station when a commotion startles me. Sheriff Norton is wailing as two officers guide her out toward a car. They are somber and I think the woman beside her may even be crying. I wait until they drive away before I get out.

"What happened to her?" I question a woman that's smoking outside the door.

The woman turns to watch the car drive off into the distance before regarding me.

"She found her daughter dead this morning alongside that of the body of our mayor," she says, breath gruff from years of chain smoking. "Very sad. They think it was a murder suicide."

I furrow my brows at her. "Did he kill her?"

The woman steps away from the wall, a cloud of her stench enveloping me, and casts a glance over her shoulder making sure nobody is nearby. "Actually," she says in a hushed, conspiratorial tone, "The poor gal killed *him* before offing herself."

She takes another drag and I frown.

"Why?"

"Everyone knows he knocked her up awhile back. Nobody, including her momma, did a damn thing about it either. They made her feel as if she'd been the one in the wrong. That girl's not been right ever since," she sighs and puffs on her cigarette again. "To be honest, he deserved it, preying on a minor. I just feel bad she took her own life too. Damn shame."

My thoughts turn to Alex with her vibrant blue eyes and dark hair. She reminded me much of myself at her age which is why I needed to get rid of her—before Hank did. Even Alex, with her young body, was in no danger of getting pregnant because of Hank being sterile. The morning after pill was something to convince him more than her. What it meant, though, was that she was in huge danger of getting choked to death by my husband.

Alex wasn't as smart as me.

None of the women over the years have been.

Their survival instincts were nil compared to mine.

Alex was exactly like them but I saved her. Even if only for a short while. I saved her from my husband.

Not like it matters now anyway. The girl is dead. And by her own hand no less.

With a sigh, I wave to the woman before pushing through the doors and enter the station. I check in and let the lady guide me into a private room where I wait. It seems like I've been waiting hours when the door clicks open behind me.

"Mrs. McElroy," a man in a crisp black suit says. "I'm Agent Rick Stoney." I remember him as the one that called my husband a cop killer.

"Yes?" My tone is curt. I don't like this man whose demeanor has changed for the better since yesterday.

"We've had many revelations in the past twenty-four hours regarding the Blue Hill murders," he starts and scrubs his cheek with one hand before sitting down. His steely grey eyes are tired and apologetic.

"And? When can I see my husband?"

He groans. "They're processing his release right now. Apparently we have a signed confession. And evidence."

The evidence part causes me to shiver. I knew Clive was creepy but I didn't know he was creepy enough to collect things that would be considered evidence at the crime scene.

"What sort of evidence?" I probe.

"I really shouldn't disclose that, ma'am. Let's just say it

was damning." He lowers his voice. "Blood from one of the victims under his fingernails was one nail in his coffin."

I swallow and suppress a shudder knowing Clive had his dirty, unwashed hands all over me last night. "So from what I gather, it wasn't the sheriff?"

He shakes his head. "No. Turns out your husband has a super fan. A stalker of sorts. He was reenacting the crimes in his books. At first glance, it was easy for us to link Mr. McElroy to the crimes since his books described in detail the murders. But, the signed confession, forensic evidence, and other substantial physical evidence blew our original findings out of the water."

"Well, I'm just ready to leave this awful town and take my innocent husband home. He requires medication that he's currently not on because of your wrongful accusations. I do pray that you hurry and release him so that I can get him back on his meds."

He stands and nods. "We're terribly sorry, ma'am and an official statement will be released to the public by our communications liaison this afternoon."

"I hope they apologize to my husband and our family as this has been rather upsetting. Not to mention, this has damaged his reputation. We'll be seeking outside legal counsel because I can't help but wonder if we have a civil case against this city."

A sigh rushes from him and he nods. "We'll cooperate however we can. Like I said, ma'am, we're sorry for the trouble we've put you and your husband through."

He strides from the room, clearly eager to escape my venomous glare, and leaves me alone. I wait for another century until the door opens again. Hank steps in and I gasp. His hair is disheveled. It appears as if he's been crying. He needs his medication.

"Oh, baby," I sob and stand.

He stalks over to me and pulls me into a hug. "Leesa, she's dead. They told me she's dead."

*Alex.*

I cry for him because I know his heart is broken. All over again. Just like when Helen was brutally murdered by their father.

Just like when I found the dead girl in his dorm room and had to help him stage her suicide by hanging in her bedroom. Maggie was her name. Once he understood what had happened, he was distraught. I was there to stroke him and nurse his mind back to health.

And the time in Adair Village when he called me crying. He suffocated a woman named Jeannette in his hotel room. That time, I drove him west and helped him dump her into the Pacific Ocean. He cried so hard he vomited in the car. Again, I took care of him.

The saddest time was when his Grandma Lynette got a new home health nurse named Sarah. He obsessed over her looking just like Helen until one day I found her blue body on the living room floor. I was so shaken up to see him clutching on to her blue scrubs and crying that I ran back into Lynette's room. That day I concocted a tale that would send the police in another direction.

Hank and I packed up Sarah's body and took her to a piece of property Lynette owns. We buried the girl and when we came back, I had to do the unthinkable. Lynette said for the police to believe it, it needed to come from a woman. And so I did what was necessary. I destroyed her bedroom, emptied her purse, and hit the poor lady I loved so much in the face. Her face bruised terribly and with our testimonies, the police believed that the nurse beat up my husband's grandma and took off with a huge chunk of her cash.

I fixed it.

Every time.

After the girl at the bar that inspired Marla, Maggie, and then later me, I wondered how he could live with himself after everything he'd done—both their successful and my unsuccessful killings. But the problem with Hank, he doesn't live with them. Instead, he forces his past acts into a part of his brain I'll never be privy to—nor do I ever want to step into. Once I learned that he locks those violent times away and attempts to disassociate himself from them in an act of self-preservation, I knew I had to be the key. When he finally pushed away the horrors he'd created, I had to be the one to lock them up for him.

Hank always relies on me.

And I always come through for him.

Sometimes the memories—the overwhelming pain—escapes from the hell hole in his mind. Each time, I shove them back into place. With medicines, my love, my constant intervention—whatever it takes.

And I fucking lock them away. Each time, praying it will be the last.

"Oh, baby. Everything is okay. I have you now. Forever. You know that," I assure him.

He nods but his tears won't stop. I'm convinced every

time that he loves those girls. Maggie, Jeannette, Sarah, Alex. Each one reminding him of his dead sister. Each one, he obsesses over to the brink of insanity. The pills help but when he goes on his writing benders, he refuses to take them.

But now?

With the death of Eli, I think we may be able to finally close that door.

"But I loved her," he sniffles and buries his face in my hair.

"I know, baby," I coo. "You love them all."

He starts kissing me, his hands roaming over my tits. "Make it better, Leesa."

I pull away from him and look up into his broken face, both inside and out. My husband is beautiful despite his issues. His father made him this way but I help him get the life he deserves. The life Helen always wished for him to have.

Had I given up on him all those years ago, he'd have gone to prison, or worse yet, some mental institution where they don't understand him like I do. Nobody can fix him like I can.

I tug at his hearing aid and remove it. Knowing the drill, he dips his mangled ear to me, always eager for the words he can't ever hear.

Running my tongue along the scarred and bumpy flesh of his ear, I grin when his cock hardens between us. He loves this. I love this.

"Hank, they don't know you like I do. Nobody will. Not even Helen knew you like I know you now. You're my twisted soul mate and I'll die protecting what we have. No matter who you kill when you lose yourself in that head of yours,

I'll dive in and save you. I'll fix you, baby."

He smiles when I pull away and put the hearing aid back in place.

"Let's go try for a baby," I smile. "I'm getting older by the second."

I straddle him and grin. "What can I say? I'm getting frisky in my old age?"

It's been hours since we left the station and I can't seem to get enough of touching my husband. I was so close to losing him this time and I don't ever want him out of my sight again.

"You are not old," he laughs.

His eyes normally twinkle and dart back and forth when not on his meds. Tonight, they're dull and steady.

Dull and steady means normalcy for us.

I crave dull and steady.

When the phone starts ringing again, I whine. "Will she ever stop?"

He shakes his head and reaches over to answer Linda, his super annoying agent's call.

"What Linda?" he snaps, clearly unhappy about being interrupted from making love to his wife.

I can hear her chattering away on the other end even though I can't hear exactly what she's saying. *HBO. Miniseries. Blue Hill Blood.* Those words I do pick up on. He grunts out approval and hangs up.

"We're having offers coming out of the woodwork on

*Blue Hill Blood* getting picked up for movie rights and it isn't even finished or published yet. Linda says her phone and emails won't quit. Apparently this book will make us very rich," he laughs.

I lower my bare chest against his and kiss him. "Who needs money, baby? We're rich in love."

His mouth steals mine and he flips us over. I shiver when I see the sparkle. No matter how strong the meds are, my true Hank always peeks out and reminds me of why I married him. I'm in love with all of him. The ugly parts both inside and out. The scars on both his face and his heart. His obsessions. His weaknesses. His affinity for killing.

Henry *Eli*ot McElroy is mine.

Not Maggie's.

Not Jeannette's.

Not Sarah's.

Not Alex's.

Not Helen's.

Mine.

# CHAPTER 24

Hank

## Eight months after Blue Hill...

"Are we there yet?" Callie whines from the backseat. "We've been on the road for four hours and the GPS says we're near Maine State Prison.

"Almost," I tell her as I turn down the road that will take us there.

I glance over at Leesa and beam with pride at seeing her huge belly. She's fucking beautiful as hell as she shines with her pregnant glow. We may be old but the moment we wanted to get pregnant again, she came off the pill and it was done. According to the doctor's calculations, we conceived while in Blue Hill. Looks like we took a little souvenir back home with us.

She reaches over and squeezes my thigh. "I love you."

I wink at her. "Love you too, baby."

"Gross, get a room," Whitney complains from the back-seat.

Callie erupts with laughter and soon we're all joining in, even Miss Crabbypants in the back.

After I park, and I leave my girls in the lobby area of the prison, I clutch my gift in my hand and check in. They run me through many rigorous procedures before they finally take me into a room with many other men and women waiting to visit other prisoners.

Today, I'll be meeting with Clive.

Leesa and I make the trip up here each month. His aunt passed away not long after he was indicted so we decided to take him in as our own. After all he did for us, it only seemed right.

The guards begin filing in the prisoners and when Clive sees me, his eyes light up.

"Mr. McElroy!" he exclaims as he sits across from me. "I wasn't sure if you were going to come this month."

"Next month, buddy. Leesa is due then but we'll be back after that. Besides," I smile and push the paperback over to him. "I had to give you your present."

His eyes widen and he gushes over the book. "Wow, it's gorgeous. The cover is deadly!"

I laugh and nod. "Sure is. Are you dying to know what happens?"

This time he smiles broadly. "It's all I've been able to think about for months."

When he flips it open to read the dedication, tears swim in his eyes and he looks back up at me. "It's dedicated to me."

**To my truest, dearest fan. This book wouldn't exist without you. There would be no happy endings in *my* book if it weren't for you.**

His ear to ear smile is immediate. "I'm so honored. This is the most amazing thing that's ever happened to me," he sniffles.

I reach over and pat his hand. "It's the truth. I can't thank you enough for stepping up for me."

His cheeks redden. "Aww, it was nothing."

But it was something. It was everything.

"Are they treating you right? Do I need to add more money to your account?"

He shakes his head. "I still have money left over from last time. Now, I have a book I can't wait to read over and over again. It's actually really nice here. The big guys don't mess with me because they think I'm a psychotic killer. And, yet, the guards are friendly to me because I don't cause trouble and spend most of my days reading. Life is good, Mr. McElroy."

I smile at him and can't help but agree that life, is indeed, good. Better than good.

"How's the missus?" he asks, a lusty gaze filling his eyes at the mention of Leesa.

It's hard not to bristle at his inquiry. He always asks about her and it usually sends me on my way so I don't end up popping him in the nose.

"She's fine," I clip out and stand.

His smile sickens me. "That she is, Mr. McElroy. That

she is. Tell her I said hi."

"See you in two months, buddy," I say with a wave.

As I stride down the hallway away from him, I shudder. The motherfucker always asks about her as if he's imagining her naked and on his little pecker right at that moment. It's creepy as fuck and it irritates me every time. For all I know, he probably whacks off to thoughts of her pretty face every night.

Little does he know, Leesa would never give some loser like him the time of day. She'll always be some sick fantasy to weirdos like Clive.

With a smug, satisfied grin knowing she's all mine—*always has and always will be*—I push through the doors back into the lobby and back to my family.

# EPILOGUE

## One year after Blue Hill...

I tap my patriotic fingernails on my notebook that sits on top of the book I brought especially for this occasion. A gold leaf, the logo for Southern New Hampshire University, is emblazoned on the front cover and I have the urge to pick it off.

I'm nervous. *Really damn nervous.*

I've never had an author autograph any of my books. But this book is special to me. So the fact that my *now* favorite author will not only sign my book but I'll actually get to speak with him is about to cause me to bust at the seams.

The speaker announces his arrival and my eyes jerk away from my notebook to the stage in the auditorium. Soon, I'll see him.

Henry McElroy.

In the flesh.

The coffee I sucked down is now my nemesis as it jitters a dance through my veins and nausea knots my belly.

*Breathe, girlfriend.*

*He's just a man—a man you can* certainly *handle being around.*

With a suck of a calming breath, I relax my mind and wait for him to walk onto the stage. I can do this. He's an author, not a celebrity.

He's Henry McElroy.

Applause echoes around me and I spot him the second his foot steps onto the stage. Slim, dark jeans encase his muscular, long legs and he wears a fitted, black Henley.

He looks good.

*Really good.*

My belly flops, this time for a different reason and heat prickles the skin on my chest.

The man eyes the crowd in an unsure manner, as if he's afraid they'll all start ridiculing him for his disfigured appearance at any moment.

*But he doesn't see what I see.*

Despite being disfigured, Henry radiates with a beauty that not many notice because they're vapid and worried about cosmetic shit.

I don't give a rat's ass about what's on the outside—*I can see more.*

His blue eyes flicker and blaze with a passion that normal people don't have. They tell a story—*several stories in fact*—and I crave to know them all. The scruff on his cheek is his way of masking what's beneath.

*But he can't hide from me.*

The creative monster that claws at his surface, just begs to be released. And I want to be the one to free him from his cage. Indulge him in his fantasies and desires.

I close my eyes the moment he speaks and for the first time in quite some time, I feel whole. Reading his words on their pages over and over again allows me glimpses into him but it can never compete with the deep, timbre of his voice that serves to send chills along my flesh.

When I finally get to shake his hand after this event, will he feel the desire and craving that surges through me at the touch of my hand? Or will his features pass over mine as he scribbles his name into the book, unknowing of my own monster that wholeheartedly seeks his.

*My heart tells me he'll know.*

I spend the entire speech basking in the way his voice rumbles through my chest, saturating itself into my soul. I've waited so long for this moment.

I love Henry McElroy.

He just doesn't know it yet.

"Thank you, and for those who purchased a backstage greeting pass, please make your way to the stage as we call out your number. Mr. McElroy will be waiting for you," an announcer says as he waves to the crowd and disappears.

The moment he leaves, my frown is immediate, and I jerk to my feet.

"Numbers one through ten, please come to the stage now."

I gather my notebook and book, about to walk away, when a masculine voice beside me speaks up.

"Hi there," he says. "Anyone ever told you that the Yankees suck?"

Snapping my head in his direction, I'm irritated to see a handsome guy smirking at me. It takes me a moment to realize he's teasing me in a flirtatious way and mentioning my ball cap that covers my long, almost black hair—a color I'm still not used to.

"*You* suck," I bite back.

He bellows with laughter and trots after me when I leave him. "Wait, I'm number eight. What number are you?"

I don't turn around to him, annoyed that he's interrupted my mission, and blurt out, "One."

I'd paid a pretty penny the day the tickets went on sale for that number. I've been waiting three months for this event. And now some guy is trying to flirt his way into the middle of my business.

"What are you doing after the signing? I'd love to take you to coffee. We could talk about serious shit—you seem like a serious kind of gal," he chuckles.

I stride down the steps, taking two at a time, and hurry to the stage. "Don't bother. Besides," I grumble, "Mom told me never to talk to strangers."

Ignoring his response, I make my way to the right of the stage, pushing past people and wave my lanyard to the person letting the first group of people in. She guides me to the front of the line and away from the pesky man.

In a nervous manner, I twist a lock of my hair with my free hand and bounce on my toes.

*So close.*

*So close.*

I've read this book from top to bottom at least a hundred times, highlighting my favorite parts, understanding truth from embellishment. Eli is such a complex, misunderstood character. I know the heroine in the book came to understand that in the end. Had she only been more patient, wiser, given him a second chance, she and Eli could have had their happily ever after.

Instead, she jumped the gun.

She made a decision that ruined it all.

But I'm different from the heroine in that story. I believe in second chances. When fate brings people together, it's for a reason.

*Henry McElroy is my reason.*

"Number one, you can go ahead," the woman tells me and ushers me down a hallway.

My legs become wobbly as I near his table where he's standing behind the chair pushed underneath. He's smiling at a picture on his phone—as I approach, I can see it's of his new baby boy. A twinge of jealousy ripples through me but I squash it away. Now isn't the time to dwell on the fact that while all the wrong women get their babies, the deserving ones don't.

*Well, at least not yet.*

I set my books down on the table in front of him and slide out *Blue Hill Blood* from the bottom. His face is still drawn to his phone, but eventually, he sets it down on the table and lifts his face to mine.

Moment of truth.

His friendly smile falls and he blinks in confusion. I bat my eyelashes and bite on my bottom lip—a lip that draws the attention of his eyes. When they finally drag back up to mine, I'm elated at the explosion of emotions that pulsate from behind them.

*Love.*

*Love.*

*Love.*

My heart thumps wildly in my chest as I wait for him to speak. He feels the connection, I can see that. His hands tremble and his eyebrows furrow together as he attempts to work it out in his mind.

"Hello," I mutter, my voice merely a whisper.

Again, his eyes are on my lips.

"Helen?"

The name is both a blessing and a curse.

I'd prayed for another one to fall from his perfect mouth but the name I was expecting was murmured instead.

I flash him a wide smile and reach my hand to him. "No," I tell him, "I'm Candace."

The name seemed fitting. And when my mother, a woman who had finally had enough of the bullshit men in her life controlling her, covered up my "mistake," she told me I was free to go on and be whoever I wanted to be.

For a while there, I was Britney and Ashley and Jennifer.

But now, I'm just plain ol' Candace.

The moment I read through the book on release day, eagerly flipping through the pages at the bookstore here in town, I knew.

I'll always be Candace.

Well, until *he* decides otherwise.

"Candace," he grins at me, his eyes drinking in every

freckle on my face, "I love that name."

He takes my hand and grips it. The warmth of it engulfs my soul. His eyes draw down over my breasts that are barely contained in a fitted Aerosmith tank top and I shiver. A pleased groan erupts from him.

"Um, Candace," he grunts out as he finds my eyes again, "Would you like to meet after the event? Maybe have a slice of pie or something?"

I beam at him, my heart fluttering around in my chest. "Married men shouldn't go off eating pie with young women," I chide, flicking my eyes at his wedding ring and attempt to draw my hand from his grip.

But he doesn't release it and instead drags me closer to him, my bare thighs just under my cut-off shorts pressing into the table between us.

"You look like my sister," he assures me. "Just a friendly chat over pie."

My skin flushes at the way he possessively grips my hand as if I'll disappear before his eyes.

*I'm not going anywhere, Henry.*

"Well," I giggle, "I suppose I *will* have pie with you after all, old man."

His eyes darken and he nods in a curt manner. "After this."

I smile and nod, eyeing our clasped hands with a raised brow. "You going to hold onto me all afternoon?" My tone is suggestive but I bat my eyelashes, feigning innocence.

He runs his thumb over the back of my hand and goosebumps scatter all over my flesh. With a scowl, he finally releases me and sits in his chair. His gaze is on my thighs and it takes everything in me not to crawl over the table and into his lap.

*In time, Candace.*

"No birthmark," he mutters to himself. "Not Helen."

I smirk and hand him my marker. "Blue, please."

He flashes me a pleased smile as he takes it from me and then scrawls out his signature on the first page in a messy flourish. When he finishes, he thumbs through the book and scribbles out something I can't see.

After snapping the book closed, he hands it to me but waves the marker. "Can I keep this? It's my favorite color."

His sexy smirk is my undoing and my cheeks heat. This man has an effect on me.

"Sure, Henry. I'll see you after," I tell him with a wave.

He nods, his smile never waning. "I can't wait."

I turn from him and hear them call out number two. With each torturous step away from the love of my life, I am deflated.

Casting a glance over my shoulder, needing to see him again, I'm pleased to see him looking past the person standing at the table and watching me walk away. Finding a place on the wall out of the way but in his view, I slide down and sit on the cold concrete floor.

He drags his gaze, almost unwillingly, from me to greet the next fan.

But the next free moment, his eyes are on me again.

Just as they should be—where they belong.

Cracking open the book, I open it to the first page and run my fingers along the lines of his name. I want to run my fingers along his chest, to finger the scar near his shoulder.

To circle his belly button and tease his cock. To graze them along his damaged cheek and over his mutilated ear. To run them through his messy hair.

I want to touch him.

Flipping through the book, I stop when I find his message.

**I want to touch you. —Scarface—**

My heart explodes in my chest and I jerk my chin in his direction, my bottom lip quivering as emotion threatens to rip me in two.

His brooding gaze is on me and then our eyes meet.

Recognition and joy radiate from him as his lips quirk up into a half-grin that effectively melts me into a puddle.

I'm not like the Candace from his book, the woman who wasn't quite strong enough in the end.

I'm better than *that* Candace.

*This* Candace is strong. *This* Candace gets her *Eli*.

The Bloody End.

A Note from Elizabeth Gray

If you enjoyed this book, please check out some of my other books published under my other pen name, K Webster. I've published dozens of books in many different genres under that pen name including: contemporary romance, erotic romance, paranormal romance, and historical romance. My stories are all different and unique from one another. Thank you for taking a chance on this book and I hope to hear how you liked it!

# ACKNOWLEDGEMENTS

Thank you to my husband. You inspired this story by something you told me and I'll forever be thankful for the spark that you caused that turned into a full-on raging fire that was this book. And thanks for listening to me quote my book over and over again when I'd have proud moments over this story. You pet the crazy little artist that resides within and I appreciate that.

I want to thank the people that beta read on this book. Nikki McCrae, Wendy Colby, Shannon Martin, Amy Bosica, Ella Stewart, Anne Jolin, and Elizabeth Clinton. (I hope I didn't forget anyone) you guys always provide AMAZING feedback. You all give me helpful ideas to make my stories better and give me incredible encouragement. I appreciate all of your comments and suggestions.

Thanks Ella Stewart for being my final, second set of eyes on this. You're a star and I'm so glad we found each other! #squirrel

Thank you to all of my blogger friends both big and small that go above and beyond to always share my stuff. You all rock! #AllBlogsMatter

I'm especially thankful for the Breaking the Rules Babes and my Krazy for K reader group. You ladies are wonderful with your support and friendship. Each and every single one of you is amazingly supportive and caring.

I am totally thankful for my author group, the COPA gals, for being there when I need to take a load off and whine. Y'all rock!

Vanessa Leret Bridges, thank you for being my editor on this book. You really understood what I was trying to achieve with this book and helped me get it there. It wouldn't have been as wicked without your help. Thanks for involving your proofreader Manda and I hope I didn't scar her mind too badly.

Thank you Stacey Blake for making my book beautiful. You are a true artist and I adore you to bits. Cheers, girlfriend!

Lastly but certainly not least of all, thank you to all of the wonderful readers out there that are willing to hear my story and enjoy my characters like I do. It means the world to me!

# ABOUT THE AUTHOR

Elizabeth Gray is the author of the psychological thriller Blue Hill Blood. When not spending time with her husband of twelve years and two adorable children, she's active on social media connecting with her readers.

Her other passions besides writing include reading and graphic design. Elizabeth can always be found in front of her computer chasing her next idea and taking action. She looks forward to the day when she will see one of her titles on the big screen.

Elizabeth Gray also writes under the pen name K Webster where she is the author of dozens of romance books in many different genres including contemporary romance, historical romance, paranormal romance, and erotic romance.

You can easily find Elizabeth Gray on Facebook and Goodreads!

Join her newsletter to receive a couple of updates a month on new releases and exclusive content for both Elizabeth Gray and K Webster. To join, all you need to do is go here. (http://eepurl.com/9AqRD).

Facebook
https://www.facebook.com/authorkwebster

Blog
http://authorkwebster.wordpress.com/

Twitter
https://twitter.com/KristiWebster

Email
kristi@authorkwebster.com

Goodreads
https://www.goodreads.com/user/show/10439773-k-webster

Instagram
http://instagram.com/kristiwebster

Books by Author K Webster (Elizabeth Gray's alter-ego)

*The Breaking the Rules Series:*
Broken (Book 1) – Available Now!
Wrong (Book 2) – Available Now!
Scarred (Book 3) – Available Now!
Mistake (Book 4) – Available Now!
Crushed (Book 5 – a novella) – Available Now!
Disgrace (Book 6) – Coming Soon!
Defiance (Book 7) – Coming Soon!

*The Vegas Aces Series:*
Rock Country (Book 1) – Available Now!
Rock Heart (Book 2) – Available Now!
Rock Bottom (Book 3) – Available Now!
Rock Out (Book 4) – Coming Soon!

*The Becoming Her Series:*
Becoming Lady Thomas (Book 1) – Available Now!
Becoming Countess Dumont (Book 2) – Available Now!
Becoming Mrs. Benedict (Book 3) – Available Now!

Alpha & Omega – Available Now!
Omega & Love – Available Now!

Apartment 2B (Standalone Novel) – Available Now!
Love and Law (Standalone Novel) – Available Now!
Moth to a Flame (Standalone Novel) – Available Now!
Erased (Standalone Novel) – Available Now!
The Road Back to Us (Standalone Novel) – Available Now!
Give Me Yesterday (Standalone Novel – Coming Soon!

Made in the USA
Charleston, SC
08 June 2016